Th

Sidew

(Bad People II)

The Second Skulk Rock Musical Novel for the 21st Century
     Story: Maximus Morpheus
     Music/Lyrics: Robbie Thinman, Andrew Cutts
"The Sidewinder" is the further story of Lucy and James and Skulk Rock.
Their histories and destinies are strangely linked in this world and the next.
Their histories and destinies are also linked to those of all of their friends
and with "Skulk Rock".

Mike Remo, Thunderman, TheGnome, Felicia, English Bob, Boris The
Cranium, Wangly Dangly, Marv, Don Estrada, OolJee, Ajei

     And introducing:
     Sophia (Speedy) Coppola
     and
     The Sidewinder and The Fatback

The story is linked by 39 original songs.

The novel is complete. The songs are complete.
Some of the songs are not yet voiced correctly.
(If it was a musical they would be sung by the appropriate characters).
For now, however, they are just "demos".
All the songs are live and linkable.
(If you read this on a PC or Tablet you can click the song links to hear them
as you read).
If you want an overall link to all the songs in the order they appear in the
novel, then here it is:
https://badpeoplethemusical.bandcamp.com/album/the-sidewinder

Hope you like the story and the songs.
Hope you like "Skulk Rock".
KOFR

The
Sidewinder

(Bad People II)

"Do you believe in a fate
Everything comes to him who waits
Chance brings you all you need
Ambition is a form of greed*

Distant Meteors, 2004

Chapter 1
The Eagle Flies

The Eagle furls its wings, it sees the red bridge through a small tunnel in the clouds and immediately falls into gravity. As it drops out of the base of the cloud the bridge is below it and it sees the human scars on the land leading to the bridge and the human virus moving along the scars. It deploys vast wings and harnesses its speed, altering course towards the human mountains. Its dive becomes a controlled glide and it looks left and right at the devastation of the humans; how did it come to this? It has no wish to travel back here? At this altitude it sees the demons themselves. It circles high over the island. Demon Ants. It focusses onto its destination tower and loses some more height gliding over the wharf. Little Harriet sees it and her gaze locks on, taking her attention from her ice cream cone,

"ig urd!!!"

"What is it Harriet? Don't drop your ice cream!"

"urd!"

"That's right", her mother smiles down from her chatting to another mother, "those are seagulls Harriet!"

Harriet ignores her mother and stares up into the vastness, watching the eagle until its flight path takes it behind a low-down fluffy white. She turns her attention back to her ice cream suppressing her frustration at not sharing this moment with her mother. She thinks to herself, "I need to work on this talking thing…".

The eagle glides to its landing area atop one of the tallest human mountains. It perches at the edge and carefully folds its wings into a statutory pose at the edge of the parapet. The only discernable movement is its eyes and momentary re-orientations of its head. It scans for the ravens.

****

Michael Remo's left eye opens. It sees a high ceiling and shifting shade as clouds flypast the penthouse flat. He turns his head looking for Felicia. She's not there. His heart sinks but then he smells coffee. Life is not so bad. He thinks of her. He could spend his life thinking of her. He has no idea how much time passes as he thinks of her legs. His imagination has not got past her feet, her shoes, her ankles, contoured calves and knees, her skin... he forces his thoughts to tell him to get out of bed. He has stuff to do with Thunderman and The Gnome later. Later, later, later. Dressed now, he sees her smiling face across the kitchen island. He's slightly uneasy in these surroundings but her presence overrules all those feelings. She weaves a hypnosis. He's happy in the trance. Her nose twitches slightly as she talks keeping the trance locked on. Her voice guides him over a vast ocean. A beacon guiding him to shoreline safety. He wakes, sipping coffee as she turns to look out of the window. She talks of the view, how she loves it, loves to see the ships progress along the bay, loves the flocking birds, the gulls and the bridges. He agree but he's only looking at her for now. She speaks again,

"I really miss Jimmy", her eyes glint in the daylight as they moisten

"Me too."

He's not even hurt by the tactless mention of Jimmy English – under the circumstances of the present.

"I sometimes feel he is still here – watching"

"His songs live on Flea – skulking!"

She turns her head and smiles, moving to her left and kissing Mike on his right cheek.

"He'd love that Mikey!"

Mike nods. Jimmy English was some kind of "messenger" for him. A messenger from Planet Skulk, An oddball little limey bastard. Mike loved him like a son. Two years on and Mike knows exactly what she means. He is still here? Maybe it's because The Dirtkickers are still working through his legacy of songs? Maybe because Lucy has joined the band? Maybe because Little Joan is so precious to them all? For now, and every time he sees Felicia, he seems to feel Jimmy's eyes burning into him. He feels it now and shudders. Her voice snaps him out of it,

"I have to be going Mikey. Got an assignment."

"Fashion or film?"

"Passion in fashion darling. Should be fun with Miranda and Yolande. It always is."

Mike's imagination soars and he sighs, deep inside,

"What about Amanda?"

"She's got a shoot in Macy's."

"Good to hear"

"She's really back now Mikey. Still asks about you."

"I got stuff with The Kickers too."

"That'll be more fun than fashion photos. I'll come and see you next chance."

He wants to linger as he gazes out to the island. We're all prisoners. Prisoners of gravity. He remembers that song of Lucy's. Fate weaves strange paths for us all. He remembers long conversations with Jimmy English as they rode back from gigs. Thunderman and The Gnome in back with the gear. They'd talk about physics. Strange theories of gravity and electromagnetic forces. From the DeArmond pickup on their old Harmony Stratotone guitars through to the orbit of the moon and beyond. All these things are connected. No-one really understands it all. It could be that two skulk rockers are destined to work it all out on the way back from a distant gig? High paid physicists on big fat grants – fuck them. This was the philosophy of Skulk Rock. Work it out for yourself. Let the force be with you. The groove is everything. Lucy Smith knows that. She told Mike about a guy called "Boris The Cranium" who lived up in Oregon. How he had crazy crazy theories about physics and the "forces of nature". Mike laughs to himself.

*

Now he's walking up Taylor Street his heart beating a fast double time. He's not sure if it's his fitness, or lack of it, or his mixed thoughts of Felicia. Anyway, he loves it. He is alive. He is more than alive. As he reaches Ina Coolbrith Park, at the top of the street and he jumps and clenches a fist. He stops and turns thinking of Jimmy English. For some reason he senses Jimmy's presence again. He often does, but he feels it strong here. He feels a tear on his cheek. He spins and looks down Taylor Street from where he has walked. He sees The Island again, with a Sausalito hill in the far distance behind. He remembers Lucy's first gig with the band over in Sausalito. That was the night some of the music clicked for sure. Skulk. He detours into the park and turns his gaze to see city peaks to his right. This is the city he loves. He will die here. He knows it.

****

Thunderman plugs his '67 P-Bass into his Dirtkickers HQ practice rig. He lets a low note hang and relaxes; like a first sip of beer. He also actually takes his first actual sip of actual beer,

"Bit early – even for you? Ain't it?", enquires TheGnome looking over his snare drum as he adjusts his kick pedal.

"When you need a drink, you need a drink Gnomey!"

"True enough Lowdown Dirtboy", the Gnome wanders over to the beer handle. Mike Remo has put a barrel of IPA on tap,

"This barrel is never ending eh?".

They both smile,

"Jimmy English!", they raise their glasses and drink. A dilated moment's silence follows. Thunderman continues,

"He was always on about fate wasn't he? Fuckin Limey Philosopher!"

"Fate and women!".

They laugh and fall back to silence. The Gnome speaks first,

"Do you sometimes feel like he is here?"

TMan looks at him vacantly. Eventually replying,

"Like now?"

"YEH, like now!"

"Yeh I do – howdy doody Jimmy!"

TMan raises his glass to the thin air,

"Here's to fate Jimmy E. We're gonna do one of your songs. Mike keeps us workin. You shouldn't'a left so many!"

The Gnome giggles,

"Fukkin workaholic! He could make up a song about taking a piss and find poetry man!"

"Gravitation and urination. His two favourite themes."

"Nah – whores and dwarves were his favourite?"

They raise their glasses one more time,

"James English!!!!!!!", as Mike Remo enters the practice area. Mike stares,

"you shitheads have started early!"

"You brought temptation into our lives Mike"

"Well, it was Ho Chi Minimum that sent the barrel over", pouring himself a glass. They raise their glasses to Ho.

"We got some more gigs at Ho's soon Mikey?"

"Next month TMan. Gotta say, that venue reminds me of those SnakeFuckers everytime!"

"Yeh Mike. What a gig that was?", they smile, and then look sad in unison.

"When you shot Les Paul!"

"I sure did!"

"Always preferred Fenders myself anyway"

"Well a strat wouldn't have stopped a 38?"

"A good old alder body one might?"

"Maybe?", Mike picks up Jimmy's old Stratotone, "This old boy wouldn't even stop a .22 set to stun!"

He plugs in the old guitar and it hums and feeds,

"Sometimes I swear this axe plays itself? Or maybe it's Jimmy's ghost?"

"No ghost Mike. He's here! Me and TheGnome were just saying that."

The three Dirtkickers smile at each other silently. Savouring the IPA. Mike Remo looks down now, guilty as he remembers his night with Felicia. He thinks,

"Firk! They could be right!".

He had felt Jimmy's presence this morning. He rememberes the Susanville gig; the first appearance of Felicia. He remembers Jimmy talking about her. He remembers the gig at The Saloon when she reappeared. She was something else that night. "Something else" didn't cut it as an explanation. Jimmy saw her first; or rather, she saw Jimmy first? Something at first sight.

Wouldn't say it was love. Could be love now, but Mike was smart enough to know that Felica would never be in love with any man. Love can never tame her? You were lucky to spend time with her. Christ, you were lucky to be in the same room as her. How lucky was he? She was an angel? An angel of the first degree? A temptation angel, so perfect she'd even spend time with mortals. Not all her time though. She was way too important in the grand scheme of the universe for that. He longed for the next time. He prayed for a next time. He was already living in Hope City.

"Mike! Are you at home?", TMan was stood now and riffing on his bass smiling at Mike. The Gnome clicks along. Mike snaps out of his dream. He smiles back at his two fellow Dirtkickers,

"We been doing this a long time boys? No point in stopping now?"

"No fucking point at all Michael J Remo!", TMan shouts, pulling down a bass riff from some white fluffy San Francisco cloud passing through his brain.

"Fucking Keep On Fucking Rocking!", The Gnome adds, stirring a snare rudiment and a floor tom condiment into a sharp groove soup, they all shout, "KOFR JIMMY ENGLISH!!!!"

KOFR

https://badpeoplethemusical.bandcamp.com/track/k-o-f-r

I'm rolling down the road - got nowhere to go
But I'm still thinking of you
I done 16 years Now I'm in the clear
Drink away my blues

The night times are the worst times
When I can't even dream
The only way I can face the day
Is when your face is what I see

It wasn't meant to be this way
We had ambition to feed

But circumstances ruined my chances
So now just watch me bleed
All the years gone by
Something about Einstein
The Stars they fly across the sky
How did we get this far?
KOFR

Five state lines - two day solid drive
I'm running on empty
My rig is old but she pulls her load
And man, she still got her speed

But every heart can bleed
The devil knows what you need
Temptation angels on patrol
Next thing you know you're on parole

All the years gone by
Something about Einstein
The Stars they fly across the sky
How did we get this far?
KOFR

I can't change But I'm not strange
You might think I'll never win
But a mountain range Can't keep me at bay
You wanna fight? Well bring it on in

I got a heart made of steel I thought no-one could steal
But I still feel the pain
But now I'm healed Tomorrow's a new deal
So deal me in again

Well evil thoughts make for evil deeds
And we all have a greed to feed
You're goin down like the devil decreed
All the fates agreed

Thinkin about the good times
Followin the white lines
Still staring at the stars above
How did we get this far?
KOFR, KOFR, KOFR, KOFR

****

Lucy Smith opens her eyes – wide in shock. There is Little Joan dancing at the side of her bed...

I'm a seal rider
Out across the waves
Out with my Momma
They're my favourite days
My Teddy's called Jimmy
Like my Dad
He talks to me
He is out there and can't get back

Lucy feels a tear run down her cheek as Little Joan carries on her dance. It has been her first night in her new bed and she had slept through to the morning light. Lucy thinks of James. Snippets of a movie run through her head. All too short a movie. She pulls herself together before letting Little Joan knows she is awake.

"Wow Joanie, what a nice song!"

Little Joan stops and smiles.

"Breakfast time Momma! Then we can go out?"

"We sure can Joanie. You want to go see the seals?"

"Yeh!"

"Wanna get the boat across to the Island where they send the Bad People?"

Little Joan looks worried.

"The Badees - Won't they get us Momma?"

"Nooooo, they're not there anymore"

"They might be"

"No they're not Joanie"

"Their ghosts are", Little Joan accentuates her serious frown.

"Who told you that?"

"TMan"

"TMan sometimes makes things up Joan"

"Nooooo, he's right"

"Oh, he is - is he?"

"He showed me his Ghost Radar on his phone!"

"What!?"

"It shows you where the ghosts are!"

"Wait until I see TMan!" ("I'll kill the fucker"), under her breath.

"You should get it on your phone Momma. He showed me and there was a big ghost light near us"

Lucy's thoughts run away. She smiles at Little Joan's serious face. What mother doesn't think their little girl is the cutest thing on the planet?

"Let's go have breakfast Joanie. Be quiet though so we don't wake Aunt Ronee."

The two Smith's sit and eat their porridge. Out of the window they can see the island. Little Joan breaks the silence,

"Al Catraz! The baddest person ever ever ever on the earth"

Lucy smiles,

"That's right"

Little Joan summons her theatrical voice,

"No-one can escape The Island! Not even Al"

Lucy cracks up laughing at Little Joan's melodrama and then reciprocates in equally serious tone,

"That's right! Once you are sent there, there is no way back. NO WAY!"

Little Joan's expression becomes seriously worried and Lucy regrets her excursion into method acting. She immediately laughs and explains once again that it is now just a museum and how Bad People are treated much better these days.

"Two wrongs don't make anything right Little Joan."

Lucy banishes her conscience lawyer who is now addressing her mental jury on the grounds of hypocrisy or similar. She's pleased that Aunt Ronee enters the room. Little Joan jumps down from her stool and runs across to hug Ronee,

"We're going to see the Bad People Ghosts Aunty Ronee!"

Ronee looks across at Lucy,
"Oh are we?"
Little Joan jumps down from her stool and dances around the room. Lucy and Ronee smile. Little Joan drags Ronee to the window and they look out on the island. Little Joan tells Ronee all the contents of her imagination..."Fairies come in my dreams..."

Lucy listens in snippets until her memory cuts in and reruns some of Jimmy's stories of Manchester England. She remembers the song he wrote about his own ghost. How he wondered if anyone would remember him. "They do Jimmy, they do!".

Ghost

https://badpeoplethemusical.bandcamp.com/track/ghost

I saw your ghost - under a streetlight
And I saw your ghost – in the rain
I saw your ghost – looking lonely
Looking for a way – a way back again

And I saw your ghost – standing in a station
I saw your ghost – waiting for a train
The loneliest ghost – in all creation
Looking for you – once again

This place is old and cold and lonely
But its got such memories
And time and tide can't touch me
It's the time and place I want to be

Ghost - on the bus home
Ghost - on the links
Ghost – with time to be alone
Ghost – with the time to think

Will yer tell me – where yer goin
And where yer bin ?
Will yer tell me

If you'll come back again ?

I saw your ghost – on the football pitch trying to play
And in the pub at the bar
And the PC in the morning is always logged on to eBay
Watching old american guitars

Ghost - come and talk to me
Ghost - don't slip away
Ghost - this is the 21st century
Plenty of time left to play

Ghost – you're a star in the night
Ghost – you're the moon in the evenin'
Ghost – You make everything alright
Ghost – Don't ever think of leavin'

Ghost – you're a star in the evenin'
Ghost – you're the moon in the night
Ghost – Don't ever think of leavin'
Ghost – don't ever say goodbye

Ghost – don't ever fade
Ghost – you'd better stay
Ghost – Don't ever think of leavin'
Ghost – don't ever say goodbye

Lucy looks over at Ronee and Little Joan now reading a book together on the couch. Things have turned out ok? She nods to herself. Jimmy's ghost in her mind. Darkness banished to the edges of her universe. She smiles to herself thinking of their day ahead. She cherishes every moment. She has gigs coming. She looks at Nick Lucas. She thinks of her Dad. Nick never lets her down. She thinks of Howard and Elizabeth. How Howard saved Nick's life when he was mortally wounded. Nick had saved her life by bringing out the worst in her? She shivers at the thought. She wonders if she'll ever see Jimmy in hell? She shivers again. She tries and tries to put darkness aside but she knows it's there. Lurking. At the edge of her little world. She somehow knows its damp dark feelers are going to encroach again. How could that be? It's been more than two years now. What's the statute of limitations here? So much more at stake now. Little Joan. All her friends. The life she's found here. Or the life that's found her? Is she in the clear? Is it fate? Is there any such thing? Or do we make our own fate? Trying to occupy her mind otherwise, she switches on the radio as she works on last night's dishes. Some guy talks about the Mojave Desert; Captain Beefheart. "Fast and bulbous", "bulbous also tapered"; she smiles. Jimmy back in her mind. But then. The guy suddenly talks about "sidewinders" – a mean-tempered snake. A rattlesnake with a bad hangover. They can appear from nowhere or from shallow graves they dig for themselves in the desert sand. Waiting for their prey. Lucy freezes before she reaches for the radio "off" button. As she does so she knocks a mug to the floor and it shatters with the sound of cracked crash cymbal. Little Joan and Ronee look across. Ronee's eyes meet Lucy's and time stops for a long brief moment.

****

Jimmy English sits on the roof. Like he most often does. Lonely, tired, sad. No; not sad. He watches over Little Joan and Lucy. He sits in on Dirtkickers rehearsals and gigs. He makes up songs. He swoops over the streets of SF. He goes to ocean beach and loves to see the rollers surfing in. He sometimes looks for Felicia. He watches bands. He never gets tired of that. He goes to watch over his Mum. Sees his Dad too. He sees his Mum thinking of him. She sits in his bedroom at home in Manchester from time to time. She sends emails to Mike Remo. She loves to know how the Dirtkickers are getting along. She's been over three times now. Once for his funeral and twice more to see Little Joan. Lucy and Little Joan love her to pieces. She listens to his songs.

Jimmy is no wiser than he ever was. His new status in the afterlife has provided no answers to any of the machinations of the universes. It frustrates him. He has no idea how he can fly. No idea how he can see people he loves so clearly; yet they can't see him. Seeing Little Joan and Lucy more than makes up for that though. He is as happy as a ghost can be (he keeps making a mental note to write that song). Life (and death) move on.

He feels guilty when he thinks of Felicia. Even guiltier when he goes looking for her. He can't resist though. He runs fingers through her hair. Watches her walk. He runs and flies and dives into the waters of The Bay when she is with Richard Guillermo – fucking Rich Guy! He knows Felicia though. He knows what she is like. He laughed when she went home with Mike Remo after a Dirtkickers gig He loves Mike, he loves Felicia but he loves Little Joan and Lucy differently. Thoughts so confused. He is so so proud as Little Joan makes up her songs and dances. He's happy. Lonely but Happy.

Missing Her

https://badpeoplethemusical.bandcamp.com/track/missing-her

Missing her
I'm missing her

Light passes so slow
This is heaven – don't you know ?
She didn't make it
I don't think I can take it

I'm missing her
I'm missing her

The earth was too much for her
And she raised the temperature
Everything tempted her
That is what exempted her
She was perfect to me
Just a little wild you see
She had – imagination
Mine had its limitations
If she let me down – I don't care

I need her here – not there

Yeh missing her
I'm missing her

This is eternity
A long time to be lonely
I appealed truthfully
To the highest authority
But they got rules they rely upon
It's the same for everyone
A sad story for sure
It's just that it's the law
But
I'm missing her
I'm missing her
Not sure I can take this forever
I never was that clever
I'm thinking of busting out
She might be lonely
She might need my company
I made mistakes before
I can make some more
Do you know where I can find the backdoor?

Cos
I'm missing her...

Jimmy Smith longs for company. The more he thinks about it, he longs for Lucy's company. But then, he doesn't like that thought because Little Joan needs her Mum. He worries more than ever because he can't be there totally. His predicament worries him. Not because he might "go down" for what he's done but because Lucy might go down. Was her misdeed worse than his? The geezer had only broken her guitar? But, on the other hand, her evil was not pre-meditated? AND, it was a Gibson Nick Lucas that the "sonoffabitch" broke? Yes, he deserved it, any heavenly jury would forgive Lucy. His misdemeanour was a lot more serious? His was pre-meditated! In fact, he'd spent a long time meditating it!! There was no way he was gonna get a heavenly reward, but if he did, he would bust out to be with Lucy. Wow, they'd never let him back in after that? What the hell - he'd be with Lucy...and Felicia...she'd never get in!!! Let's face it we are all Bad People!

Chapter 2
Come Back When
(Your Soul Has Been Saved)

Deidre loads a trayful of IPA's, she smiles at Mike Remo as she sets them down on the table. Mike, TMan and TheGnome smile back. Lucy looks at them all – suddenly silenced? As Deidre retreats, Lucy smiles,

"Never known you three so quiet?"

The three Dirtkickers look at Lucy as if to say,

"What are you talking about?".

Lucy giggles as the moment passes. They raise their glasses,

"To Jimmy!".

Then the Skulk Rock Salute. They hold the moment. Mike speaks before Lucy's sadness takes hold.

"Two gigs this weekend. We all ok on the setlists?", they all nod.

TMan enthuses,

"I love that "Everyone Leaves" song. One of Jimmy's best."

"Pity we never got round to it when he first brought it?"

"He brought so many!"

Mike looks at Lucy. He sees sadness drift into her expression and moves the conversation on.

"Did you get in touch with that guy you know in Oregon? Long time since we had any gigs up 101."

"English Bob. I did he's working on a venue. We can trust him Mike. Maybe he will visir SF and you can meet him."

TheGnome chips in,

"Hey Mike, I saw Marv the other day and he was askin for a gig?"

"I'll give him a call and set it up."

The late set sun hits the point of the year and day where it sits atop the hill and fires red light directly into the bar. They watch the light sparkle and flicker through the cheap shit crystals of a skewed junk shop chandelier. The light show is suddenly extinguished by a large shape passing slowly outside the window. The Gnome is leaning back on his chair and, for some reason, he momentarily loses balance. He looks around nervously as he corrects himself. No-one else seems to notice. The shadow presently passes and as the light returns the double entrance doors begin to creak open. The first thing to appear is a wolf's head belt buckle, followed by a strained and stained T-shirt under a leather jacket the size of tent. A smiling face on a big round head ducks under the door and Lucy has to stop herself staring. The smiling face clocks The Dirtkickers and the mouth moves,

"Michael J Remo and his Shitkickers!!"
TMan sighs as The Gnome smiles at the apparition. Mike stares at the face for a silent moment, the whole bar watching. He lets the moment ride before replying,

"Tiny! Where you been? Your smile has not brightened my life for many a long day."

"I been up North Michael J."
TMan ventures,

"We thought you must be deceased Tiny?"

"Ain't no grave big enough to hold me – LowdownSound-Man", Tiny's smile broadens.

Mike Remo moves to the side and pulls up a stool inviting Tiny to sit. Tiny hooks a foot around a nearby stool and positions it next to the other stool before carefully placing his bulk between Mike and Lucy. As the spectral light dances over them both TMan is reminded of some kinda science fiction scene. Tiny looks down at Lucy,

"Hello young lady?", he smiles.
Lucy's mind flips, she suddenly remembers the inhabitants of Lincoln City insisting on calling her "young lady". Her thoughts whirl as her memory takes her back to her nightmare journey. She senses panic at the outskirts of her mind. Mike Remo breaks the silence,

"This is Lucy. She plays with the band now Tiny."

"Comprendez!", Tiny smiles. He looks back to Mike,

"Hey – I heard about Little Jimmy. Sad Mike. He was a sweet singer."

"Sure was Tiny".

Somehow a silence takes over. Jimmy floats by. Spectral lights dance over Lucy's face. Jimmy smiles.

Tiny breaks the silence, offering a hand to Lucy,

"Nice to meet you Lucy! Feel my gravity?"

Lucy ventures a hand that is immediately swallowed by Tiny's vast grip.

TheGnome smiles,

"That's a lot of gravity Tiny!"

"You always did warp space-time Tiny", adds Mike

"And you always warped singing Michael J!"

Deirdre now appears at Tiny's shoulder,

"You drinking little man or just here to bullshit?"

Tiny turns his head,

"Deirdre! I knew you couldn't resist my gravity either."

Deirdre puts two beers in front of Tiny and he smiles,

"You know you're still my favourite bar manager Deirdre! Wanna climb on board later?"

"I'll need Sherpa Tensing's help to climb on you Tiny!", she walks away, "I put the drinks on the shitkicker tab!".

The Gnome leans forward,

"Get in on back o' the queue Tiny boy!"

Somehow, Tiny's gravity is strangely reassuring and the assembled oddballs move into a conversation about the usual motorbikes and music. Tiny asks about Marv. He needs a new bike and will eventually need some work. Lucy begins to like Tiny and she finds his "gravity" comforting. She finds herself siding with him as he enthuses about Morrissey's singing,

"You don't get to fill stadiums without being a good singer! People describe him as a lyricist, which is fine, but he could sing the phone book and peops would love it"

Lucy jumps in,

"Damn right Tiny!"

The Gnome finishes a pint and slams the glass down,

"Best singer roulette – best singer roulette!!"

TMan giggles,

"Oh Christ here we go!"

Lucy looks across,

"And…errrrrrm………how does that work?"

"Easy – first person suggests a singer and the next person has to say a singer who's better. If you don't agree you can challenge and if you get a democratic majority from the others you get a point. If you don't, the person you challenged gets a point."

"Democracy eh? I love it"

"No-one can think of a better system Lucy!"

Lucy briefly considers expounding her theory that a benevolent dictator of supreme intelligence could be given total control but she figures a game of "Best Singer Roulette" might be more fun? She stares competitively at The Gnome,

"Who starts?"

"I do. I suggested it!"

The table falls quiet as The Gnome retreats to silence and a question mark above his head signifies his thought cardinals are in session. Eventually,

"Tom Jones", The Gnome slowly turns his stare to TMan,

"Tom Fuckin' Jones?! Too easy…", he thinks, "errrrrrm…Rod Stewart!!", he turns to Lucy.

Lucy suddenly feels pressure,

"Ohhhhh so it's a Brit's round is it?"

"Not necessarily Missy"

"Morrissey!", she blurts, turning her stare to Tiny who begins to twist his mustache whiskers. His eyes twinkle and he stares down at Lucy. The two guys on the next table are now listening intently. They smile at Tiny muttering,

"challenge, challenge!"

Tiny thinks carefully before slowly speaking,

"Dav-id Bow-ie!"

TMan is next and he immediately "challenges". The Gnome commentates,

"TMan with a challenge, TMan with a challenge, TMan with a CHALLENGE……………", as he gets louder Deirdre looks across from the bar and rolls her eyes upwards, smiling at new customers.

Meanwhile, Mike Remo goes around the assembled participants and eventually announces,

"As electoral official I can officially announce that Stephen Patrick Morrissey wins the vote and is declared the round 1 best singer and the point goes to… TMan!"

TMan stands and takes a bow. The Gnome announces,

"TMan to start round 2."

"Frank Sinatra!", he pumps his fist as if he'd run the length of the pitch for an intercept touchdown, looking around at all the others. Mike Remo is next and he stares at TMan,

"Mr SmartButt TMan eh? No-one can beat Frank?…?"

TMan smiles and intensifies his fist pump until Mike continues,

"…except …maybe…Bob Dylan?"

TMan is deflated and intensified,

"CHALL – ENGE!"

The tension mounts as Mike collects votes,

"Lucy?", she thinks hard, amazed at how much concentration she gives to this bullshit,

"Bob!"

They all laugh.

"Tiny?"

Tiny twiddles his mustache again before earnestly responding,

"Frank."

Mike turns to "other guy number 1", he responds immediately,

"Frank."

Other guy number 2 winks as he smiles at Lucy,

"Bob!"

Lucy gives him a big smile and fist pump.

Mike looks over to The Gnome who relishes the spotlight. He milks the moment with an impression of Auguste Rodin's Thinker before,

"Welllllll…I gotta say…Bob!"

Now it's Mike Remo's turn for a victory salute. TMan doesn't readily buy it though,

"How the fuck do you work that out Gnome?"

"Easy – Bob only got famous in the first place because there is a whole world in his voice – and that's just his first voice. Then he had all his other voices man!"

"Frank had a first voice too and then he developed?"

"Yeh but Bob did it over and over. The '66 voice. The sweet country voice. The '70s voices!"

TMan feigns disbelief,

"Bullshit The Gnome! You're just siding with Mike – like you always do – fuckin' yes-man!"

The assembly stare at TMan and slap themselves laughing at his petulance. TheGnome continues the wind up,

"I particularly love his early voice eh Mike?"

"For sure The Gnome!"

TMan is gone. Red in the face by now. Everyone loving it. The Gnome up on his feet and breaks into song in some bullshit Bob Dylan caricature voice, whilst breaking into one of his dances.

> "As we marched down
> As we marched down
> As we marched down to Fennario
> The Captain fell in love
> With a lady like a dove
> And the name she had was
> Pretty Peggy-O"

Mike Remo drums on the table, everyone smiles, TheGnome continues,

> "The Lieutenant he is gone
> The Lieutenant he is gone
> The Lieutenant he is gone – Pretty Peggy-O
> The Lieutenant he is gone
> Long gone
> He's ridin' down to Texas – WITH THE RODEO"

The Gnome gets loud as he transmutes his dance into a rodeo riding dance. Tiny's eyes water with laughter now until the moment is abruptly ended by Deirdre's authority,

"Gnome-IO – getting loud-IO!!"

The Gnome slowly de-escalates his singing and dancing,

"OK Deirdre-O!"

He smiles at everyone's beaming faces,

"I'll get the beers in", before sashaying over to the bar as Deirdre gives him her disapproving eye.

As the Dirtkickers, Tiny and others eventually spill out to the street everyone is IPA happy. The two guys from the bar wander off down the hill. Tiny gives a BIG hug to everyone and promises to attend a Dirtkickers gig as soon as. Mike reminds them of a rehearsal tomorrow and TMan puts his arm around The Gnome's shoulder,

"Sorry about calling you a Drummer-Brain."
TheGnome giggles,

"None taken my friend. Anyway, it's a compliment!"

"Are we walking? Or a cab?"
TheGnome looks down at the ground, with hands in pockets, as if searching for words. The three other Dirtkickers are now waiting, as if for a newsflash, or a request to borrow money, or a suggestion to do a Frank Sinatra song. He eventually speaks,

"You know what? I kinda promised to help Deirdre clear up", his voice tailing off at the end of his sentence. Mike breaks the ensuing silence,

"Sure thing Gnome-IO! See you tomorrow. Save some energy!"
The Gnome breaks for the bar door and is disappeared. The remaining Dirtkickers wander off up the hill giggling.

They leave Lucy at the end of her street and she inwardly laughs to herself as she begins the slow walk from the crossway to her door. She avoids looking at the bright yellow sign saying "Dead End"; a silly superstition she had developed. Jimmy had told her about his superstitious constraints and it had made her laugh. Now he'd gone she found them populating her mind more often than she'd like. She looked up at stars through windows between the drift clouds; there wasn't much breeze tonight. Jimmy in her mind. He'd've loved the Best-Singer-Roulette! She knows he would. She smiles. She loves Mike and TMan and The Gnome. She figures there is not an ounce of evil in them. She brings the evil to this band? She shivers. For some reason she thought confesses to Jimmy. It's the IPA she thinks. Where does Deirdre get her beer? As she approaches the house, she looks up at the roof. A bright star sits just above her ridge tiles. She thinks of BorisTheCranium and giggles. Maybe she'd see him again if English Bob could fix up a gig and Mike could schedule a mini-tour up 101. She fumbles for her key and looks once more at the star before entering the shadow of the porch.

Inside the house it's quiet. She looks in on Little Joan sleeping quietly with arms flung out at random. She blows her a kiss. She makes a coffee and sits in the lounge. Nick Lucas begs to be picked up and she plays quietly. A star flickers outside her window and she smiles to be under its countenance. Nick's voice calms her, excites her and takes her to their special place. A place she shared with James, however briefly. Nick speaks in the voice of Bob as she idly strums a D chord and sings some Mr Tambourine. She giggles again (IPA) as she remembers what Tiny had said to her in the bar earlier; that a journalist once asked Bob "Is it true your new song is called Mr Tambourine?". Bob had replied, "It's Mr Tamboureeeeeen MAN!" and the journalist had said, "That's what I said – Mr Tambourine!". Lucy stifles a laugh. She channels her pride at proving to the assembled jury at the bar that Bob is the best singer. He is too. She remembers his voices all the way back to early Bob. She loved his early fingerpicking songs. He didn't have Nick then, of course. He had a Gibson J50. Didn't matter, Nick sounds sweet as she starts picking. She wasn't too good at that, but James had been teaching her. Well, he had encouraged her. Convinced her that audiences loved it – they do too. She thinks of The Gnome and hopes he's having fun with Deirdre! Men! She sings to herself and once again time stands still and soon she is looking at a scribbled song on the pages of her trusty notebook.

Come Back When

https://badpeoplethemusical.bandcamp.com/track/come-back-when

When I spent long nights drinking
And all the women were smiling
And my mind began to sinking
Under dark thoughts I was thinking

And now I know the devil is deceiving
Told me only so much time until I'm dead
And told her I was leaving
And this is what she said

Come back when – you learned how to behave
Come back when – your soul has been saved
Come back before – you're lying in your grave
Oh – oh come back then

She said, go to your whore - Don't darken my door
You didn't break no law - So stay away some more
Go have your fun and think what you have done
Your soul is gone no matter how far you run

And then the sun sank down
The sky so grey and cold
Cruel wind circled round
Her words biting at my soul

Come back when – you're counted amongst men
Come back when – You're sane again
Come back when – you think of your children
Oh – oh come back then

Sin is such a tragic trap
Sometimes there's no turnin back
You can sink so fast
If you fall for all that

Because the devil made temptation
It is his most deadly weapon
The dreams that steal your imagination
It's how he ruins every nation

Come back when – you're long forgotten
Come back then on your own – And see your children grown
Come back when – You're born again

Oh – oh come back then
Come back when – you learned how to behave
Come back when – your soul has been saved
Come back before – you're lying in your grave
Oh – oh come back then

She sighs and wishes James would "Come Back"! She wonders if her soul will be saved? Could it EVER be saved? How many commandments has she trampled to death?

Lucy Smith sets Nick Lucas down in his corner of the room. As she closes her notebook she thinks of Howard and Elizabeth. She looks out at the star and thinks of James. She sets a kiss off into the night sky and it floats on up – towards her star. She loves San Francisco. She thanks her lucky star that she made that fateful snap decision to set "The Dog" on course for SF. She could have gone anywhere but not in her wildest dreams would it have turned out like it did. Some good, some bad. So much has happened since. She has a feeling that so much more is going to happen? She hopes it will be more good stuff. What can she do? Destiny has brought her here. The destiny star is in her sky and she is looking down its laser barrel. (Fucking IPA!).

James wipes a tear from his eye and thinks of Little Joan.

Chapter 3
Speedy Cop

Lieutenant Lathan of the SFPD wakes to a bright spring day.
He thinks to himself, "Lieutenant D Lathan!" Promotion. It
eventually happened. He knew that "playing it by the book"
would eventually pay off. He has always been "hard but fair".
Unequivocal. He was going to bring all those qualities to his
new position. He feels glad to be starting a new job and getting
away from his previous colleagues. They bored him. Their
constant cutting of corners. Taking the interstate without
understanding the highways. Not for him. He has one rule. "If
they break the law, they take the fall." He could never understand why others seemed reluctant to press that point. Life
would be simpler. One rule for all too. The Commander had
told him he would be a "Lone Wolf" in the new post. That
doesn't bother him one little bit. He has felt like that all his
career. Anyway, he can call on help from any other department
as he sees fit. The Commander has given him that authority.
Responsibility for his own actions at last. No-one to hinder him
now. He looks out of the transport window onto the city. His
domain.

He gets off the BART and proudly walks a couple of blocks the
hill to his new office building on Bryant Street. He breaths fresh
spring air as he scans for any hint of lawlessness on the San
Franciso streets.

The Office Commander welcomes him and walks him along a
corridor to his new private office and then takes him around the
corner to meet Jane his acting administrator. Jane is obviously
busy and gives him a smile and shakes his hand,
    "I put the first batch of case files on the shelf in your office.
If you need more let me know?"

She quickly resumes her work and Lathan finds himself sat
alone in his office. He takes time and sits looking around the

office before walking over to the pile of case files. He picks a few from the top. "Hardest job is starting!", as his father always used to say. Setting the files down on his desk he opens the top one. He scans and quickly closes it. The process repeats a few more times until he opens a file that seems to grab his attention.

****

"Speedy" Cop, otherwise known as Seraphina Coppola, doesn't mind her nickname. She catches more traffic offenders with her trusty speed gun than any other officer out there so there is nothing sarcastic about the nickname "Speedy". She likes it. She is popular and always up for a laugh and a few beers with her friends. She never takes her job too seriously but she loves that she had the best percentage of expensive car owners in her "hit list". Her catchphrase was "Don't want a Porsche, Don't need one, but you been hit, by my Speed Gun." Nothing dampens Speedy's enthusiasm.

This spring afternoon she slumps at her desk. She sees a fluffy white skip by through her only source of daylight; a high window to the cluttered office she shares with two deadhead new recruits. These guys are not cut out for the job. They got no life force they can divert to the task. They don't understand that dumbhead drivers who figure speed is cool are dangerous to innocent people. Every needless death or injury due to road traffic is cursed by Speedy. She runs a personal vendetta against shitheads in sports cars or SUVs. Especially BM-fucking-Ws. Anyway, this particular afternoon she welcomes being in the office alone so she can process the evidence from her speed gun. As her office door slams behind her she spins and draws her speed gun holding it two handed and pointing it at the door,

"You're looking at the most powerful speed gun in San Francisco – you feel lucky? ...punk!"

(Pause)

"Or should I save time and just give you what you deserve?"

(Pause)

"Did your Daddy buy you that Porsche?"

(Pause)

"Well I'm gonna bury your spoiled ass in it!"

She fires at her imaginary quarry and re-holsters her trusty weapon. She giggles to herself and then sighs,

"They need me on more complicated cases. Traffic violations are too easy."

She knows she'll get a break one day. Just got to keep her head down and work. One day she'll get that career break and then she can bust even bigger criminals in their BM-fucking-Ws!

****

Lathan hates drugs. He hates the obscene quantities of money associated with this business. And so, he greedily turn pages of the file he now examines. A 4x4 High Roof Mercedes Sprinter conversion. This was the van of his dreams. He could tour his own magnificent country in one of these when he retires. German engineering is so far ahead of the rest of the world. He looks at the pictures of it wrecked and tumbled at the base of sandy cliffs. Three bodies on a beach some 20 yards from the van. Staggered footprints leading to the bodies. Each killed with a shotgun blast; one at close range. Four more sets of footprints on the sand and motorbike tracks along the sand. Traces of cocaine around the bodies. Easy to see why this was written up as a drug related incident. Jake Snake, Edward Snake and Simon Snake, all from out of town. Montana? What were these guys doing in San Francisco? Drugmen around here would not use such a van. They'd use a Chevvy. This must've been a drugs buy gone wrong? Were these guys trying to buy drugs? They were some kind of musicians after all? But why the heavy weaponry the police found? A Mini Uzi? These had an automatic fire rate of 900 rounds a minute. Hardly the weapon musicians would carry? Too many questions. The more he reads the more he realises that this case is unfinished. In fact, it's not even started. He can break this case and gain some credit with narcotics. He knows what has happened here; it's an oddball case; nobody downtown with enough time to devote. This is the kind of case to start his new career with a breakthrough.

The morning hours pass. Lathan chain drinks coffee reading the file notes. There's only been minimal investigation so far. The van has Montana plates and no-one has even been to interview next of kin. Strangely, no next of kin has been to identify bodies. Lathan spares a thought for the busy officers in Narcotics. He decides to pick up this ball and run with it. All the way to the End Zone. This needs some real detective work to tie up loose ends. He decides to see what movements have been associated with the van. It's an unusual vehicle for criminal activities for sure. He walks out of his office to catch Jane the administrator. He stands at her desk shuffling until she looks up from her computer screen. She looks at him without speaking. He breaks the awkward silence,

"Can you get me someone in Highways and Traffic?"

"They're on the system."

Jane looks back down at her screen. End of conversation. Lathan begins to speak but there are no words. His mouth slowly closes again and he retreats to his office. He closes his door quietly, at pains not to show his annoyance. He turns to his computer screen and finds the number for the traffic department. The puter throws up a list of names. His eyeballs suddenly become static as the name Coppola S jumps out of the screen. They called her "Speedy Cop" at the academy. Oh wow, she is gorgeous. His mind wanders to how he used to sit in lectures and watch sunlight illuminating her dark hair. He sings to himself; "Her dark hair could weave a snare – that I would one day rue." Maybe it would be an idea to re-kindle their relationship (although he isn't sure she ever noticed him) and chase up some information on this "SnakeVan". She would notice him now he has a promotion and a Department. She might even be better company than Jane – there was a good chance of that! Lathan notices his fingers trembling as he dials her number.

****

Speedy watches a cloud drift by outside her office window as she downloads her recent haul of speeding offence data. She watches a container ship move slowly across the waters. It inches across to The Port of Oakland across the bay. She loves the sound of shipping on misty days. Distant foghorns; distant places the ships have been? What cargoes they will discharge? Exotic spices for Chinatown? Containers full of cheap Chinese goods? They might be cheap but that don't make them poor quality. Her ex-boyfriend reckoned he had a Chinese Les Paul guitar that was way better than his bandmate's real Gibson. Where would the drugs be hidden? She could find them! She's wasted in traffic enforcement. Speedy's mind wanders. She wonders if her law enforcement career is marooned in the traffic backwater? Fucking cars – she hates cars. People think it's their human right to ride around in cars. Have they not heard of global warming? They don't care about the state of the planet after they've gone? Not even for their kids and their grandkids? That's human nature for sure; we need less selfish fuckers and more selfless fuckers! Simple! She enjoys her work but she feels she has more to offer than just indicting pain-in-the-butt rich people in stupid cars. She resolves to talk to her supervisor about any possibility of a transfer when there is a knock at her door and Lieutenant David Lathan enters her office. He had rung earlier and said they had been at the academy together. Speedy looks him over and quickly realises she doesn't actually remember him at all. Lathan approaches, hand outstretched,

"Officer Coppola. Good to see you again."

"Yes, you too."

"How is life in Traffic Enforcement?"

Speedy hears a slight tone of sarcasm in his voice; she puts it down to her own sensitivities.

"It's fun. Seven butthole motherfuckers in Porsches yesterday. Booked! Just gotta file the evidence now!"

Lathan is rocked back a little by her vehemence, eventually managing a smile.

"I'm in charge of the cold case review project now!"

"Super cool."

Lathan smiles at her enthusiasm and continues,

"Some tough cases and I'm pretty much alone", he pauses for effect, "...could do with some help with vehicle information?"

"I'll try my best. I know the information systems here inside out."

Lathan shows Speedy the info on SnakeVan. She quickly logs the plates and chassis numbers and gives him basic information. His tone is elevated now,

"We know all that. I was wondering if you had any info on previous involvement of this vehicle in offences or any means of checking movements of this vehicle prior to the date the owners were murdered."

"Murdered? That's terrible!"

"It happens Officer Coppola. Down to us to put the headshits away!"

Speedy stifles a giggle at his clumsy use of bad language. Somehow it didn't fit with his character. Too much bad language about these days for sure. All down to the motherfuckers who make movies and modern film stars. Eddie fuckin Murphy? You wouldn't get John Wayne coming out with dirtmouth shit like that. She warms to Lathan; just a little.

"Yeh – let's put the suckercocks away! And soon!"

Lathan doesn't know whether to laugh, smile, ignore, rebuke. He doesn't do any of those and just carries on,

"If I could map movements of this van before the murder incident then I might be able to locate their business associates. This may have been a deal gone wrong?"

"You mean drugs?"

"Yeh.....", he sighs, "headbutt drug dealers if ever there were any. Probably deserve what they got. I don't give a..........", he pauses, "I don't care about that. I just see it as a possible means of interring some more arsepain drug dealers", he catches a wave of enthusiasm and tries to surf it a while, "Put as many of the fuckermothers away as soon as possible!"

His voice tails off as Speedy stares at him open mouthed for a long second,

"Too right Lieutenant!"

Speedy Coppola sees a chance here. Her mind is always alert. This guy is naïve and needs help. This could be her chance to make a move outside of Traffic Enforcement.

"Can I get to see the vehicle?"

"Well, the incident was over a year ago. Homicide and narcotics have been over it."

"They don't understand vehicles like I do. Maybe I can find something they missed. They are busy guys!"

Lathan recognises the coded language for "they don't care" as the same thought pattern he had followed a few days ago.

"Sure, you might be lucky and find it out at the SFPD scrap lot."

"Great – leave it with me and I'll get back to you. Can you have a word with my Commander and get him to release me for this ……investigation?"

"Consider it done", Lathan gains in confidence, revels in his own presence. He adds,

"Give me a call and come over to my office. Lunch is on me."

Lathan leaves feeling good, feeling like it all went well. His first collaboration on a case. If he can just identify potential perps by an aggregation of evidence and good old deductive reasoning it would be a "feather in his cap" for sure. Officer Coppola – Speedy – seems efficient and somebody he could work with. She's also a very good looking woman. He skips on the sidewalk.

Speedy reads this new situation and relishes the freedom it could bring her. This could be her chance? Lieutenant Lathan seems very straight but what the hell. She could soon be instrumental in drug busts and murder cases, aswell as kicking ass for traffic offences. They're all "fuckermothers!" She giggles at Lathan's mixed up swearing. What the hell? He seems harmless and he could be her ticket to more interesting police work. She brings her thoughts back down to earth; saying to herself that "police work is hard work". It's not like the movies. Life isn't like the "shitbull" movies. She sits and turns to her computer screen and sings to herself, "I'm better off in my dreams!"

Better Off In My Dreams

https://badpeoplethemusical.bandcamp.com/track/better-off

I didn't shoot no-one in Reno
I don't want to see anyone die
I'll tell you one thing about me you already know
I'm just a boring guy

I'm a hound dog for your love
You're no angel from above
But I'm inconsolable
You're so unobtainable

Better off in my dreams
Better off in my dreams
Better off in my dreams
Better off in my dreams

And once I thought I saw yer
Across the misty skies
I'm always looking for yer
When I open my eyes

And once I thought I saw yer
Across a crowded hazy bar
I'm always looking for yer
Wherever you are

And I still prefer fiction
There's a good life in dreams
They tell me I should be moving on
But I like it 'round here

I didn't shoot no-one in Reno – I just let him be
If I wanna see somebody die – I switch on my TV
They got knives and bombs and machine guns
They got machetes
Yeh – if I wanna see somebody die

I turn on my TV
Any night

Granpa died last week
They buried him in the rocks
He stood next to me at his funeral
And told me the afterlife sucks

He said......
you're better off in your dreams......
better off in your dreams........

And I was walking in Memphis
I'm an Elvis obsessive
On a rock and roll chain gang
All of my life

I'm Better off in my dreams
Better off in my dreams
I'm Better off in my dreams
Better off in my dreams

Chapter 4
Skulk Lock

Ho Chi Minimum appears from between an array of cooling condensers and kitchen extraction units at the rear of his terrace of restaurants and above his lowdown basement "Dive Bar". It's become something of a Skulk Rock hotspot since word got round about Mike Remo shooting Les Paul. Ho walks over as The Dirtkicker Van pulls into the rear loading area.

"Mike Lemo – Skulk Lock Lules!"

"Sure does Ho – locked and loaded!"

Ho continues,

"Locking out tonight Thunderman! The Gnome and the lovely Lucy!"

He hugs them all. There is nothing not to like about Ho. The gig over two years ago when Mike shot Jake Snake's Les Paul guitar has developed a legendary status amongst fans of the Dirtkickers. The fans now call themselves "Skulks" and even have their own 'zine called "Skulk Zone". Along with "KOFR", is their oft-quoted mantra.

"Dlinks are on me Kickers!", Ho is as enthusiastic as ever, if not more so.

The Dirtkickers are well used to this venue and soon carry in the necessary equipment and get set up. It's an easy gig as there is always a well maintained house drum kit and PA set up. They run a quick sound check and retire to the side room to wait for punters to begin arriving. Ho's waitresses bring the jugs over and Ho joins the group.

"How is business Ho?"

"Dive Bar doing vely well Mike Lemo, thanks to Skulk Lock!"

Thunderman enthuses now,

"It's the new wave Ho!"

Mike Remo knows what is coming. He knows Ho always remembers Jimmy and he knows that will get in Lucy's mind. Mike smiles across the table at Lucy before Ho speaks,

"We all miss Jimmy English here", Ho looks sad.

Mike quickly replenishes all the glasses and raises his,
"To the Limey Bastard – Wish he was here!"

What they don't know, although some might suspect, is that Jimmy English IS there. He hovered in a few moments ago and now circles the table. He looks at Lucy, smiling, wishing, hoping, pleading they can be together once more. He misses gigs more than anything. This is torture for him. Gigs at Ho's were always such fun, except the last one when he was ill and everything seemed to get out of control suddenly. Now he has the torture of seeing all the people who really matter to him in the situation of doing what he wanted to do all his life.

They all raise their glasses, slam them down and execute the Skulk Rock salute. Mike takes Lucy's eye and nods. They recognise the moment before Mike speaks,
"Hey Ho...................(laugh)..........Hey Ho, we do need to get to work on our set list."
Ho retreats as Mike gets out a pen and paper from his trusty leather brief case. The Gnome requests "Whores and Dwarves" and Mike moves his gaze to Thunderman.

James giggles at The Gnome's suggestion. He always loved that song. The Gnome always drives it so well – he loves The Gnome.

Thunderman requests his song "Fall"…………..

James smiles. He remembers bass line that Thunderman came up with for that song. He thinks back to the exact moment in The Dirtkickers practice suite, all those years ago, when he saw Mike Remo smile and then he first knew he could create songs other people could like. A Skulk classic for sure. This was the first song of his that The Dirtkickers ever did. He remembers the elation of knowing his band mates liked his song and, even better, how they all had ideas for it. Creation! One of the best feelings in the world.

He looks at Lucy as it's her turn to choose. His sadness sweeps over him. He wants to hold her and Little Joan. He is the proudest ghost in Rodgers and Hammersteindome.

Lucy thinks hard, her eyes moist. He looks deep into them. Lucy chooses "The Cowboy Drunk."

(If a ghost can stagger) James staggers. He remembers singing Lucy that song in his apartment. He doesn't realise the Dirtkickers had moved it into the set. He remembers making up that song. He had received a letter from his old friend Pete Royle back in Manchester. How Pete had been to a Leonard Cohen concert and none of the gang would go with him so Pete had gone alone; described himself as a Lone Wolf! James would've gone with him like a shot. Anyway, somehow that one thought had been enough to trigger a song. It brings back Manchester memories. James makes a mental note that "Manchester Memories" would be a possible song title. He files it, as a ghost tear runs down his cheek. A chord also rings in his mind; he remembers Lucy telling him that she sometimes got the feeling when a song appeared that a ghost had visited and donated the song – somehow? Seemed crazy at the time but she believed it. The thought crystallizes that here he was in the perfect position to test that theory. Maybe this was a way to send communications. He'd try anything – so much he wanted to say – needed to say. Problem is, he thinks, he won't have ghosts visiting him unless it's in person and that might destroy the magic? He suggests to himself that there might be ghosts from the next next world who would visit him. His brain begins to hurt. Fuckin fuck!

Mike Remo smiles. Lost in remembrances himself. He remembers the time he first met Jimmy at an open mic. Jimmy was nervous and lonely. Mike had not been struck by his songs or his singing at that stage but by the fact that he was the other side of the world from his home and so obviously alone and, therefore, songs must burn in him. Little did he know how much they did burn in him. He thinks of all the times they had taken long road trips back from gigs or on tours and he'd be driving with Jimmy sat wide awake while TMan and The Gnome were asleep in back of the van. Mike remembers Jimmy being transfixed by the American landscape. Flat-Top mountains: "We don't have them in England!". Lonesome Highways: "We don't have them in England!" Jimmy would go on and on about everywhere in England being crowded. His nightmare was always being stuck in a line. He would say, "Too many people in England. There's space over here." Mike remembers Jimmy talking about a friend of his dying as they stared at the highway on a long drive back to SF from Bakersfield. Their agent had booked some crazy distance between venues. He remembers Jimmy telling him about that song and somehow it pops into his mind. Mike Remo thinks to himself, "Our lives are only footprints in the snow."

Inside My Head

https://badpeoplethemusical.bandcamp.com/track/inside-my-head

There's a place – inside my head
Where some treasured thoughts are kept
Of things you said
And things we did
Even though – we were only kids

Remember that time we went to Wolves
And we decided not to drink
And then you told me how the world revolves
As you puked into the kitchen sink
And then you pushed it down the hole
And John Richards scored the goal

And you brought me Astral Weeks
And changed my life around
You're a ballerina on big feet
Whenever I spin those sounds
Boring people never confess their dreams
But you - ventured into - the slipstream

And one last time in the Auld Hoos
Why did I wait so long
I could listen to your stories
All night long
I wish you hadn't gone
I could stay with you for days
And piss the weeks and months away

But time was too much distance – don't you know
And our lives are only footprints - in the snow

Dark air is blowing
Blue skies are falling
As time dims away
Faint stars still glowing
Old light is crawling
Around from day to day

New glasses show me ghosts you know
But that is why I need them most - as I go
Driving home into the dark
With a busted beat up heavy heart

It's a - cliché I know
But I don't care – it's what I want to say you know
G, C and D you know
But I don't care – it's what I want to play you know

As Mike Remo suggests the song James immediately remembers the same drive. He loves mike Remo. They used to talk about the old west, new west, music, physics, more music. James blesses the day he walked into that open mic and fell under Mike's spell. He found home with The Dirtkickers. Skulk Rock was his foundation all those years. He remembers his mother once saying he could never make a living playing the guitar. He corrects himself, she had said it was "highly unlikely he would ever make a living playing" the guitar. Well he'd put his money on an outside chance and it had paid off. Paid off big style. There's more important stuff in that life than money and houses and holidays and "stuff". His Mum would have been delighted to admit she was wrong though because his Mum had always been supportive. Seems so long ago now. He is glad to know his Mum seems happy and has even been over to see Little Joan a few times. Mike Remo has seen to that.

James watches the venue fill. It warms his soul that Skulk is getting more and more popular. Must be down to Lucy (he thinks). Well she is a bit on the gorgeous side. He smiles as he watches a group of "skulkers" sharing "The Salute". They circle their faces and heads in an accelerating upwards spiral until their clenched fists make perfect landings on top of their heads. James remembers inventing the salute in Deirdre's Bar with TMan and The Gnome one November night. Oh how he would love a taste of IPA right now? He sees The Dirtkickers rise from their table and move through the rear door to the stage.

As Mike Remo and Lucy Smith reach the front of stage and adjust their mics the assembled crowd begin the salutes. It looks like a ripple across a sea of heads. Lucy plugs in a battle scarred black telecaster. She hits a big overdrive chord and her amp shimmers.

James Smith smiles. Oh wow, that's nice. She always said she wanted an old Tele. Unusual with the rosewood fingerboard. Is that a humbucker fitted in the neck position? Could be one of those Valco reissue types wound by a guy up in Portland. James loves the axe. It suits her, visually and sound wise. Way to go Ms Smith. He could look at guitars for eternity. He probably will, he sighs.

The Dirtkickers kick into "Nothing You Can Do". Oh Christ, he remembers that song. He'd been diagnosed by Doc Charlie and had a calling to go see The Ocean – explain that? Anyway, the song had come to him. One of his best. Mike takes the vocal and Lucy nails a guitar break; kicking on an overdrive pedal and driving her 6L6 power valves. The best sound in rock and roll – ask Neil Young!

It's Lucy's first gig with her new (old) Telecaster. She is nervous. She has been using James' old Harmony Stratotone but it is getting a little frail. She loves that guitar and will be heartbroken if it gets broken or stolen so she has invested in the ultracool look (and sound) of a vintage Telecaster. This one could take being dropped or falling over and will stay in tune better too. As it comes to the guitar break in their first number she stands on her overdrive pedal and palm mutes the strings. James had taught her that. As the band takes it down behind her she hears the Tele ring loud and clear. The sound makes her want more. It feeds her confidence. She likes it. She loves it! She is surfing in a feedback loop of energy. She builds the solo and wazzes in some jazzy (dis)chords as a climax. She sees Mike notice and look over at her. He smiles. Tonight feels good. For some reason her mind flashes back to the moment she decided to head for San Francisco. She was sat in The Dog; frightened, scared; alone, until Morrissey came on the radio. Best decision she ever made. SF had turned out good. Mike Remo's intervention at her first foray into SF Open Mic Bars; then finding James. In that moment, just after her guitar break, she sees him. At least she thinks she does. She staggers momentarily. Mike notices. She blinks and looks again at the back of the room where he had seemed to be. Stood on something as he was above the crowd. Keeeerrrrrist, how much IPA had she swallowed? She can't find him now as she stares to the back of the venue, her eyes searching the alleyways of the shadows as they open and close with the flow of people.

The gig takes over. Lucy lost in her performance. The Dirtkicker's songs tonight somehow more emotional and the crowd respond. It seems to get to them on a different level. Word seems to spread somehow and more people expand the crowd. Lucy sees a sea of heads. She loves it. Strange how thoughts come in the middle of songs though. She thinks of Little Joan, as always but now she sees James or at least she begins to imagine his presence? Later, on a longer number TheGnome and TMan take it down to a low groove and she suddenly finds herself at her mic rapping words she had never written before,

I'm looking from a window but I can't see no trees
I'm in a starlight city in the land of luxury
A woman in a fur coat walking down the street
She got the all light in all her eyes but she can't see me

James watches and nearly falls from the air. Those are lyrics he was putting together in his mind this week. How did Lucy get them? Somehow, he doesn't feel quite so alone in the crowd now. Not quite as if he doesn't exist. He floats to the ceiling to think.

Mike Remo takes the vocal on the next song. He looks out over the crowd thinking to himself, "Skulk IS the next wave – no bullshit!" As this thought passes, his sensors detect a crowd ripple; at first he thinks it must be some outbreak of dancing at the rear. That's always a good sign. A positive groove indicator for sure. This time though, the singularity seems to move slowly, inexorably towards the front. A shaft of light momentarily reflects from dark hair. A strange dark, it seems to reflect all colours like some kind of black body that suck in light and re-radiates it as light cocktails guaranteed to intoxicate. It's Felicia! A heavenly brass section blows a fanfare. The sun rises over a perfect tropical island. His first taste of IPA after 7 lost lifetimes in a desert on a distant planet. Mike feels a rush. Sugar rush, IPA rush, speed rush – all rushes at once. He looks across at TMan. He has noticed too. His bass drops into a groove, his fingers on autopilot. The Gnome and the crowd respond. They fall and rise. TGnome and TMan control the groove. It's a great groove from Planet Skulk but Mike also knows their sound so well and he can tell that they too have picked up Felicia on their radar. The ripple is the crowd parting as her aura affects the people in her zone. This is the fifth force of nature and it will take more than quantum theory to explain it. The best brains on the planet had better get working.

James watches Lucy from his position near Ho's ceiling. He watches her movement, her fingers and her hair swaying under the photon bombardment of Ho's atmospheric lighting. This truly is the centre of the Skulkverse. Like Mike Remo, a few photon-metres previously, James notices the groove modulation and then the "disturbance" and then Felicia! He falls to the floor, his gravity shields disrupted. How the fuck does that work? There are more mysteries of the universe of the next world than in the last one. There will be no rest for physicists. He finds himself lying at the feet of Skulkers. He thinks of laughing but his mind so devoted to regaining an upright position he swims in his aether for an eternity. Eventually his navigation systems regain some control and he moves towards her. He circles her, he can't resist. He feels guilty as Lucy hits aggressive percussive dirt chords on her Telecaster. He sees Felicia look at Lucy. Does she sense his presence? He sees the line of her neck and cheeks and nose once again. The way she tosses her hair. Her fingers her hands. Intoxication and he is intoxicated. He cant help it. This is the finest work of creation. Sir Isaac Newton, JMW Turner, Rembrandt and Vermeer and an army of similar could never get close. "She's delicate and seems like Vermeer" – is that a Bob Dylan line? Even if Bob joined that army they couldn't get anywhere near to this masterpiece of creativity. A singularity for sure. Anyway, wasn't it "She's delicate and seems like the mirror"? That's a line that had always fascinated James from way back and fuelled his interest in the mythical land of America. How can they pronounce "mirror" like "meerrr"? The young James had always thought America only existed in the movies. John Wayne could never really exist. He'd never seen flat top mountains or red dirt deserts or giant redwoods or buildings that pieced the stratosphere. How could they really exist? Now he knew different. The hair. Oh the hair. He stares. "Her dark hair might weave a snare" – this was a snare he would hurl himself into. He'd start a run up from the other side of the galaxy with the destination as the heart of her snare. Set the navigation systems - ETA as soon as possible.

Lucy Smith also notices Felicia's entry to the venue. Her eyes follow progress through the crowd and she also notices the band shift the groove. She also radars Mike glancing across to Thunderman. That's about when she puts jigsaw thoughts together and realises who this is. Her expression hardens. She knows of the legendary Felicia but she has never seen her before. It's a subject she has not addressed her mind to since the last times with James. She looks away, then looks back. Then – their eyes meet. A conduit is established; information passes; it's encrypted and impossible to translate to words. Lucy goes back to her business. So do the rest of The Dirtkickers. They kick the gig up a notch and the atmosphere simmers. Once again Lucy's stare pierces the shadows of the room. This time her expression has changed. Her gaze is like the FBI closing in. CIA Black Ops on the case. Her mental SWAT team on red alert. She is set to defend the homeland. Homeland Security. She has a license to kill. She has killed before. That thought bounces around her skull as if an evil spirit in her head trying to unleash itself on the outside world. She fights to control it –

the future of mankind is at stake and she is a defender. God says to The Devil "You really wanna try that Pal?"

The gig continues to rise until Ho gives Mike the sign to wind things up. The Dirtkickers play their "last song" and then their encore. They return the Skulk Salute to the audience and depart the stage. Mike catches Felicia's eye and points to the door to the side room. She nods. Ho has left a large jug for the band and they flop, apart from The Gnome who brings his strange dance to the party. The Dirtkickers leave him to it. As he pirouettes past the side door it opens and Felicia appears in front of him. She takes his attention and his movements gradually subside under her spell. His gyrations slowly diminish until he is stationary and he manages a "Howdy". Felicia gives him a hug and,

"Great gig, thank you!"

"My pleasure. Come and have a beer?"

"Don't mind if I do"

They both walk to the table. Felicia takes a seat next to Mike and The Gnome sits the other side of her. He is strangely tongue tied. Thunderman smiles at him. Mike realises Lucy has never met Felicia and does the introductions. There's a definite tension as the two women shake hands across the table. Mike breaks the silence,

"How are Iolande, Miranda and Amanda?"

"As ever, all working too much. Amanda loves her new nose and so does the camera!"

Mike nods, remembering the night down here when her nose was smashed. Justice had sure been served there, although the thought that the punishment was a little too severe crosses Mike's mind. He sighs,

"Over 2 years ago now?"

Felicia nods,

"You're still my fave band!" She gives the Skulk Rock salute. The Gnome reciprocates, smiling at her perfection. She smiles back and The Gnome reddens slightly as she mimics his dance from a sitting position. The Gnome drifts off to paradise with a satisfied smile on his face. Imitation is flattery? He gulps at his IPA.

Mike Remo smiles and asks,

"Where you been anyways?"

There's a long pause. Murky waters. No-one really knows how much anyone knows about Jimmy's last few months or about The Snakes demise or about the money that came along. Lucy's flat and The Dirtkickers new touring van. These thoughts cross Lucy's mind now as she silently sits at the table trying not to scowl. Felicia eventually replies,

"Been working on a film."

"Of wow – big time?"

"Nooooo – small time. Very art house."

"Tell us more. Do you need music for it?"

Felicia smiles. The Gnome and Thunderman look at her hoping for a positive response. She self-deprecates,

"It doesn't merit The Lowdown Dirtkickers! It's just an arty evocation of memories. That kinda thing."

The Gnome wishes he had more memories involving her. She continues,

"...All filmed in old Super8 and I'm blurred most of the time. Somehow it all seems so sentimental and colourful...it's a kind of reminiscence... kinda sad...", she meanders a little and the assembled males run out of responses.

Lucy inwardly giggles. Part of her tries not to like Felicia but Felicia has a personality to match her physical manifestation. You can't not like her. Lucy still tries to though, but finds herself making mental notes of the film Felicia is describing. Her Dad used to take Super8 film of family holidays and as Felicia talks, she remembers how the film quality and the memories contained always used to trigger sadness in her mind. Like days and memories of things that cannot be regained. Memories can be lonely places. You want to share them, but its degree of difficulty is way too high, even if you could find someone to share them with? People need "fellow travellers". That's what love is? Lucy's mind wanders. The conversations drift. Thunderman and The Gnome begin dismantling equipment. Lucy packs her rig and guitar. Mike and Felicia still sat at the table talking. One of Lucy's inner selves tell her,

"This bitch is gonna fuck things up?"

The Dirtkickers are quiet as they return from the gig that night. All descending from a good gig? Maybe? Or maybe they are quiet because Mike has offered Felicia a lift and she sits up front as he drives. The Gnome and TMan in the back with Lucy. An interloper in the van and the normal equilibrium has been disturbed. Felicia could disturb a dead man. Lucy looks at TMan and TheGnome as they sit lost in thought. Mike takes a different route tonight so he can drop The Gnome and TMan and Lucy off. Nobody mentions this but it's a gravity shift, an orbital correction and these things are interwoven with fate in a yet unknown physics theorem. Well, not totally unknown; The Dirtkickers know it but they just haven't written it down yet. Lucy descends from the van at her flat. It's late but she is wide awake. Little Joan and Ronee are asleep and once again she shares some memories with Nick Lucas. Scribbling in her notebook as a full moon hangs over Alcatraz.

Drink To The Memories

https://badpeoplethemusical.bandcamp.com/track/drink-to-the-memories

Those ghosts they sit around and wait
Trapped forever in the land of Super 8
Road dreams sunset flat mountain tops
Invade my mind and the film - it never stops

That time belongs to them and they keep it so precious
The world spin by and back again and time can be so vicious
Distant lands and a golden sun - they still belong
To you and we can never share the chances are all long gone

But I drink to the memory
And raise the glass to defy
The cruel fate of gravity
Wickedness and lies
Let's get high

So this is my religion time is locked forever in a light beam
parallel ray

And lives can glow and fade but never disappear away
And memories are like ships that float slowly to horizons
And clouds collide in skies that I never flied in

So don't you worry don't you wait you always got a date with
destiny
You make no sense with any theory of philosophy you're tellin'
me
I don't surrender nothing - I keep it locked so safe
No highwayman doubts or logic louts can draw me from this
place

But I drink to the memory
And raise the glass to defy
The cruel fate of gravity
Wickedness and lies
Let's get high

Chapter 5
Ajei

Ajei descends from The Dog. She checks her rucksack and then retrieves her bass guitar in its case. She looks up at James. Pale even for a white man. This one talks funny. Where is he from? Across an ocean somewhere? The country of the white parasite. Her mind fizzes. Jake, Sly and Si gone. Gone to a spirit world. Her main thoughts are worry. What will Ooljee say? What will it mean for the two of them? They may need to move off the farm? That wouldn't be a problem for her; it holds so many bad bad memories. Ghosts even. She takes a last look at him and gives him a pouch of Medicine Powder. Whatever pain he is in, then it will help. She does feel gratitude for his behaviour. At least he tried to save her? Maybe his intervention did save her? The motorbike whites were wild. Braves on bad medicine. As she turns to walk away she looks into his eyes. She sees a strange land. Places she has no knowledge of. He is not a buffalo killer for sure. There is gentleness there. She tries to smile. Maybe he is not a fucking parasite?

Now she gathers herself, turns her back on him and walks over to where the buses gather. She drapes her hair over her head wound and steals herself for this journey. She soon finds she is in the wrong place but is directed to the Greyhound Bus Station. She hands over the cash for bus tickets to Sacramento and Portland. Once there she can get a train eastwards to Wolf Point Montana. Then she should be able to hitch a lift back to the nation. Home in two days. Easy. She gets food for the trip and tries to shut the crazy white man city from her mind. She gazes up at the tall whiteman towers and sees the eagle soar from the top of one. Her eyes follow it as it circles before finding a thermal. It diminishes in size as it rises before wheeling away northwards. Ajei sings a native Nakoda religious song to herself. Two long hours pass before she wanders back to the bus office and boards the bus. She is nervous it's the right bus and asks a white man in uniform. The Bus Soldier confirms this is the bus for Sacramento and then Portland Oregon; from there she can get an iron train to Wolf Point. He is helpful. She boards the bus longing to see some open space. Fucking parasites.

The Greyhound slides up the ramp to the Bay Bridge. Ajei looks at the glass jungle either side of her. Then, crossing the big water she sees a ship loaded into the air with metal boxes. What are they bringing? Is it necessary? Do they have to build these big machines to bring in all that they have destroyed? She has learned about "world trade" in school. They burn fuel and destroy the air so they can rob distant lands of their buffalo too? The parasites call it "globalisation". They bring in more vehicles on one ship and send out other vehicles on another ship. The ships pass each other and destroy twice the air. Fucking parasites.

Through Oakland. Cars – cars – cars and on to Sacramento. Same – same – same. Next the bus links onto Highway 99. Look at them all. They drive around like it's their country. It might be, it's not my country but I wouldn't trash it like they do. Highway 99 becomes Interstate 5. Progress? The elders wouldn't think so and I agree. It's the old Siskiyou Trail. I bet not one of the parasites knows that. It was our foot trail. Now look at it. Fucking Hudson Bay Company. Fuck them.

Ajei calms herself down. She blames her recent experiences. Jake, Si and Sly. They were shitheads full of shit but did they deserve that? What sort of afterlife had they gone to? What is Ooljee going to do now? Not her fault. There will be trouble though. Jake had business with criminals from Helena. BossX. Evil genome if ever. Evil ancestors who roamed the dark paths of dark forests with no shame. No responsibility. What the whitemen call psychos. He would kill a buffalo just to watch it die. She'd seen him at the farm. Ooljee was unhappy when they came. Thoughts, thoughts thoughts. A new era was dawning. Her grandfather always told Ooljee and she that nothing lasts forever. The more evil it is, the shorter its life. But evil keeps returning like a tide of darkness. Like a dead animal poisons the water. It is the way of this world. Bad people.

The bus roars on. Passengers come and go. Now she sees the Cascade Mountains on her right. "Louwala-clough" – The Smoking Mountain. She looks for its smoke but no sign. One day the earth will rid itself of parasites. Smoking Mountain might help? 1980 was just a warning. She sees snow capped peaks now. She takes some medicine powder and dreams; half-awake, half-asleep. Hooves beat across the plains. The rumble of the herds. The eagle soars and dives through clouds. She stands on a hilltop and sees the valleys laid out below her. Now she is descending from the hilltop as the bus approaches Portland. She begins to wake.

As the bus pulls in she checks her rucksack and gathers her guitar case. She feels self-conscious in the city crowd and avoids anyone's eyes. She takes the short walk to the train station. Again she waits; avoiding any eye contact. This city is just like the last. Like them all.

Now the train moves. Ajei panics, it's heading north. It crosses the river and she is relieved as it swings east. She sees an airport to the other side of the mighty Columbia River. The first nations have survived on and around this river for centuries. Who would ever build an airport – a fucking airport! The train rumbles and climbs along and up the River gradient. She sees the cars on highways next to the rail track and remembers what her grandfather taught her. "The parasites will burn their own air so their offspring cannot survive and they are born greedy and will die greedy but hungry because their stores will run bare of food and they will not know how to survive on the land and if they did there are too many of them. Fucking parasites!" Her Grandfather isn't big on short sentences or punctuation, but he sure could make a point. He wasn't afraid of using bad language to emphasise his point either. "Their civilisation takes trade too far and will only bring smallpox or similar in the end. The end, for them, will be soon." Listening to her grandfather could result in a sense of doom. She giggles, maybe she will see him again soon?

Now the hills rise up to her right across the river. She feels better to be out of cities. She dozes and opens her eyes as the train rolls past a cascade of water, rounds a slow bend to open a view of a high bridge across a river gorge. So high it sparks a memory of the legendary Bridge of Gods. A high rock natural arch connecting both sides of this river and cast asunder by the gods in conflict. This bridge must be the white man's version. "Those who emulate the gods will surely perish", was one of her grandfather's favourite sayings. Where did he get this shit?

Her head hurts and she eats some fruit she bought on Portland Station and takes some powder and some water. She dozes. The train on high plains now. She wakes and pays attention as the train gently swings northwards around a long bend of the Columbia River. Then a long low bridge between two cities on either side of the river. The bridge must be a mile long and she watches the surface of the water. The random signs of the wind. This is a mighty land. She feels better to be moving homeward. The train rumbles on to Spokane and waits there for a long while. Ajei keeps her seat and her countenance. Maybe they attached another locomotive because she knows the Rocky Mountains are ahead. She loved these mountains and as a child they used to travel there in spring and would fish and hunt. Life before The Snakes.

It's early dawn as the train moves off. It climbs steadily as slanted light enters the deep valleys from the low sun. The winding track and stark sierras form a light display of sorts. Her heart lifts. The dominating peaks make everything else insignificant. Ajei is convinced by her grandfather's assertions that the planet could free itself of human parasites should it ever decide upon that course of action. Or should the stupid humans cross some threshold. If there was such a threshold they must've crossed it by now? It could be soon. Ajei finds herself desperate under the burden of these thoughts and thought of her mother and grandfather waiting. Soon she would see them. The train now through the mountains and the plains begin to lay themselves out on either side. This was Blackfoot Country now. She looked with interest at the town they pass through. Glacier Peaks. The Snake Brothers Band had played The Glacier Peaks Casino. There were usually music lounge bars and the gigs were always lively. All of a sudden, she missed Jake and Si and Sly. Tears appeared in her eyes and then ran down her cheeks as gig memories flooded into her mind. They were evil but the music was good. She offers a prayer to The Gods. "Wherever The Snakes dwell let them enjoy music. Forgive their sins. Everyone has difficulties in life to fight." Ajei dozes now as the high plains miles roll under the train. She wakes as the train pulls into Malta.

Ajei looks, sleepy eyed, at the flat town of Malta. She remembers the Snake Band playing gigs here. So many gigs, it all blends. There's a casino here as well as one or two lively bars. A high plains flat town where people liked to party. Was this where Jake almost killed a guy who didn't have the money for his bag. Jake was a dinosaur for sure. His stuffed body should be in the Dinosaur Museum a few yards away across Highway 2. Soon the train would rumble on to Wolf Point. She would find Jimmy Newshoots at his office and see where Ooljee was.

****

Jimmy Newshoots is pleased to see Ajei. Her mother has told him Ajei is away with Jake and the band and what his motive for San Francisco was. Jimmy asks questions but not too many. He is a good friend of Ooljee's side of the family and knows not to ask too much. He is pleased to see her back, his face and demeanour tinged with worry.

The front porch light switches on as Ooljee hears the truck approach. She waits on the porch, shrouded in the dull light of the single bulb. Ajei feels relief to see her mother once more. She thanks Jimmy Newshoots and descends from the high passenger seat of his truck, reaching over to retrieve her bass guitar case from the rear. She walks slowly to the porch smiling at her mother. She feels relief to be home and emotion and tiredness creep over her.

Ooljee is calm and does not fire questions; she waits as Ajei settles before she tells the story of the ill-fated trip to San Francisco. Ooljee shakes and closes her eyes as Ajei relates how Jake and his sons passed from this life. Ooljee clenches her fists as she sees that, once again, her visions have turned out true. Sometimes she dreads her visions. Nobody truly wants to see the future. It can be good, but it can also reveal dark turns of fate that are best left shrouded.

Ooljee has a lamb stew simmering and Ajei sits and eats now as Ooljee watches smiling. Both women know there is darkness ahead. As Ajei wipes her plate with her cornbread Ooljee speaks calmly,

"Tomorrow, there is no time to spare. We must go see Father and adjust things."

Ajei nods as Ooljee carries on,

"Xylo has been agitated. He never trusted Jake and there is money running through all this. He will be in touch soon. Too soon!"

As Ajei stands, she staggers and Ooljee cleans her headwound before sleep. Ajei soon passes into sleep and Ooljee stands in the bedroom doorway staring at her sleeping daughter. Her mind fizzes with worry.

Xylo. Nobody knows his real name. Maybe it is "Xylo Somefucker" or "Somefucker Xylo"? All Ooljee knows is he is a miserable fucker. Whatever business the elders concluded with him all those long years ago was big. All she knows is it involves land at the boundaries of the Reservation. There are some crazy deals for land and darkness is forever trying to spread into the territory. Jake was part of Xylo's plans. Xylo had many plans, many tentacles. Jake Snake was just one of them. Land, drugs and, most of all, money. Whiteman's greed consumes everything. Land and homesteads were constantly being bought and sold. She didn't understand it all. She had been stupid in the past and that's how she had become locked to Jake Snake. It was a long dark shadow and she would still be roped to its darkness for sure. Now Jake was gone, the shadow of

Xylo could grow. She feels panic inside. Whatever Jake's evils, and there were lots, he was not in the same evil hierarchy as Xylo – or BossX as he liked to be known. Ooljee knew him – knew him too well. Jake had made her be with him at meetings. She shivers. He was old now. She wishes him dead. There may be opportunities here for some freedom; some independence; but she doesn't hold out much hope. She would discuss with her father first thing tomorrow. Ooljee watches the full moon through her bedroom window tonight. She shivers between her sheets. Sleep hasn't come at all as a pale grey morning arrives.

****

Morning and they drive out of the farm. Ooljee is nervous of every approaching vehicle; she checks her rear view mirror as if taking a driving test. Ajei smiles at her and talks of her trip and the big whiteman city.

"Jake chose his life and now the life he chose has chosen his death."

"Same for the brothers?"

"Not sure they all deserved it?"

They sit in silence for a few miles, each weighing up the last statement. Eventually Ooljee speaks,

"The white girl had some steel will?"

"Perhaps we'll never know what happened?"

"Perhaps better if we don't know. I fear BossX will want to know"

Ajei is aware that Ooljee is nervous.

"This BossX must be a piece of shit for sure?"

"You speak the truth there Daughter – although not particularly elegant language!"

They look at each other vacantly and then giggle. Another long silence follows as they look at the long shadow of their truck cast by the sun directly behind them as they travel north.

"We will think of something Mother!"

They turn off the highway as it passes a small valley in the plains. The track winds through the trees until they see various cabins arranged in no particular pattern. A large oak tree stands in the middle of the cabins. The cabins are well kept and children play at the other end of the valley. A slim but noble figure emerges from the closest cabin to where they park. Ajei smiles,

"Grandfather!"

He walks forward and embraces her as she walks to him. Next he walks to Ooljee, he smiles and holds her shoulders,

"No man could want for a better daughter."

She smiles and looks down. He continues,

"Nothing can right the wrongs you have endured.........but things are beginning to change."

Ooljee nods, trying to smile.

The Elder looks up at the sky. The eagle circles, gaining height. All their eyes follow it in silence for a few minutes until he speaks,

"Anukasa has told what happened in the white man city", he looks at Ajei, "None of it was your fault Ajei. Snake men brought it all upon themselves. White man greed!"

They look at the elder in silence, waiting for his next wisdom,

"Fucking arsehole white men. Fucking parasites!"

Ajei giggles. Her grandfather's grasp of English has always been good. She is not sure how long he would survive in white man culture but, he has certainly mastered their poxy little language. He rants a little more,

"Ooljee fell under whiteman spell that turned out to be a Snake spell."

Ooljee interrupts,

"OK father! Let's turn to the future?"

They all pause as the elder gathers his thoughts. He opens his mouth slowly and Ooljee and Ajei turn expectantly. He pauses again.

"Xylo will want information soon and I fear he won't be pleased", he looks at Ooljee.

"BossX never pleased father. He just wants more money."

"Always. He is as greedy as the next immigrant arsehole!"

Ajei giggles at her grandfather's inappropriate expressions. He should be a politician. He would never get elected to anywhere - but he would get her vote. He looks at Ooljee now,

"Daughter and Grandaughter – brightest stars of my sky – free eagles of my eye – love without no lies…"

"Fuckin fuck Grandad – get to the point…"

"…you must both go Utah!"

"Utah – you're fuckin joking!"

"Ajei – you talk like a dog who has eaten bad flesh!!"

Ajei glares back at her mother. Grandfather continues,

"Until these dark clouds pass!"

Ajei opens her mouth to speak but Ooljee silences her with a touch to her leg and a stare burdened with tension, pain and acceptance. Her Grandfather speaks again,

"BossX is a turd from a shit stained dog's ass. But BossX is not well. This I know. His evil son LynkX is worse, he is a diseased turd from a poxhog's fevered ass and he will soon take over. We must hope they take possession of the Snake Farm and that will satisfy their lust for wealth and you will both be forgotten. Things will settle and you can return."

The two women stare at him and bow to his senior countenance.

"I will speak to BossX and stall the storm. Feed his greed."

He bows his head as though his thoughts were all too heavy.

"Leave tomorrow. I have some whiteman money waiting for your journey. Your truck will travel. We have Navajo friends who will be hospitable. I have arranged jobs…and even a contact so you can play music Miss Ajei!"

He smiles and Ajei cannot help but return the smile. She loves her grandad since forever she can remember. He taught her to shoot, to skin, to throw a knife, to speak the whitemen language and to play the whiteman music. He loved Bo Diddley and sowed the seed of her groove.

"Tonight we feast and set our minds to the future!"

****

The sun two hours into the big sky as they drive off the farm. A silence is maintained. Ooljee drives west on a dirt road at first before turning south on another deserted highway.

"Just in case BossX visits this morning. We don't want to pass him on the highway do we?"

Now they hit Highway 2 and turn west. The sun behind them is the same sun that watched Lucy Smith nervously push The Dog onto this highway nearly a year ago. The women are silent until they reach Malta. They gas their truck and stop for a coffee. Ooljee smiles at her daughter. At least they are free of The Snakes. Freedom tinged with sadness as Ooljee remembers her early days with Jake. How could someone fall into darkness so badly? She holds her daughters hand on the table. For all the worry and apprehension of the future she feels some weight has been lifted. Things have changed. Life is simpler and they might enjoy their time in the Navajo nation. At least it will be warmer in Utah.

Back at their truck Ooljees Stratotone Mercury Guitar and Ajei's P-Bass wait patiently. Their prized possessions. The women climb in and set their minds for a long journey south. They hang left onto Highway 191 and the road dives under the railroad track. Ajei remembers sitting in the station here a few days previously. She is so glad to be with her mother once again. She feels the same tension Ooljee feels but she is young and resilient and ready to change the fuck out of this world. Once again, her circumstances changed by those around her, outside of her control. Her plans, not greedy, not selfish but, in the end not achievable because of others around her. Her young mind seeks justice as her dreams fade once again.

Raindrop Dreams

https://badpeoplethemusical.bandcamp.com/track/raindrop-dreams

If you see a crowd
Go the other way
They could all be going down
You wanna live another day

They all got their raindrop dreams
They all fall at once

You can only ever catch a few
The rest forever gone

Raindrop dreams – fall away
Raindrop dreams – run away
Raindrop dreams – never stay

Me, I got so much to do
There's a world to save
Wasted time was all without you
All I got coming is a grave

And I'm thinkin
Where did I go wrong ?
I'm still living
But I don't got long

Raindrop dreams – fall away
Raindrop dreams – run away
Raindrop dreams – never stay

Do you dream in the next life?
Do you dream of this life?
Do you dream that things turn out right?
Do your dreams get you through the night?

I cross the dream Himalayas
On a dream elephant
I'm a dream detective looking for yer
In every dream incident

I soar like a dream albatross
There's a dream world below
On every dreamboat I come across
I look for your dream shadow

Raindrop dreams – fall away
Raindrop dreams – run away
Raindrop dreams – never stay

All of the raindrop dreams
Raindrop dreams become rivers of tears
Raindrop dreams become rivers of tears
Raindrop dreams become rivers of tears
If you got a memory
If you got a memory
Did it happen ?

Chapter 6
Investigating Officer

Speedy Copp looks at herself in the mirror and smiles. She loves motorbike days. She wears her vintage leather biker trousers and leather jacket over her favourite Triumph Motorcyles T-shirt (oh yes, Highway 61 Revisited is still her favourite album and she sings Queen Jane Approximately to herself in the mirror this morning) under a long sleeved paisley shirt she got up in Haight. That was many years ago, but it's still a fave. She feels invincible in her biker boots. She ties her hair back ready for her helmet. Her Department issue revolver under her left arm and her badge in her right hand side inside chest pocket. A "plain clothes" day. This is a new experience. As she leaves her kitchen now she glances at her new uniform and trusty speed gun left on the shelf for the next two days. Lieutenant Lathan has authorised her to investigate the "SnakeVan" wreckage. This could be a chance. Speedy is not fooled by Lathan though. He tries to sound slick, efficient and tough but he is a hayseed for sure. She's met them before. All too often. If it came down to it he would fold straightaways. She doesn't hold out much confidence that this opportunity is likely to lead to anything. Still, a couple of days out of the ordinary and a chance to go "out of uniform" on her favourite transport – her motorbike.

Speedy opens the door to her lock up and smiles as she sees her beloved Kawasaki W650. It's been her pride and joy for 4 years now. She knows this bike inside out. She does her own maintenance and has even carried out minor customisations herself. She likes that it's like a Triumph Bonneville, the bike Bob Dylan rode when he had his accident? Speedy is a careful rider though. No speeding. That would hinder her career in traffic enforcement for sure. She likes Kawasaki; she has a contact in the trade who imports parts for her. She loves keeping her bike in perfect condition. It's a beaut bike and anyone with malicious intent to her bike is on notice to leave this planet with their death being a painful memory. Speedy would circumvent legal niceties, conventions and protocols if it ever came to that. It is her religion and they better respect it. They better fuckin' respect it!

Speedy mentally pinches herself. Two days of investigative police work and the weather is fine. Why not enjoy it. This is a paid holiday. She is going to ride on up to the impound where the bust up SnakeVan had originally been towed. Admin there will help her with finding what happened to the vehicle after that and then she will ride on out to find it and "comb it for evidence". She knows nothing will come of it but Lathan is a soft touch and she may as well make the most of this opportunity. Speedy gets the buzz, like she always does, as she steps over the machine and one quick kick and Kawi purrs into life. Speedy listens to the music of the twin cylinders. So smooth. She listens for a while, sitting and feeling the minimal vibe as the machine warms to the task ahead.

She swings onto the 280 and heads for the city. Kawi is purring. Doubly satisfying to be able to ride as part of her job. This is her city and she guides her trusty mount through the traffic and into the spring morning of law and order. The freeway swings east and she is riding alongside a BART train for a while. She feels the eyes of the passengers on her. They are admiring her Kawi for sure. She intersects the mythical 101 and heads north now. One day she will ride 101 a long way north; she has been as far as Crescent City and vowed to venture further one spring or summer. Maybe up and over the Cascades and thence to the Rockies. Kawi could manage that. What a trip!

Now she cruises up the incline of Portrero Hill and as 101 swings over the top she sees the city 'scrapers ahead of her. She should ride Kawi to work more often. Shitbrains sweep past her, exceeding the speed restriction in their VW shitbrainmobiles. It crosses her mind to nail some of them but today she is a detective and not traffic enforcement; they have had a lucky escape. She glides down the exit ramp at 7th and Bryant and into the vehicle impound. She makes her way to an administrator called Veronica and together they seek to find the current whereabouts of the SnakeVan.

"It was in the scrap impound until three months ago and was released as scrap to a dealer down in San Jose", Veronica frowns, "Looks like Harry Crushner got it in a scrap consignment."

"Harry Crushner?"

Veronica smiles,

"Oh yes, San Jose's premier breaker. Harry don't mess about. Probably a crushed scrap cube by now? Or even recycled?"

"Oh well, it is what it is. I'll have a run down there and see if they still have it? They may have kept it for parts?"

Veronica smiles. Speedy has a winning way.

Now she heads south. Kawi rocking out the miles. She sings "Do You Know The Way to San Jose" to herself. Highway 101 Revisited. Probably a waste of time but hell it's a day out. She can cut over to the coast on the way back. Nice ride. 101 guides her through San Jose until she exits west and finds Monterey Road. Cruising south the Harry Crushner sign comes into view and she eases the Kawi into the yard and stands the bike in front of the main office entrance. She feels the eyes of the scraphawks upon her as she enters the office. At the counter an Indian guy looks up and at her from under the greasiest baseball cap she has ever seen.

"I'm looking for Harry Crushner?"

"Harry Crushner - Harry Crushner, Crushner Crushner - Harry Harry – Turn your scap car into money – hurry hurry!-hurry, hurry", he sings. His white teeth beam back at her. Speedy is rocked back for a moment. She smiles, but before she can speak,

"Who wants to know?"

"Officer Coppola SFPD", Speedy forgets where she put her badge and loses some degree of authority during time spent interrogating her various pockets. He looks her badge up and down.

"At your service", he bows emphatically.

Scrappers aimlessly examine parts laid out on Harry Crushner's shelves but really they examine Speedy. She is already bringing glamour and intrigue to their world. The silence indicates their attentiveness as they wait for her to speak.

"Mercedes 4 x 4 Sprinter Van conversion? You got one recently?"

"Recently? No, no,no,no,no,no..........that was 3 or 4 months ago. A long time in the metal and parts reclamation business"

"So it's crushed, re-cycled, sold?"

"No, no, no no, no, no, no....................."

"So? It's still here?"

"No, no, no. no. no. no......................."

"So where is it?"

"Parts are on my well stocked shelves – in the VW section", Harry throws his arms out wide in the direction of shelves and trays at one end of his empire. Speedy turns and looks. Customers suddenly look busy.

"But it's a Mercedes?"

"German section!" Harry smiles.

"And the chassis?"

"Chassis and shell in yard somewhere."

"Can you show me?"

"Glad to be of assistance Officer Coppola", Harry lifts his counter flap and steps through. He gesticulates for Speedy to follow. Eyes follow her as she walks out. They walk out into the vastness of Harry Crushner's scrap metal empire. Harry absent-mindedly sings his song as he marches around haphazard piles of scrap vehicles. Speedy follows. She can't not like Harry. He walks with a bounce. He sings. He smiles. He is happy in countenance over his empire. Eventually they find the rusty black remnants of what was once the majestic SnakeVan, sad now in its resting demise. Harry breaks the silence as they stare at the shell,

"Not much left I'm afraid. Some good spares from this one." Speedy walks inside the shell. Wires hang from the cannibalised dashboard. She notices one side of the vehicle is really bashed in. Not so much the other side. She thinks it must be from the crane of whatever. Eventually she emerges, none the wiser.

"Could you roll it over Harry so I can check chassis number?"

"Sure thing Officer Coppola!"

Harry walks off as Speedy stands contemplating the huge depression in the side of the van. She's seen collisions in her time with Traffic Enforcement and this is a severe side on impact? Her thoughts interrupted by the sound of heavy machinery approaching. Harry skids around the corner of piled car-casses in a mobile crane. Speedy takes a few steps back as Harry deftly puts the boom arm against the van and flips it onto its side. He reverses, switches off the motor and jumps down from the cab smiling, as ever. Speedy walks around to look at the underside. Harry walks alongside her,

"To be cubed soon Officer Coppola. Lucky you got here just in time!"

Speedy is resigned to finding nothing but goes through the motions of examining the chassis. Maybe she'll look efficient taking a chassis number. She's not sure why she tries to impress Harry and she giggles inwardly at herself. She feels Harry's eyes on her leather ass. She giggles again. She takes the number and stands back for one last look. Now a cylindrical attachment to a front chassis member catches her eye. It doesn't seem to serve any purpose. Her interest in motor vehicle mechanics takes over and she steps forward to examine from a closer coign. Speedy's finger soon dislodges caked dirt to reveal a shiny black cylinder. She quickly removes the rest of the grime. She grips it hard and pulls and twists and it is loose in her hand. She staggers back in surprise.

"What you got Officer Coppola?"

"Not sure. What you reckon Harry?", Harry looks.

"Never seen anything like that on a vehicle. German or not!"

Speedy pauses, deep in thought. She holds the device at an angle to the light and sees etched words…."V-Track Mk1".

"It's a tracker!"

Harry looks over her shoulder. She repeats,

"It's a fuckin' tracker Harry!"

"Can I sell it?"

Speedy turns and stares at him,

"It's state's evidence now."

She laughs and feels a buzz. HA! So this trip has been worthwhile after all. Something to go on. She stands back. Harry breaks the silence,

"Was this a big accident?"

"No accident Harry. Homicide", Speedy inserts some melodrama into her voice.

"Looks like a collision to me?"

"Well Harry the bodies were found 20 yards from the vehicle each with fatal shotgun wounds. Well, except for the dog! Van had gone down a cliff!"

"What happened to the dog?"

"Shot with a 38!"

"Evil bastards!"

"We might get them yet."

"Get who?"

"The perps Harry."

"Still a collision involved! You not wanna see the other vehicle?"

Speedy gazes at the tracker trying to think ahead. How she can progress this, until, eventually, Harry's last statement barges into her conscious thought. She thinks she misheard him,

"What's that Harry?"

"We also have the car that collided with this van."

Speedy turns to face him – puzzled,

"How do you know that Harry?"

Harry jumps into his mobile crane, starts up and quickly sets the van upright again. He walks back to Speedy and points out the caved-in side of the van.

"See the impact line Officer Coppola?"

"Yeh?"

"Vehicle with a bull-bar on the front."

Harry walks forward and points to lacerations in the sheet metal.

"Sharp edged bull-bars too. Three feet 6 inches wide."

Speedy stares and nods. Harry gesticulates for her to follow him. They walk around two more corners and there is a big old shed lounging in a corner of the lot. Harry opens the doors and there is a Dodge truck. It looks old and lost and lonely but still proud. Strangely, Speedy's eye is drawn to the word "Dog" on the front. "Dodge" has lost its "d" and "e". She giggles. Harry points to the bars, obviously modded to the front of the vehicle.

"Three feet six inches wide Officer Coppola! If I don't miss my guess?"

He carries on as Speedy stares,

"Remnants of black paint on the bars Officer Coppola!", Harry stands proudly with arms folded, like a top lawyer resting his case.

She walks around the Dog now. Opening the driver's door she sees a strange bucket seat and harness,

"What's with the seat Harry?"

"Looks like someone was worried about collision?"

"Maybe it was used in that Demolition Derby shit?"

"Could be Officer Coppola."

Speedy is motionless. Processing information. Eventually,

"Where'd you get this vehicle Harry?"

"From the impound. Same time I picked up the van."

Silence again until Harry breaks it,

"You mean you guys didn't work that out?"

Speedy is wounded.

"I'm new on the case Harry."

Harry laughs,

"Detective Harry Crushner – Head of Homicide!"

Speedy laughs,

"I didn't know Indians got irony Harry!"

There's a silence and she eventually announces,

"This vehicle is State's Evidence now Harry."

Harry nods,

"I wasn't fixing to sell it quite yet anyways."

Speedy holds his gaze,

"Thanks a lot Harry Crushner. You are a servant of justice"

They walk back to Harry's office. Speedy deep in thought; there is so much to go on here. The tracker; what info might that hold? Lathan said he wanted to know about the van's movements. Looked like specialist equipment? What was it doing on the van? Then "The Dog"! Speedy giggled to herself at the name. A vintage old truck like that was certainly not the first choice of drug dealers. Harry is quiet too. He glances across at Officer Coppola. The early afternoon Californian sun reflects from her ponytailed hair. He looks ahead. He glances at her again now. This time he notices her slender hands and fingers; a cuff of paisley shirt creeping out from the sleeve of her leather jacket. He pauses momentarily to look along a row of stacked car wrecks and glances back to look at her perfectly fitted leather jeans over shapely legs ending at her biker boots Police officers are not normally like this. As he catches up to her he sees her cheekbones leading his eye to her nose. Harry realises he has enjoyed the past hour more than any hour he can remember recently. He tries to think of something else to say but the usually dominant part of his brain gurgitating inane conversation has switched off. Or maybe he has switched it off trying to mutate into a different character? A character Officer Coppola might like? She seems to like him; he detected fondness in her last comment? "Ask her out for a drink Harry", his inner voice suggests. As they reach the steps up to Harry's main business area his mind panics in search of words,

"Wanna coffee Officer Coppola?"
Speedy is deep in thought. So much new evidence to process. She needs to ride and think this through and work out her next move. This was progress. She looks back at Harry,

"Thanks Harry. You have been a great help. Really!", she holds out for a handshake.

Harry shakes her hand his mind racing but getting nowhere. Circles. His inner self kicking his ass for not asking; for turning mute; for being a complete airhead. By this time Officer Coppola has swung one of the legs of his dreams over her Kawasaki 650 (Harry even loves her bike choice). She revs the Kawasaki and rolls away. As he watches her sweep out of his yard he wanders back inside staring at the ground. Harry Crushner is one of life's heroes. He's lonely but he keeps on pushing. Harry is a giant amongst men. All men, especially pain in the arse celebrity men. He walks to the music system in the corner and turns up the local radio station he always plays. The DJ announces a song by The Lowdown Dirtkickers.

The Wrong Time

https://badpeoplethemusical.bandcamp.com/track/the-wrong-time

Fate's cruel tuition
She's on a mission
She's got a plan
That I can't understand
But she don't give a damn

In the arms of catastrophe
How did this happen to me ?
Lady Luck is a whore
She leaves you wanting more
But she is the one I can't afford

These are the wrong days
These are the wrong days
These are the wrong days ... for love

Like crucifixion
Gives you time for thinkin
The tightening of the rack
She's not coming back
And that's a fact

Sinkin low to the killing floor
Running straight at a plate glass door
I been here so many times before...

These are the wrong days
These are the wrong days
These are the wrong days ----- for love

Now I dream with Morpheus
The old ghosts all pity us
The cracked memories
The faded imagery
The sky is empty now
The stars too far away

The past forgotten
And nothing left to say

These are the wrong days
These are the wrong days
These are the wrong days ... for love

Like a faded film star
Loud colours and long cars
Life has a dark texture
Since I ever met yer
But worse since I left yer

These are the wrong days
These are the wrong days
These are the wrong days ... for love

Harry Crushner thinks to himself, "It's always the wrong time!". He sighs.

Chapter 7
Nurse Cupid

Mike Remo jumps down from the driver seat and helps Lucy Smith out with her guitar and amplifier.

"Just take the amp back to HQ Mikey?"

Mike nods. They don't dwell. He holds her shoulders,

"Great gig Lucy. Keep those songs coming!"

"Sure Mike....................Thanks."

Lucy knows Mike now. She trusts him. She trusts him with any crowd, any song and any important decision. She's not sure she trusts him with Felicia though. She giggles to herself, "Men!"

Mike jumps back to the driving seat and looks at Felicia,

"Where to Miss?"

"It's not Miss anymore Michael Remo!"

Mike smiles. Her eyes sparkle before she speaks,

"I'm not tired."

"Are you hungry?"

"Always"

"Thought you models had to be careful how much you eat?"

"I'm lucky…and nervous…burn it all off"

"Ok…well…I know an all night café in Sausalito. A lot of musos use it during recordings and after gigs. We're in no rush?"

"No rush at all Mike."

Mike relaxes. He's blessed tonight; he has the company of an angel. A good gig and he is energised. His veins full of electricity. Felicia doesn't talk but it doesn't bother him; he senses she is content. She stares out the window as San Francisco streets roll by. He heads west on Jackson Street now before a right on to Van Ness and 101. Now he heads north towards the moon. They swing west before 101 sweeps them up. Now they see The Gate looming. The Two Towers proclaiming the western entry to the greatest city of the greatest country in the world. Crossing the bridge always an adventure. Tonight the air is still, the waters dark and the stars look down. These moments are priceless. Especially tonight. He glances at Felicia as she surveys the majesty. She is the mythical goddess of the west. Mike's blood soars and his mind surfs.

Over the bridge they hang right and drop to Sausalito, along the waterfront through the town and Mike pulls into an industrial area and parks outside an inconspicuous diner entrance. Inside the conversation hums. Mark Sandman's cool vocals fill the space. Groups of people inhabit the seating booths and many of them give Mike a wave. The usual wave of dropped jaws, forgotten words and general missed heartbeats follow Felicia. She rearranges wherever she passes. They find a quiet booth and sit. Beer and burgers. Mike Remo thinks life cannot get any better. No point trying to be someone you are not, and he is blessed to be the someone he is.

"Is everyone in here in a band Mike?"

"Most. Some after gigs and some are recording."

Pictures are hung haphazardly around. Felicia looks at a few in wonderment.

"Is that.......?"

Mike nods.

"Isn't that.......?"

Mike nods. This time he takes her hand and leads her over to a chimney wall. He shows her an old picture of The Dirtkickers around a table. She peers into the photograph until she whispers to herself,

"Jimmy English."

Time pauses until they both look away and their eyes meet. Felicia's eyes are moist and glisten as well as sparkle.

"Jimmy never stopped talking about you Mike Remo."

"How I never paid him?"

"Nothing of the sort. He would've taken a bullet for you Mike."

"Dunno what I ever saw in a nervous dumb limey with a stupid accent!"

They giggle before falling to silence. The burgers arrive and they eat in silence until Felicia speaks.

"His Mom was so upset at the funeral."

"You met her?"

"Only passing by. What can you ever say?"

"She came over again a few months back. With Aunt Clara. Wanted to know all about his music and life out here."

"Wish you'd told me."

"Didn't have your number and hadn't seen you around much."

"His Mom was a nurse. Retired now."

"Really? I remember him really being into a nurses uniform I once had a modelling assignment with."

"Not sure that would've necessarily related to his Mom having been a nurse Felicia."

Felicia stares at him. Mike stares back; his soul elevates in her countenance. Eventually they both giggle,

"He used to call me Nurse Cupid."

"Oh Christ!"

"Oh yes…He wrote me a song."

"Oh…I bet he did!"

Felicia smiles and sings to him,

> "She went shang-a-lang-a-lang-a-lang-a-lang on my heart
> And wang-a-wang-a-wang-a-wang-a-wang in my mind
> I been hit by a love dart
> And it's true love this time"

Mike looks at her,

"It's hooky! I like it!"

"You're the prince of Skulk Rock Michael Remo – do not bullshit me – but get me another beer!"

Mike returns with the beers singing,

" shang-a-lang-a-lang-a-lang-a-lang on my heart!"

"It's a hit record Flea!"

"Fuck off!"

"Nurse Cupid and The Medicine Men!"

"Fuck off!"

"Sing me some more…?"

Now she laughs, and sings,

> "Nurse Cupid is my favourite nurse
> She saved me from the hearse

She said I was looking sooooo pale
She's my Florence Nightingale
She said Dr Cupid made me well
And she checked me over and she can tell"

Mike Remo now semi-serious as he joins in the chorus,

"She went shang-a-lang-a-lang-a-lang-a-lang on my heart.."

A leering face now appears over the booth divide,
"Mike Remo IS in lerv…!"
Mike hits the face with a ketchup coated french-fry and it disappears to an orchestration of laughter.

Mike Remo does not want this night to end. Felicia is full of life. She never tires. Mike drives them to the pier viewpoint past Fort Baker and under the gate. They watch the dawn come up over the city and across The Bay. It rides on in across the Bay Bridge in the distance. Can life get any better?

****

The Gnome practices his press rolls and shouts across to Mike,
"What we doing today Boss?"
"Gnomio, an old Jimmy English song has been unearthed."
"Unearthed?"
"Oh yes a re-discovered masterpiece!"

Jimmy English sits on top of a speaker stack listening with interest now. Must be one Lucy has brought in? It's one of his current pleasures to listen to The Dirtkickers kicking life into his songs.

Mike runs a recording he's put together.

Nurse Cupid
https://badpeoplethemusical.bandcamp.com/track/nurse-cupid

I woke up in a strange room
My heart was beating boom-bang-a-boom

A sign said Heart Department
And a nurse said "your case is urgent"
Dr Cupid's gonna start deployment..

We never seen such a bad case (We're sorry you had to wait)
But Dr Cupid says "it's never too late"
You need a Wang-Dang-Doodle
And a triple by-pass reversal
And then a wedding night rehearsal....

She went shang-a-lang-a-lang-a-lang-a-lang on my heart
And wang-a-wang-a-wang-a-wang-a-wang in my mind
I been hit by a love dart
And it's true love this time

I never seen such a beautiful face
And her uniform made my heart race
Dr Cupid can stay at home
I want Nurse Cupid all alone……..

She goes shang-a-lang-a-lang-a-lang-a-lang on my heart
And wang-a-wang-a-wang-a-wang-a-wang in my mind
I been hit by a love dart
And it's true love this time

Nurse Cupid is my favourite nurse
She saved me from the hearse
She said I was looking sooooo pale
She's my Florence Nightingale
She said Dr Cupid made me well
And she checked me over and she can tell

She went shang-a-lang-a-lang-a-lang-a-lang on my heart
And wang-a-wang-a-wang-a-wang-a-wang in my mind
I been hit by a love dart
And it's true love this time
She goes shang-a-lang-a-lang-a-lang-a-lang on my heart
And wang-a-wang-a-wang-a-wang-a-wang in my mind
I been hit by a love dart

"Fuckin fuck Mike. That's different! Do we do pop tunes?"
"Might make us some money? You never know!"
"Where'd you find this shit?"

Jimmy swoops over to The Gnome and tells him, "Deirdre will love it!" The Gnome doesn't hear him (of course). Jimmy remembers this song and he remembers Felicia modelling her nurse's uniform. He turns a slow backward somersault in the air with long sigh. His memories flood back. Death is such a pisser.

"Got it from Felicia."
The Gnome looks at him and opens his mouth to speak but holds back his words as TMan arrives.
"We got a pop toon hit TMan. Let's get rockin!"
Thunderman smiles at The Gnome. His enthusiasm and good nature is a force for good in the world.
They play the run down version again for TMan. He listens quizzically. Mike speaks,
"Just an idea? We could try a video to go with it. Felicia says she will get Amanda, Iolande and Miranda to try backing verbals? They'd be good for a video for sure?"

The two musicians look at Mike in silence before TMan asks,
"Are you rockin with Felicia Michael J Remo?"
Mike smiles before TMan continues,
"You be careful Mike. Her husband is loaded and connected. Jimmy told me that she told him that Mr Felicia has some heavy friends. You know the type?"
Mike Remo thinks to himself,
"She's worth it", before replying,
"I can look after myself!"

Chapter 8
BossX and The Chief

On Highway 191 Ajei's eyes follow the white line that marks their track south. The high plains stretch out on either side and the white line guides them. Ooljee deep in thought as she grips the wheel. They don't realise, but they pass the point on the highway where Lucy Smith decided to make for San Francisco on her flight from Montana some months earlier. History repeats or is it the DNA of fate? Some people are connected by fate? Or is it a twist of fate? A hybridisation. These thoughts don't trouble Ajei's mind as it wanders.

To their right now The Missouri Badlands – The Breaks! Ajei has learned about the flight of the Nez Perce and the lessons return. She shivers. A noble people pursued and herded and victimised and humiliated and crucified and decimated and abused by the parasites. This was the way of the world. Everyone fights for survival, but the parasites fight for more. Their greed is their power. They lay everything at its altar. They sacrifice the Buffalo, the land, peoples and even, eventually, the whole world. Or will the world sacrifice them? Ajei knows that one dark day their greed will burn their hearts out and the earth will return to an equilibrium. Like a lot of what she knows – she could be right, or she could be wrong. Grandfather says that she has Nez Perce blood from the last century. Their ancestors had sheltered fleeing Nez Perce from the evil bitchson white generals, and the bloods had mixed. She doesn't mind the idea that Chief Joseph's blood is in her. She feels the strength and valour energise her as all her muscles and thoughts flex. Our next time will come. The highway leads them west now towards the illegal town of Lewiston. Built on the mirage of gold. Hin-mah-too-yah-lat-kekt would piss on their gold. What worth is it apart from a vain pursuit?

Ajei gets sleepy as she always does on journeys. She sees the truebrave warriors seated on their spotcoat appaloosa and thunderhooved buffalo herds leaving dust rainbows above the plains. The realgold sun, bathing the whole scene like no artist could ever capture. Her eyes widen now, staring, as a different dust appears from the east. A dust of greed, of industry, of evil weaponry that not even the young braves can resist. Dust and darkness of evil of blue armies like a plague. Rocks like meteorites, black and burning rain upon it all. The blue soldiers scream and cry; some sink to their knees to pray to a false god while others shout for their mothers. In the sky, a light of colour never seen before and a wind that paints blood across the sky in strands. Men scatter and fall with each thunderclap as the earth is cleansed.......

BurnEmAll

https://badpeoplethemusical.bandcamp.com/track/burn-them-all

I'm comin
and hell's comin with me
It's drinking up time
In this old saloon

You had an ugly world
But now it's over
And not a moment
too soon

He stood on a mountain top
In a ghost city of soldiers
This time it's got to stop
This time it's over

Burn 'em all   (cocksuckers)
Let's burn 'em all (motherfuckers)
God said to the Devil
Let's just burn them all

What makes people do
All the things they do ?
They can never steal enough

And now they just ran out of room

They die for fun
Burned out like the sun
No pride no dignity
They've even got suicide bombs

He stood on a mountain top
In a ghost city of soldiers
The devil said to Jesus
Where's your mother tonight ?

Burn 'em all   (cocksuckers)
Let's burn 'em all (motherfuckers)
God said to the Devil
Let's just burn them all

So let your fires burn the night
Paint darkness on the morning light
Make this place history
Like iron stars in the sky

Their hearts beat start to pound
So they can't hear nothing else
Hear them pray so loud
Just to save themselves

Listen to the thunder
As the lightnin' strikes
They're going under
It's happening tonight

Burn 'em all   (cocksuckers)
Let's burn 'em all (motherfuckers)
God said to the Devil
Let's just burn them all

Ajei kicks her mind to life and snaps herself back to her current time and sweeps visions and dreams from her mind. She looks across at her mother who grips the wheel bent to the task of delivering them. Things were changing; maybe for the better? She smiles in hope but then shivers in despair – things could get worse too? Does anyone know?

****

"What does everyone do around here Pops?"

"Exists!"

"It's a miracle they do that!"

Lincoln Xylo gazes from the tinted window of the large black Chevvy as 6 litres effortlessly pulls them up a long incline out of Great Falls on Highway 87. His eyes glaze over. The two men sit in silence for miles before Lincoln speaks again,

"Can't we delegate this shit Pops?"

"Told you before son, we do good business with land and casino's up here and sometimes business needs the personal touch", he pauses, "…and you gotta learn about the personal touch son!"

"Me and Skinny are good at 'The Personal Touch' Pops", Link nods towards the driver who sits staring at the road. Face expressionless.

More high plains miles pass before Link again breaks the silence,

"So this stoopid Snake sonbitch owed us how much?"

"At least $200,000."

"And now he's dead?"

"Yes"

"So we just begin working through his family until they pay?"

"Not that easy Son"

"Why not? It usually works?"

"Well this time most of his family got killed with him…at least the ones that would matter to him…two of his sons"

"There must be others?"

"His other son was killed in a fire six months earlier"

- 79 -

Link thinks.

"He got a wife then?"

"Yeh, but she is from the nation"

"So?"

"Well nobody knows who she is. No records. She was actually part of a major land deal and other arrangements a generation ago."

"When I'm in charge I'll simplify business Pops!"

Skinny looks in the mirror and his eyes meet BossX's as LinkX gazes back across the high plains.

Bostan Xylo is 78 now. He is misnamed after the city where his ancestors arrived from eastern Europe in the last century – Boston. His business (some would say criminal) empire is based in Helena; at least that's where he resides and where his administrators are based. His building there is modestly tall with four floors administering his business interests all over Montana, North Dakota and Wyoming. He has never been identified in any criminal proceedings and, during the last 40 years of his tenure, there has been very little adverse publicity. Business through the books is mainly property. The company rents properties in various cities and town on and around the high plains. The company also operates haulage contractors from many depots around the same area. The top floor of his building houses his "legal team" in very private offices adjacent to his own. Accessed through a separate and, hardly noticeable, door and elevator the staff in this office have little or no contact with other staff. His "soldiers" are based around the high plains and in the haulage depots. Everything has operated relatively smoothly for the last 40 years since he took over from his father. The worst decision he ever made was marriage and, although Anne is long gone, his son, Link, is his biggest worry. A movie cliché for sure. A son without the business sense to run the business – but with the false family pride that will not allow him to surrender the control that one day must be his to others more able. BossX wishes to himself that young Lincoln had found some other way in life, but he had long since been seduced by money, cars, drugs, women and weapons. Bostan Xylo sighs to himself, "Oh fuck!"

Lincoln Xylo, son of Boston Xylo, known as LinkX or, sometimes, "The LynkX" is a sonoffabitch! Anne must've been a bitch.

Skinny is BossX's driver, bodyguard and chief enforcer. Probably a borderline psycho but faithful. Bostan recruited him from the army special forces sometime after "Nam". Nothing he doesn't know about "black ops". He's totally faithful to Bostan but Bostan wonders what fuses will be lit in Skinny's mind when he is not here.

"Why didn't we fly Pops?"

"Because it's only a six hour drive Lincoln"

"Four hours plus piss stops Pops!", LinkX laughs at his 'joke'. BossX looks away as Skinny pulls into a highway diner. BossX groans as he gets out of the Chevvy with Skinny's help. LinkX swaggers to the counter, as BossX heads for the Rest Room cursing his prostate.

****

At Big Timber Ooljee, still driving as if in a trance, guides the truck onto Highway 90. She's now zoned with coffee and some of her father's magic powder. The fact that they follow the route Lucy Smith took some 8 months before is not known to them. That tree that fell in the forest of destiny started this fate avalanche of which they are now a part. It's late afternoon and they pull into a Bozeman Motel.

A watery sun in the eastern morning greets them as they depart the Motel after coffee, cereal and muffins. Their compasses set south and they pick up Highway 191 again. The mighty Rocky Mountains. Ajei's mind wanders again to the fleeing Nez Perce and she puzzles as to how they navigated this terrain keeping ahead of the blue uniform filth. She feels emotion and banishes it. She changes her focus and wonders about the music scene in Utah. She knows there will be bars and casinos and Ooljee has told her of a time when she used to work the music scene down there. She will see. She admits to herself that she is beginning to miss The Snake Brothers for the music – but nothing else.

They gas the truck in West Yellowstone before turning east on Highway 20. Soon they pass into Idaho. The Targhee Pass. The second time in as many months Ajei has left Montana. Rocky peaks loom ahead, shrouded in grey clouds. The clouds envelope her mind too now as she senses mountain peaks all around them. She thinks of her grandfather.

****

As Ajei's thoughts return to her grandfather, Skinny turns BossX's Chevvy off the highway and into the same small valley in the high plains plains where the Chief now lives. As they slowly drive toward the closest cabin, LinkX idly surveys the scene with some arrogant disdain. His eyes are drawn to the large oak and halt abruptly as he sees a large bird sat at the top. As Skinny opens the door for BossX the two men are startled as they hear a shot. They turn to see Link fire his handgun at the eagle. It dives from the branch and elegantly glides before using its vast wingspan to ascend. The three men's eyes watch the bird before BossX speaks,

"Lincoln!"

"What Pops?"

"Did you file the front sight on that piece?"

"No Pops – Why?"

"Because it will hurt like a motherfucker when I tell Skinny to insert it in your ass!"

"Awwww Pops. The bird was looking at me!"

"It was thinking it's never seen such a peckerbrain. Now put your toy away."

LinkX slowly puts his gun back under his arm but jolts in shock as he looks up and The Chief is stood in front of him. The Chief stares. LinkX finds himself backing away from the Chief's countenance before checking. He looks over to his father and to Skinny. They stand smiling as Link almost falls over backwards. The Chief speaks,

"Indian wisdom says: …Bad shit comes to people who shoot at Eagles."

LinkX tries to hide his embarrassment. He mutters to himself but somehow the Chief's character dominates easily. Link puts his gun away, clumsily. The three older men exchange glances before entering the Chief's trailer and he brings out a bottle putting four small glasses on the modest table they now sit around. Lincoln looks around unable to disguise his discomfort at his surroundings. BossX starts the conversation,

"Good to see you again Steaming Buffalo"

"You too Bostan Xylo"

Silence follows and each man slowly takes a drink. Lincoln coughs slightly.

"Jake The Snake had our money. A lot of our money!"

"Jake was a stupid shitpiece!"

"He never missed a payment until now."

"Death disrupts many schedules and commitments Bostan?"

"Nevertheless, he represented our interests around here. Considerable interests."

"A business is only as good as its employees Bostan."

Bostan falls to silence, as if carefully considering his next statement. He sips his drink deep in thought. Finally…

"We do need recompense Chief. I have partners too."

Now The Chief is silent. Link interjects,

"Fuckin right we do Pops!"

Bostan sighs before replying,

"Son – you are seldom right. That's why you need to learn – and learn fuckin quick. The quieter you are, the more you can listen, the more you can listen, the more you learn! Understand?"

Link begins to draw speaking breath but falls silent and red in the face as Bostan puts a finger to his lips.

Now The Chief speaks,

"You can take his farm."

There is a finality in the Chief's offer. Bostan falls silent in consideration.

"Contents and machinery?"

"There is lots"

"Then we have a deal Chief", Bostan offers a hand across the table.

Time dilates. A singularity moment. Numerous fates hang on this one moment. LinkX slowly looks at his Father, opens his mouth but doesn't speak. Skinny stares at The Chief. The Chief stares at Bostan. Up above the eagle soars but suddenly, as if it has come to a decision, furls wings and dropglides under gravity through a cloud. As the two men shake hands the eagle settles silently in another large solitary tree with a view of The Chief's trailer.

"Another drink Bostan Xylo?"

"I would love to Chief but we have a long drive", (Bostan's thoughts turn to his prostate).

"Then let us say goodbye once more Bostan Xylo. It was good to see you again."

The four men rise and move to the door. The Chief holds the door and steps to the ground himself as the visitors move towards their vehicle.

Slow time becomes fast time now as a swift shadow passes through a watery sun and the eagle is suddenly attached to LinkX's head. He squeals like some kind of pig as its talons tighten. It's a whirlwind now as Link kicks his feet trying to maintain contact with the ground but he is airborne. The eagle swings him around and into Skinny who is by now drawing a weapon. Skinny falls to the ground and the eagle drops LinkX on top of him before wheeling away to the air. Skinny gets off three shots at the eagle but is hampered by LinkX holding his head in total panic. The eagle swoops down behind the large tree before ascending when out of range. It circles and looks back as if mocking.

Skinny helps LinkX to his feet and looks at his head wound. Bostan speaks, calmly,

"How bad?"

"Hard to tell Boss it's covered in blood and Eagle shit!"

****

Highway 20 rushes south now. Not much traffic. Ajei chats to her mother as they both begin to calm from the pressure of the last few days, the last few weeks, the last few months and the last years. They even manage to recollect funny stories about Grandfather and, even Jake Snake. Ajei looks at her mother in silent amazement as Ooljee explains that he was not always like he was towards the end. Ajei's sad childhood memories run in her mind and Ooljee sees them too. She reaches out and holds her daughter's hand and the talk moves back to Grandfather and time on The Reservation.

Highway 20 falls to a high plain and Ajei gazes out at farm-steads. Towns and Cities; Ajei doesn't know the difference; she doesn't care. She suppresses a curse on the white man invaders. Her mother has told her, "This is now! The past is in books and long memories only." Rexburgh, Rigby, Ucon before they reach Idaho Falls. Gas stops and diner stops. She loves to observe different people. What stories can they tell? What ghosts are in their houses? What heavenly reward or torturous hell awaits them or is already in their lives? Do they all think and dream like her? Do they want live happy lives or do they just bide their time until whatever end fate has decreed for them? She misses playing her bass. She wonders what Halchita will be like? They have relatives there. There must be some beautiful creation happening down there? She'll find a band. A happier band than The Snakes – that's for sure.

Flat plains now. They criss-cross The Snake River. She shivers like Lucy Smith did. The truck eats miles. She is hypnotised by the white line and seduced by the distant horizons, her mind buzzing. This is a re-configuration. She's alive. Enjoy it. Fuckin rock and fuckin roll.

Now they climb. Another mountain pass before Salt Lake City. She's heard of the white tribe that stumbled across this whole country to carve a life out of the desert and salt flats. They climb again. Into clouds now. Soldier Summit, Castle Gate. The mountains ominous and shrouded in mystery, they clamp the weather around them like the fingers of the earth clawing at time. Slowing it down. Begging forgiveness.

Through Castle Gate the mountains begin to retreat. Ajei dozes. As she wakes the land is different. Drier, distant, dusty. Flat top ridges play perspective tricks on them. At Crescent Junction they turn south. Highway 191. She panics thinking she is back in Malta. The railway and the highway. She smiles at her mother. She needs to know she is not alone. Red rocks now, like she has never seen before. Moab, Monticello, Mexican Hat. They stop for a meal. She thanks her mother.

"What for?".

"I don't know, but thank you!"

Her mother smiles. Life might well be a different now. A lot different. Maybe better, maybe worse. They would stare it down, walk through the storms or die trying. The American landscape has told them they are here. Don't let up. Ever. Ajei thinks to herself, "Keep On Rockin! Keep On Fuckin Rockin!!"

Out of Mexican Hat they cross the San Juan River, Red Desert around them. They hang a left towards Halchita and a new life awaits.

Chapter 9
You Can't Stop

Speedy's mind buzzes big style as the Kawi purrs its route out of San Jose. She swings west on Highway 84 towards the Pacific Coast with purpose to check out the beach where the Snakevan was wrecked. Might be a time-waste but it doesn't matter, she has tamed this highway before and it's a great ride, although now she is full of purpose. She's uncovered new information. Progress. Lathan will be pleased. She hopes.

The highway twists and turns. She zones to the ride and leans the Kawi. It's running like it's enjoying the work out. She works the rises and surfs the drops. At the coast she turns south towards the crime scene. She gasses the Kawi, forgoes coffee in her haste. Now she cruises down to the beach where the wreck and the bodies were found. It's a quiet spot. Why here? Speedy parks the Kawi and begins to look around. She has studied photographs of the wreck and body site. Lathan had not even worked out there was another vehicle involved. Or, if he had, he just assumed it was the vehicle of another drug dealer – whatever. Speedy realises this is "different". She looks around and sees the dirt track where Jimmy had waited and soon pieces together how this went down. Ambush! The van has been pushed off this cliff on purpose?

She walks slowly down to the beach imaging events in her mind. Wait! That explains the safety seat welded into the Dog Truck. An ideal truck for an accident! The other vehicle – or at least the other driver would come off worst. On the beach now it all makes sense to her? Although, wait, the three bodies were all killed by shotgun blasts? Then she remembers the motorbike tracks mentioned in the crime scene report. The van was rammed at the top of the cliff and other parties on motorbikes finished off the occupants on the beach? That all fits. Crime scene investigation should have been way more thorough. Photos show a lot of footprints and should've been analysed to determine the number of people present. The strange dog was killed with a 38 but no ballistics report? Fucking amateurs – Speedy giggles to herself as she walks back up to the Kawi.

Officer Coppola is "on the case" as she rides back to SF along the coast. All the new facts ticking over in back of her mind. This is her best day of policework yet. Speedy has always been like this, once she gets interested in something it tends to take over. It was the same with her traffic police assignments, same with her motorbike.

"OK, I'm an obsessive!". She talks to herself,

"I'm a fucking obsessive. It's the only way to get results. Like Einstein, like Bob Dylan, like Joni Mitchell. You got to be prepared to sacrifice normal things until you do what you got to do. You can't stop. The mysterious forces of the universe will not let you stop."

You Can't Stop

https://badpeoplethemusical.bandcamp.com/track/you-cant-stop

It's a nightmare - Started out as a dream
Now it's an obsession - A crazy scheme
Like a dog on your leg – you know what I mean ?

Won't let go
Till one of you dies
You got to keep
The dream alive

You got to give it - all you got
Once you start – you can't stop

If ambition - is a form of greed
I'm not gettin - all I need
I'm beggin – I'll even plead

Like a racehorse
Round a track
Keep on ridin

Don't look back

You got to give it - all you got
Once you start – you can't stop

To the rhythm of dripping blood
I'd learn a martial art if it would do me any good
Up against a demon from the Devil's ass
He won't let me through – won't let me past

On a mission – From high command
No-one's listening – I don't understand
They think we're pissin – into the wind

Don't let go
Till you die
You got to keep
The dream alive

You got to give it - all you got
Once you start – you can't stop

Speedy has a restless night. She pieces together various crime jigsaw scenarios. She needs to work out how the tracker fits in? If she could find suppliers in the area they might be able to shed light on who bought it? She can ask her friend Martha in road traffic IT if she knows of these things?

First light sees her kicking the Kawi to life once again and cruising onto the highway amongst the early morning traffic. Speedy is so pre-occupied she doesn't even notice all the surrounding traffic offenses. Speedy is waiting at Martha's desk as she arrives for work that morning.

"Speedy Copp herself!", Martha smiles, "What brings you to my headquarters?"

"Got a big case!"

"Don't tell me you booked another Police Captain for speeding?"

"Well that sure was fun. Even if it fucked up my career?"

"Well maybe slowed progress a bit! You need to run a plate? I love that; it's just like the movies."

"Not this time Martha. Got bigger fish to fry on up."

The two women laugh. Speedy shows her the Tracker.

"I've seen these. Not all that hi-tech. They just send out a radio beacon so that a vehicle can be followed. Department don't use them now because any savvy crims, perps, pimps, pushers or otherwise self-respecting law-breakers can easily scan for them. These would be used by husbands who want to follow their wives or vice-versa; maybe private detectives?"

"Where would I get one of these in SF?"

"Start with E-Emporium, just off Columbus. They stock lots of electronic shit like this and if they don't do them they might know who does?"

"Hey Matty. While I'm here can you look up an old Dodge truck that was in the pound a couple of years ago?"

"Sure thing Speedo. Got a plate?"

Speedy references her notebook. Martha types in the details and turns to Speedy,

"Oh wow. Was the vehicle of a guy who killed himself up in Crescent City."

Speedy walks around and they both view the screen.

"James Smith"

"English guy"

"Shot himself"

"He was living in SF"

"That's why his vehicle was brought back"

"Why Crescent City?"

"Vehicle wasn't even registered to him"

"Wasn't registered to anyone – it was that old!"

"Hey look! He was a musician"

"Played in a band – The Lowdown Dirtkickers"

Speedy rocks back in her chair,

"OMG! I've seen them. They were good. You know what Matty, I once met him when I was on duty over by The Wharf."

"What you mean 'met'?"

"I remember talking to him on the street one day. He seemed nice...but pre-occupied? Worried almost?"

"Says here he was terminally ill. Autopsy showed a weird drugs cocktail. They assumed it was drug related. Put it down to some weird muso overdoing the hallucinogenics!"

"Can I get a print of this stuff Matty?"

"Sure thing Detective!"

The two women smile.

"Police work can be fun Matty!"

"You be careful Speedo!"

Speedy pauses and takes her gaze. She appreciates the concern. She always got on great with Matty at the academy. Most were too serious about police stuff but she and Matty were always up for a laugh.

"Thanks Matty – as usual. Drink sometime?"

"Sure thing Speedy Copp! HEY!!! You take care!!"

Martha manages to blow a kiss to Speedy as she walks away. Martha thinks,

"Kerrrrrist Speedy – take your time girl?"

The Kawi purrs across town. Speedy passes City Lights Bookstore; she thinks of Bob Dylan and Allen Ginsberg stood outside. She passes The Saloon; long time since she's been to a gig there. Eventually she swings right and finds the store and politely waits in the line as the geeky store attendant deals with a HiFi addict in front. Speedy sighs to herself,

"Keeerrrrrissst, these guys are all the same, chasing the ultimate HiFiRide?"

She waits,

"Patience! You'd be the same in a motorbike spares outlet?"

Funny thing about electronics shops is, no matter how specific your request, they always ask one more detail,

"Could I get a 17 Watt, 22 Gauge, 48 Oz, 25.6 Amp, ¼ Inch Jack Plug please?"

"Certainly Miss – What polarity?"

"FUCK – I don't know!"

Speedy's musing ceases as the HiFi buff turns and leaves, unable to decide between ¼ Watt or 1 Watt resistors, or some such like. The geek turns to her. Speedy retrieves the "tracker" from her bag,

"Do you stock these?"

"We did. I think there is a much better alternative these days. These are way out of spec nowadays."

He smiles.

"Did you sell many?"

"They were very popular – yes!"

"I need a list of buyers – if that's possible?"

The geek looks confused. Speedy repeats,

"I need a list of buyers – if that's possible?"

"I don't have that!"

"What do you have?"

"I don't do administration."

"Well who fucking does for fucks fucking sake?", Speedy immediately regrets her impatience and apologises,

"Sorry, but I'm pressed for time."

He looks red in the face,

"You'd need to speak to the manager!"

Speedy fails to retain her patience, but does manage to divert it to mild sarcasm, as she shows her badge and speaks as if to an alien,

"Take me to your manager!"

The geek reddens some more and walks in back returning with a tall slim balding man in dark rimmed glasses. Speedy fixes him with a stare,

"Officer Coppola, SFPD. I need some information on past buyers of these devices", she lifts the tracker. He looks nervous,

"I'm not sure our clients would appreciate me giving out that information?"

"It's confidential at this stage, although I could return with a warrant and some more officers to look through your records?"

Silence reigns. The manager retreats to silence. Speedy interrupts his thoughts,

"Your name?"

"Norman Birdcock"

"Well...Mr B...Well Norman...Perhaps it would save us all some trouble if we went to your office a looked at your records? You might also tell me of any other stockists around SF?"

Norman thinks for what seems like minutes and eventually beckons her to an entrance door. The geek looks on as Norman shows Speedy to the "Admin Office". He's nervous,

"We run an honest business here Officer."

"I don't suspect otherwise Norman."

"It's just that trackers can be quite popular with people who want to track their spouses?"

"Don't worry Norman, this is not a divorce case or anything that might backfire on you. In fact I'll make sure it doesn't."

"We like a quiet life here. We just sell components and interesting electronic innovations. Our typical customers are radio, HiFi or other analogue electronics applications. We do get some weirdos in who want to build pedals for their guitars but I think they are harmless? The trackers were a bit of a departure for us. I was undecided when I bought them in and it was Eric, my assistant's idea. Young men you know; always wanting to be ""up to the minute"". I thought they had some good potential but had some issues with the quality. I try and keep my customer base happy with quality. These things attracted a whole new type of customer though..."

Speedy listens to Norman as he can't stop himself talking. She actually begins to like him. What's not to like about people who are obsessive about the things dear to them? It's obvious Norman is obsessive about electronics. She can understand that. All power to him. Where would we be without electricity and electronics? Stuck in some cold mechanical world? Her mind wanders. Norman still verbally meanders,

"...I didn't take to some of them."

Speedy's concentration snaps back to this domain,

"Who didn't you take to Norman?"

"Some seedy guys wanted them billed to their business and the business address was a detective agency. Didn't like those guys! We even sold one to a Hell's Angel!"

Now Speedy's mind shifts to red alert. She remembers the motorcycle tracks at the crime scene. She smiles and looks at Norman,

"How did you know he was a Hell's Angel?"

"His motorbike and his fashion sense."

"Can you describe him?"

"Well...a sleeveless denim jacket over a leather jacket...leather jeans too...blonde hair...big moustache...older...but well...you know...?"

"Do I?"

"Scary!"

"Did he leave a name or invoice address or any ID?"

"Cash...I took the sale myself...peeled the bills from a roll"

"Why scary?"

"Well...you know...they don't care...they might just kill you for fun?

She laughs,

"I don't think so Norman. I know a few myself, I love motorbikes too."

She pauses,

"I've arrested a few bent electronics dealers though?"

Norman is quiet now. His circuits don't enable response to teasing. He is flustered and can only manage an embarrassed smile. Speedy halts his torture,

"It's ok Norman. I'm teasing. Actually I have never detained an electronics dealer...But, there's always a first time!"

They both laugh, although Norman's is hesitant.

"I'll print you copies of all the sales receipts."

"Thanks Norman", Speedy sits and waits as Norman sorts data, eventually printing off twenty or so sheets of paper. He sorts sheets and then hands them to her.

"Anything else you can remember about the HAMC man?"

"HAMC?"

"Hell's Angels Motorcycle Club"

"Oh...not really...sorry."

"Thanks anyway Norman. You have been an outstanding servant of justice!"

Norman smiles and Speedy walks to the door. As she opens it Norman speaks,

"Red Bandana!"

She looks back at him and he repeats triumphantly,

"He wore a red bandana!"

Speedy looks back and smiles,

"OK Norman. Thanks again. You take care."

Norman smiles to himself as he sits to his desk and sighs.

Speedy walks from the shop. She can't resist swinging her hips as she feels Eric's eyes follow her. As the door closes and she walks to the Kawi she exclaims to herself,
"MARV!"

****

Speedy's mind races as she shifts gears along The Embarcadero. A Harley flying a large stars and stripes behind sweeps alongside her and then right up Mission Street. His traffic violations don't worry her now. She has made progress today. Plenty to go on. It swamps her mind. She has a list of people, but she is also pretty sure the "angel" described by Norman must be Marv. Man, he is famous in the realms of San Francisco motorcyclists. They say he's been around since the 50s but a BIG WHEEL ever since the 60s. Famous for his red bandana. He used to be in band that just missed a shot in the big time, but that was way back. Speedy has seen his band play a couple of times but the clientele get a bit too rough for her. Even if it was Marv, it doesn't mean he's guilty but there is the evidence of motorcycle tracks at the crime scene. She's good at this; more progress in two days than two years of trained detectives. Still main part of an afternoon left. How best to use it? She knows where Marv and the bikers hang down in Dogpatch. Marv's Motors; there have been a few violations but they were never on her traffic hit list. She likes bikers and they kill a lot less people on the roads than young rich kids in sports cars or BM-fucking-Ws. Maybe she should swing down there and see if she can catch the man himself? She knows where he hangs down in Dogpatch. Marv's Motors; famous in the motorcycle sales and customisations; if you liked Harley's and similar.

Her mind whirls. Why not call in there? After all she's been on a roll these past two days. This investigation has PROGRESSED since she's been on the case. She guns the Kawi and carries right on by headquarters and down into Dogpatch. Now she descends the freeway ramp and crosses a couple of blocks and stands the Kawi. Speedy observes Marv's Motors for a time, trying to work out a strategy for her questioning. She could go in as a biker? But how would she broach the idea of "The Tracker"? No, that wouldn't work. She will have to be the police officer; but that will make Marv, or whoever, completely clam up? She needs to be more subtle. Maybe she could take a chance and suggest it was found on a vehicle that passed through Marv's Motors? Could work? Worth a try! Chances are Marv will deny everything she'll just have to try and make some kind of impression? What are the chances of that? Slim! She thinks again. If her theory is correct, the tracker was found on the Snakevan which was rammed by the Dodge pickup which was an older vehicle. Her thoughts pile up! She slows herself down. She could go in and feign an interest in older Dodge pickups? Ask if they know anything about them? See where it leads? Speedy Copp kicks the Kawi to life and glides into the yard of Marv's Motors.

"Prospect" Al looks up from the Fat Boy he's working on. His eyes lock on to Speedy and he downs his spanner wiping his oily hands. He's at her side as she switches off.
    "You wanna trade that for a proper bike?"
Speedy holds his gaze.
    "Nobody disses my ride oil-boy."
She is calm and leans towards Al. The moment extends and extends and extends (at least it seems like that to Speedy) until Al breaks into a smile.
    "That's the 'tude we need."
Speedy relaxes and steps off the Kawi. Al holds her gaze and says nothing. This time Speedy loses and she gives him a smile.
    "You got a problem with the Jappo shit lady?"
    "She's sweet oil-boy. Nobody touches my bike but me!"
    "So you're here to ask me out?"
    "Nobody touches me either!"

Al smiles. An unusual event. His eyes shine. He changes. Deep inside fate makes a move; his chemistry changes; some DNA sparks to life; a gravitational impulse interferes with his rhythms; who can say; who has yet worked out these equations, linkages; the push-pull of the universe. Speedy notices. She doesn't notice that she notices but something electromagnetic sends a wave that drives across a void and moves energy; it's all energy; it's all connected; small moments that happen all the time, all connected, knots of fate-lines; nodes and anti-nodes. None can escape this web; no outlaw, no politician, no genius, no master, no servant, no God, no supermodel, no film star. It has happened, it happens, it will happen. It's a fact; we are all fact.......................

"What's with the music?", Speedy nods her head towards sound emanating from behind garage doors.

"Marv's band rehearsing."

"Sounds good."

"They are good!"

"What they called?"

"The Marvos."

"Imaginative!"

Al smiles. He has the conversation rocking! He thinks carefully,

"I'll buy you a drink?"

Speedy pauses. She was going to affirm but then remembers she's "on a case". She pauses again and hears herself speak now,

"I might do that."

Internally she is unsure of the voice tone she achieves in that statement. She tries to get herself back on track,

"I need to pick up a couple of bikes from north and I'm looking to buy a truck?"

"We don't do a lot of 4 wheel vehicles Miss!"

"A friend of mine told me he got a nice old Dodge truck from you?", Speedy looks around the yard as if looking for a suitable vehicles. Al's expression changes. He suddenly tenses.

"Don't remember nothing like that lady."

"James Smith. Guitar player?", Speedy looks for any change in his manner.

"No, no...NO. Can't recall anyone like that", Al overacts.

Now she realises Al is not going to give anything away but his "denial" gives away everything. The Dog has been through here; she is sure of it. A silence hangs. Al smiles at her. She can't help but smile at him; he's quite handsome! The music has stopped now and a door opens. She suddenly sees a red bandana and the imposing figure of Marv begins to approach them across the yard. Speedy is suddenly nervous. Al speaks first,

"Young lady wants to buy a truck Boss!"

Marv draws on his cigarette,

"So she comes to Marv's Motors?"

"Sure Boss! A friend of hers recommended us!"

"Oh and that would be?", Marv's eye burn into Speedy's brain. Now she knows how Frodo felt with the eye of The Dark Fuckin Lord upon him as he fumbles with his ring.

"James Smith?"

"We don't know no James Smith!"

"He was a musician too", Speedy tries to smile. She wants out of this conversation now.

"Was?"

"Yes. He died", she looks down.

"How?"

"So you don't remember him?"

"Nope!", Marv's tone is flat and aggressive. Speedy summons her courage and is undeterred,

"It was a ""Dog"", it said Dog on the front", she tries to laugh.

Marv doesn't look remotely like sharing any sort of humour. Speedy's mind empties. No signals from brain to mouth. Al interrupts the black hole silence,

"Anything else we can help you with?"

"Guess not. Thanks anyway."

She turns and walks to the Kawi. She feels the eyes burn into her. Glad to be leaving, her heart beats fast double time. She was out of her depth and struggling to get back to solid ground. Her mind races. She kicks the Kawi into life and is so glad it fires first time. She only looks ahead as she swings out of the yard and off towards Cesar Chavez. It's all a pity because she had felt quite an attraction to Al. That doorway to an alternative universe had been closed by another force. Marv! What the hell? She needs to get back to her office and work out exactly what she has got?

****

"What the fuck was that Al?"

"An Angel Boss!"

"More like a fuckin nightmare? I don't like anyone asking about that shit. You know what went down! What did you tell her?"

"Nothing Boss. Don't know nothing do I? What truck? Who's Jimmy English? Never heard of him! What Money?"

Marv smiles. Al always has a humorous countenance. Nothing gets Al down. Marv puts an arm around his shoulder,

"You remember that Eagle though Al?", Marv splutters through laughter.

"Caught me off guard Boss!"

The two men laugh together before Marv walks back into the practice room. Al is thinking of Speedy as he hears the band kick into a song.

Don't Know Nothing

https://badpeoplethemusical.bandcamp.com/track/dont-know-nothing

Did you say robbery?
I'm sorry I can't hear properly
I been in bed with a cold yeh?
And I already told yer

I don't know nothin
You must be jokin'?
Robbery is awful
It's so unlawful

But – I Don't know nothing about it
Nothing at all

I was out with my girlfriend
We'd been surfin'
We were returnin'
She's only learnin'

Don't know nothing about it
I wouldn't give you no bullshit
Give me a break officer
I'm sayin' like I said before

Don't know nothing about it
Nothing at all

There's no such thing as a victimless crime
I hope you get them to do their time
I got nuthin' to hide
I hope you put them inside

There's no need to shout
I don't know what yer talkin' about
I got no information
I bin away on vacation
And I'm sorry I broke my probation

I'm not tryin' to be funny
I only do work I can take a pride in
I could do with the money
But I'm law abidin'

Don't know nothing about it
Nothing at all

You got no reason to hold me
My solicitor told me
No matter how hard you try
I got a cast iron alibi

I don't know Jack shit
I wouldn't give yer no bullshit
That's about the size of it
I'm no culprit

I'm a vic and you're a perp
Do you think that you're Wyatt Earp?

Give me a break
Your giving me earache

Don't know nothing about it

*****

Back in the uniform of traffic enforcement now Speedy feels strangely deflated. She has enjoyed her two days as a detective and the looming mundanity of gunning down BMW driving shitbags with Doppler bullets did not seem too enticing a comparison to return to. She tells her Commander she will need to pop across to Bryant Street and report what she has uncovered. On the internationally accepted "scale of interest" she estimates his mental activity as "fucking disinterested". She needs a change.

As she walks north she turns details of the case over in her mind. She figures she has done pretty well. A cool breeze and bright day uplifts her mentalities. There is a Spring spring in her step.

She asks Jane, "Is he in?". Jane nods, lifts an eyebrow, tosses her head in the direction of Lathan's office and gets back to her admin. Speedy knocks and enters. Lathan is staring at his PC. He motions her to sit, as if he is landing a space shuttle on the moon, before a little flourish on his keyboard prefaces him turning to her smiling.
    "How did you enjoy your work experience Serephina?"
    "Call me Speedy. Everyone else does."
    "I'm not everyone."
    "OK Dave."
    "Most people call me David."
    "I'm not "most people"."
Speedy worries that this meeting has already taken a wrong turn. She tries to alleviate the mood with a smile. Lathan leans back smiling too,
    "So tell me what you found? If anything?"

Kerrrissst this guy is annoying. She bottles her feelings as she recounts her "investigations". His forehead creases,

"So this guy was some kind of musician?"

"Yeh. They are quite a well known band on the scene."

"Sound like bangerheads to me Sereph...errm, Speedy."

"No they are good. I've seen them a couple of times myself."

"Sounds like they are drug crazed low lifes to me ...Speedy."

Speedy thinks,

"Keeerrrriiisssst...talk about jumping to shit conclusions. I'll have to translate this to wankeranto language."

She slows down her delivery and explains,

"No...I think a lot more complicated. The poor guy was terminally ill and who knows what complications there were around all this?"

"The usual complications? He fell in with a crowdbad and probably deserved all he got?"

"No I think it was more complicated."

She details her reasoning and her follow up on the tracker and the possible involvement of a biker gang.

Lathan sits and thinks before blurting,

"I hate bikers. This is a chance to stick-shit some of them?"

Speedy thinks,

"How can someone so dumb think they are so smart?"

She summons her patience,

"No, it's a lot more complicated."

"So how do you think we should proceed ..errrrm..Speedy?"

"I don't think we should?"

"How so?"

"So long ago now. Complicated. Sometimes best to let things lie?"

"Let things lie? Didn't we swear some kind of oath ...Speedy"

"To protect the State against all enemies!"

"Exactly! So these musicians and bikers are our enemy. We got a chance to asskick them here!"

"Not that simple here Dave. You can't turn back time?"

"No but we can weed out some perps?"

"And maybe stir up trouble?"

Speedy begins to make unreasonable demands on her reserves of patience.

Lathan stands and walks slowly round to her. He leans forward and takes her hands and lifts her to her feet,

"I could make a case for funding for another officer in my department...Speedy?"

Her eyes close momentarily. His grip tightens.

"You have shown a lot of promise here?"

She opens eyes to look at his face in front and above hers now. He releases one of her hands so he can stroke her hair now.

Speedy's Dad had always taught her to "pick a spot and punch it through at least a foot". So that's exactly what she does. The spot she picks is Lathan's nose. He staggers backwards from the blow. He is dazed and receives her boot between his legs. She asks,

"Where do I get the application form?"

She turns and walks out smiling at Jane who has heard the outbreak. Jane smiles at her. Speedy tosses her hair back,

"He ought to look where he is going?"

Chapter 10
English Bob

A '63 Mustang cruises onto The Gate heading south. English Bob looks to his left at the city. He feels a buzz. Who wouldn't as this view opens up? Lucy Smith has been writing semi-regularly and he loves getting her letters. After she passed through Lincoln City, must be 3 years ago now, Bob had found himself thinking about her from time to time. Well, most days actually; the hair is grey, the face lined but the mind is still "immature"! So, when her first letter dropped in his mailbox it was springtime and, that made it the best springtime he could remember for long seasons. Some people are destined to be lonely and he was one; didn't mean he didn't want a fellow traveller. He did! Sadly, they didn't seem to exist. His full analysis of why life had panned out this way was incomplete at present. A project he returns to from time to time. His obsession with music had often distracted him from "relationships" and the theory that it could get, and had got, in the way of actually living with others was a central pillar of his current theorem. Maybe he just never met a woman with a complimentary mindset? Or maybe "likes would repel"? These theories are woefully incomplete; more fun to play the saxophone than be a sociologist? Nevertheless, he had returned to his theory more and more since Lucy's letters began arriving. The time she turned up at his open mic session in Lincoln City still re-runs in his memory; as do her songs. No other performers at the open mics have come close to getting through to an audience like she could. At least that was what his memory was telling him. Some people just provide that "something else" as they sing. They may not be the best singers, or the best instrumentalists or the best looking but, somehow, a style, an intensity, a quirk or quirks and, a drive, a drive more than anything makes them soar above the ocean. Bob's mind always wanders when he drives.

What news Lucy wrote in that letter? Almost a year after she passed through Lincoln City. She was singing around SF. She was in a band. She was going to have a baby. Then, a dreadful letter on a gloomy sea mist day; her partner James (another English muso guy) had died. Bob had dropped the letter onto the floor in his kitchen in shock. He didn't know what to do. Why had she told him? Of all people? He was pleased she had but, confused now. He didn't know what he could do? Almost on autopilot he had quickly packed a bag and jumped in the Mustang and gunned it south. Bob found the address she was staying at over in Haight Ashbury. He hadn't known what to expect. A young woman called Ronee had opened the door and was very cautious when he had asked for Lucy. When in the house he had found Lucy picking at her trusted guitar and staring out the window. She smiled to see him. Bob had said, or at least he'd thought he said all the normal things but, somehow, those conversations are always at the edge of the solar system. He always knew there was other "stuff" in Lucy's story and he didn't presume to understand. He had learned, long since, not to make assumptions so he had left it with the usual quotes of "…If there's anything I can do? ", "…Let me know if you need anything?…". He really knew his orbit there was awkward at this time so he'd left. He had touched her hand and she had smiled. He was glad he'd gone.

He'd sat in the mustang outside staring for a while, not wanting to just turnabout. For some reason he felt he was not alone. He can still remember it now. So strong he looked back at the window to Lucy and Ronee's house but no-one was looking. His eyes were drawn upwards; no-one at the bedroom window; then to the roof. Nothing. He looked back to the street ahead wondering what to do. For some reason, and he couldn't stop it happening, he was back in Manchester, looking down his old street. Time machine thoughts. He was blowing his new saxophone. His beloved Yamaha 23. He'd just bought it a few weeks before and used to rush home from work to play it. He loved the sound. Sadly, his neighbours didn't. Neither did his then partner. She'd split soon after he brought it home. Bob laughed to himself, "If they'd been married she would've cited the saxophone in adultery proceedings!". He corrected himself for an unfair thought. She was kindhearted and well meaning. Just sometimes things never fitted. Fate had no connection points to fasten them together. He was shaking now sat in the car; reminiscences could be so painful. Normally, when his thoughts went this way, he would press the pause/stop button and get on with other stuff but this time his mind insisted on re-running this memory movie. He was playing a blues-riff, just working on his sound. The sax sound was everything – a weak wandering tone was no use. There was a ring on the door and he had laid the Yamaha carefully on the couch before answering. There was a gang of children at the door. He had smiled. One kid spoke,

"My Dad says you sound like a ship on the canal in fog!"

"I'm working on that!, Bob had smiled until another kid had blurted

"My Dad says you sound like shit!"

The gang had run off laughing at this. Kids can be cruel bastards. Bob had looked up the street as they ran. He turned back and one kid was still stood there staring at him. Bob spoke,

"Hello pal?"

The kid stared.

"Don't tell me! Your dad thinks I sound like a bull hippopotamus?"

The kid looks puzzled.

"Dunno Mister…………..but I like it!"

"Thanks Pal! Don't think your mates do!"

"They are shitheads!"

"Well – creating sound is not to everyone's taste!"

"Can I see it?"

"Sure thing Pal. In you come."

The kid had eagerly walked into his front room and stared at the golden saxophone as if some other-worldly object that he dare not touch. Bob had spoken,

"It's a Yamaha Tenor Saxophone."

Bob picks it up and shows the kid how the fingering works. The pads "pop". The kid looks at him and smiles. Bob asks,

"Wanna hear it?"

"Yer!!!!"

Bob stands back and hits his riff. He expects the kid to back off or even run out the door. Nothing of the sort. The kid's face widens to a fullscreen grin.

"Wow Mister – that's ace!"

Bob had smiled and played some more, the kid showing no signs of leaving.

Why was this movie playing now in his mind? Now? Of ALL times. Memories so clear he felt a reminiscence-tear on his cheek. He couldn't stop shaking.

Eventually Bob had suggested that the kid better go home. His Mum would be worried? The kid had seemed reluctant to leave. Bob had asked,

"What's yer name Pal?"

"James"

"Well James, thanks for lisnin! You can come back any time!"

"Thanks Mister!"

"Well I'm Bob!", Bob had offered a hand and the kid had smiled as they shook.

"Oh and tell your pals and their Dads from me that they are the shitheads around here!"

"I will Mister"

Bob had smiled at the kid and watched him skip off up the street.

The kid never did come back but, as far as Bob could recall, that was maybe because Bob had made the move to America about that time. It had been a bad time at the steelworks and his girlfriend had left. Somehow the unkind comments of the kids had gotten to him and, who knows, if not for the last kid he might've given in to social pressure and wasted his life stood around at soirees and in pubs and in shops and walking dogs and on package holidays and in the fucking Lake District and on "home improvements" and new cars and mowing his lawn and having dinner parties and package holidays and patios and patio furniture and barbecues......well.............FUCK ALL THAT!

Here he was now. Must be twenty years later. Sat in his Ford Mustang in San Francisco like Frank Bullit himself. He could see that kids face as clear as anything. Bob wiped away the tear and spoke to himself,

"Thanks James!"

He had wondered what ever happened to that kid? Little did he know – that kid was now sat in his passenger seat – also wiping away a tear – he spoke but Bob didn't hear,

"Thanks Bob!!"

Bob didn't hear, perhaps partly because James didn't exist in exactly the same time-space continuum, although there is some overlap. But James did give Bob a song which Bob found himself singing on the way back north. It arrived kind of crystal clear and Bob was mighty pleased with himself too.

Back Home In England

https://badpeoplethemusical.bandcamp.com/track/back-home-in-england

Ferry my dreams back home
I want to be – back in England
My world is there alone
I'll be back in spring and
Do my travelling in my dreams
Nothing else means a thing and
I just want to be back home – In England

I've seen the Golden Gate
And I've seen the Empire State
And I just can't wait
To be on my home plate

I've seen Point Reyes
Laurel Canyon summer days
Route 66 to Highway 99
The Nashville Skyline
Highway 51 to Highway 14
Cincinatti to New Orleans

Woodstock to West Saugerties
But there's one place I want to be....

Ferry my dreams back home
I want to be – back in England
My world is there alone
I'll be back in spring and
Do my travelling in my dreams
Nothing else means a thing and
I just want to be back home – In England

I've seen a Nebraska Highway
And I've seen Thunder Bay
The Charles River Basin
Grand Central Station
Poughkeepsie to Tallahassie
Albaquerque to Cold Turkey
It keeps coming back to me
That there's only one place I want to be....

This time though, as he drives once more over the Golden Gate, Bob feels happier about meeting up with Lucy. She's invited him to meet at The Lowdown Dirtkickers HQ/Studio/Yard and he is slightly nervous of meeting her bandmates. They might think he harbours "romantic intentions". He's not that sad? Is he? Anyway, he has other reason to visit SF this time. Boris The Cranium is giving a talk at the Academy of Science Member's Forum and he is travelling down to meet up with Boris and Wangly. Bob is to meet them for a Dirtkickers gig tonight (Friday) or on the Saturday afternoon for the talk. Boris has been on about this for months. He's been working on equations linking Electric Charge and Mass. If the fundamental quantity of the universe is Energy then Mass and Charge must be fundamental quantities of energy. Bob thinks he understands Boris's theory as far as he can. He understands that there is much fuss about Einstein's Special Theory that tells us the Mass/Energy relationship but not so much that tells us a similar Charge/Energy relationship. Ok? So, if Mass can distort space-time, as it does to create gravitational attraction. then Charge must also distort space to create electrical forces. Fuck yes! Furthermore, it must distort space-time a sonoffabitch more than Mass because electro forces are that much stronger? For years Boris has been wrestling with this. He disappears sometimes and when he does manifest, he always looks tired. Bob worries about Boris and wishes he could help more. Unfortunately, his knowledge of maths can't keep up with Boris's. It all gets complicated because you got to account for electricity forces being repulsive as well as attractive as well as so much stronger. Rock on Boris. You gotta keep pushing the perimeters. Bob smiles and stares down the mysteries of the universe. God didn't put us on this earth to blindly follow some "faith" and hope for heaven or fear hell? Did he? He didn't give us inquisitive minds and mathematics just as mental exercise? Did he? He didn't give us independence and a beautiful planet just to listen to us singing his praises? Did he? In fact – truth be known – God didn't put us on the planet? Did he? The Big Bang did that – although Boris reckons he's also got a way of mathematically explaining Singularities! He calls it QuantumElectroCalculus. FuckinRockFuckinOn Boris!

Bob cruises the streets of SF now. He can't resist. He guns the Mustang and it seems to love the hills. Frank Bullitt rides again. Bob has seen that movie so many times. He smiles. Too cool for the blues. He hears the ride cymbal accompanying the muffled power of the Mustang. Life is not too bad. Bob's mind drifts back to 1968 when he saw that movie and all these years later he's in the remake. How cool is English Bob? He opens the window and his lungs seem greedy for the San Francisco air. He feels his chest expand with each breath. He's intoxicated. He reins in his imagination slowly before heading over to where Lucy told him she will be rehearsing with The Dirtkickers. Bob is nervous as he parks the Mustang and rings the bell at the yard gates. Lucy Smith answers,

"English Bob – no less!"

"Well well well – my favourite singer!"

Lucy hugs him, her mood massively different from their last meeting. Leading him into the yard she notices he is carrying his saxophone case.

"Never travel without your Yamaha eh Bob?", she smiles.

"You know me!"

Mike, Thunderman and The Gnome wait in the practice area and Lucy introduces them. There's a nervous few silences until The Gnome declares,

"Never too early for an IPA Mike?", and the beers are served. Bob asks,

"You still turning out songs Lucy?"

"More and more these days!"

"Great!"

"We have a gig tonight – you gonna come along?"

"Wouldn't miss it! Need any tenor sax?"

Lucy looks across at Mike. Mike nods,

"Well, if we can work something out, we'll do it! We have all afternoon."

Bob unpacks his Yamaha as Mike looks on.

"A ""23"" English Bob, nice horn! They say they can be a blank canvas to release the player?"

The Gnome whispers to Thunderman,

"Fucking noodlers!"

Mike gives TheGnome a finger.

"Otto Link?"

"8 double star"

TheGnome looks at TMan,

"Am I in a parallel uni-fuckin-verse?"

The sax players carry on, undeterred,

"Royals or standard?"

"Always use standards Mike!"

"Me too!"

Lucy giggles now.

Eventually English Bob blows some life into a riff or two and TheGnome feigns being blown back from his stool his back against the wall now. Bob smiles as TheGnome exclaims,

"Big sound, big sound BIG FUCKIN SOUND...."

Mike laughs and explains TheGnomes behaviour to English Bob,

"He can't handle beer at this time of day!"

TheGnome sit's back on his stool now and lays out a Texas Shuffle like only he can and leads the band into a few blues tunes. Bob hits the ground running. He loves it. The band give him the space to play as they slot into the grooves. Lucy smiles at Bob. They take a rest and TheGnome gets Bob a beer. Mike asks,

"You got any songs Bob?"
"A few"
"Wanna try one?"
"Sure would love to Mike!"

Bob looks at Lucy and steals himself. The 23 riffs hard with a Fela Kuti like sound and TMan and TheGnome fall in line. Michael J Remo smiles as Bob links into a vocal.

Tempted

https://badpeoplethemusical.bandcamp.com/track/tempted

Walk by a lowdown river
In and out of the mist
Bad memories this place delivers
The chances that I missed
Shadows and sad stories
Ghost ships and washed up time
And I'm like Peter Lorre
Contemplating a crime

I'm tempted
I'm tempted
I'm tempted I admit

Bullet holes in the mirror
Where I shot myself
7 years is over
But I'm still stuck in hell
I was talkin' to a pilgrim
He taught me to understand

No-one can stop us dreamin'
And we got a bust out plan - and

I'm tempted
I'm tempted
I'm tempted I admit

I like to think
So I exist
I like to drink
I like it – I like it – I like it – I like it – I like it when I'm pissed
I like it I like it
I like it I like it
I like it I like it
I like it like this

The Devil spoke to me
He said "You like it here
You like the women
And you like the beer
Well there's a space at my table
For a new Demon
And I think you are more than able
Do you want promotion ?

I'm tempted
I'm tempted
I'm tempted I admit

I like to think
So I exist
I like to drink
I like it – I like it – I like it – I like it – I like it when I'm pissed
I like it I like it
I like it I like it
I like it I like it
I like it like this

Mike Remo smiles at Lucy as they finish the song up,

"Whoooooo-eeeeeeee – that's in the set tonight alright!"

Bob smiles. Cooler than Steve McQueen right now. Right now –
right now – right fuckin NOW!

"What's the gig?"

"Bar in Haight. Should be ok. Good crowd. Hell's Angels,
crackheads and Skulk Rock. You got a gun English Bob?"

Bob looks nervous for a moment before they all crack up laughing. As laughter subsides, so does the light, dark truth seems to
invade but, as they look around, it is only Tiny, stood in the
doorway. Mike serves coffee before they begin to load up the
van.

Strange how fate's webs encompass people. Oceans apart,
generations apart and, as it turns out, universes apart, there are
bonds that cannot be broken. Like one of Boris The Cranium's
theories, perhaps? Web theory? James looks at English Bob and
smiles. He remembers his sound. "You don't got a sound, you
don't got nuthin!", he remembers The Rock and Roll Doctor
telling him that. Some mantras stick, some mantras are bullshit,
some mantras are true. Keep the ones that work for you. Hearing Bob's sound again is a magical memory but it cuts. It cuts so
bad because it's time gone. He's stuck here with memories. As
The Dirtkickers busy themselves packing equipment Bob
slowly packs the Yamaha he stares into space as James stares
into his eyes. They both travel back to Stockport England. Both
wear sad smiles for now. At least English Bob can cheer himself
up with a beer and a groove tonight. It should be a good gig.
James remembers The Coochie Lounge very well. A big venue
and a good earner for The Dirtkickers. The crowd could indeed
be edgy and he vividly remembers his nervousness at playing
that venue for the first time.

The Dirtkicker Van pulls up to the Coochie Lounge as early
evening dims. English Bob looks out at the clientele swarming
at the entrance. He gulps. Gigs in Lincoln City are never like
this. His uncertainties swell up but he stamps them down. He
looks across at Lucy and she smiles. No backing out now! Bob
remembers talking to an old jazzer back in his Stockport steel-

work days. That band would draw a big crowd. The guy told him,

"When you are on the stage – it's your gig – no point trying to be controlled or like anyone else – you just got to chase your sound – impose it on them – you know best!"

His words ring in Bob's mind now. The English Bob sound is coming to the Coochie Lounge! Fuck Yes! Run for cover Motherfuckers!

The band and Tiny load equipment into the venue. Tiny is immense. Mike deals with the owner. There is a House PA and Mike and Tiny look it over. Mike shouts over, "Hey Bob, check the sax mic will you!". Bob hurriedly gets on stage and unpacks the Yamaha. His hands shaking but he keeps a lid on it. He stands up to the mic and blows a riff. OH WOW – the sound swells and surfs around the room. It seeks out corners, it rattles the hanging lights, it sparkles, his breath fills the room, the Yamaha has never sounded quite this good. He trills high but then descends to a low B. Bob loves the tenor bell notes, stretched around the Yamaha bend, their wavelengths shimmer, the harmonics play nervously at the edges, tension, they trip close to the edge. Bob pauses and Mike asks him if it's ok? He nods. He is a Dirtkicker. He loves Mike Remo. Everyone loves Mike Remo.

Jimmy English hovers and watches the scene. Sadness in his eyes, He watches over Lucy as she soundchecks. Her faded black Telecaster rings. Her Fender amp provides a distortion that is so musical. It overloads the bottom end as well as the sparkling highs. A slight scoop in the middle range. This guitar combination is THE sound. Lucy has one sound but it's a great one. If she plays softly it's clean but if she hits harder it soon develops "edge". Not quite like his old Stratotone into a similar amp but it is A SOUND. He loves it.

Finally the whole band soundchecks. The Gnome punches a Texas Shuffle and TMan wanders the Bass around his musical universe. TMan owns the lows. He fills, he glues, he pushes it to unique edges. Mike smiles at them. He's been with these guys forever. The groove is everything. Keep on rockin. Keep on rockin. Keep On Fuckin Rockin. KOFR!

The band sit and relax now in a corner of the room. They watch the early arrivals enter the room. A buzz builds until Bob realises he can't hear people the other side of the table. The conversation fragments and he just chats to Lucy who is sat next to him. He looks up as the room-buzz diminishes suddenly and noticeably. The mosh crowd that has formed suddenly parts and Marv appears through the crowd. For the first time Lucy notices he has a strange limp, his right foot at a strange angle. He sees them and smiles, sachaying over. Lucy giggles. She's met Marv a few times these days and his initial scariness has subsided to that of a likeable rogue. Lucy knows that he is more than that though? James told her about "The Snakes on the Beach". Her mind whirls momentarily and she's back in the terrible nightmare of 3 years ago. She knows Marv is well capable of violence. He smiles across at her and gives English Bob a salute before he sits deep in conversation with Mike Remo. Lucy closes her eyes and corrals her thoughts back to the present. As her eyes open Don Estrada has appeared behind Marv and his gaze transfixes Lucy. She smiles. Keeeerrrrrist, what a couple? She used to be a quiet suburban girl and look at her now. A fierce killer (if provoked) associating with characters like Marv and Don. In fact, Don is the father of Little Joan's favourite "Aunty" Ronee and even sometimes babysits for Little Joan. No malevolent force could get to Little Joan with Don Estrada on sentry duty. Lucy's mind reverts to the concept of fate and she wonders how twisted fate can be. Could you ever cut its strands? One strand might do? It reminds her of a conversation she had with Boris The Cranium when she was in Lincoln City. She turns to Bob,

"When are you hooking up with The Cranium?"

"Well – him and Wangly travelled down yesterday. I did tell them where the gig was. Who knows?"

"Be lovely to see them again."

Mike Remo gives the signal and TheGnome, TMan, and Lucy stand. Lucy squeezes Bob's shoulder as she stands and moves to the stage. They make their way behind the PA stacks. Switch on. Toon up. Bob fumbles with the Yamaha and his neckstrap. Checks his reed. Mike Remo on Jimmy's old Stratotone. This is living. Not many people have brought Skulk Rock to the stage. Fact: only five. Tonight they were disturbing the breathable once more. Living can't get better. A time capsule you climb inside and become suspended from real life. It all runs on groove though. Lose the groove and crash and burn. Nothing is nothing without the groove. The best guitar sound ever is nothing without the groove. There is no poetry without the groove. TheGnome and TMan know it, Mike Remo knows it. TheGnome calms his energy and organises it into Roman Legions that he will soon send out to conquer the world. Imminent now, he will unleash hell. Not the entropic hell of savages, heathens and people who can, and need, to be conquered. This will be ordered. Set to equations. The Great Equations of the Universe. Not many have this knowledge. TheGnome has it though. His drum licks form into ranks and wait for the orders to go forth and conquer. Electricity connects the Skulkers who now press to the front of the stage. TheGnome is the million FirkaWatt connection terminal. He's plugged in and ready. He looks at his three bandmates. Aligns them with his gaze. He knows they are plugged in. Locked on. He finds time to smile across at English Bob. Bob gets it. The positrons glow in his veins. Charged and ready. A small moment that makes a big difference. Bob is ushered into the Skulk Rock capsule. He's safe. These guys are presidential. Four clicks and it begins.

The Downside

https://badpeoplethemusical.bandcamp.com/track/the-downside

So this is love and don't forget it
It wrecks your life if you let it
Everybody's got an asking price
And with you I asked so nice
I gave you my life – I told you once I told you twice
What is a guy to do?
So meet me in Kathmandu
I always choose high altitude

For such an important rendezvous

This is the downside
The underside of the landslide
Keep your eyes open wide
Cos all of the prophets lied

But run and hide is our current task
Colour my dreams while they last
Camouflage just don't look right
And meet me in the morning - Meet me at night
Any time of day will do
But none of this means I'm in love with you
I just moved into a room with a view
I always choose high altitude
For such an important rendezvous

This is the downside
The underside of the landslide
Keep your eyes open wide
Cos all of the prophets lied

How did we get marooned
Cloured red and blue
The compass doesn't have a clue
So send for the superhuman crew
Send for the sad-eyed prophets too
The magazine husbands who
Wanna make their magazine love to you
While I'm on top of K2
Wearing my platform shoes
I always choose high altitude
For such an important rendezvous

This is the downside
The underside of the landslide
Keep your eyes open wide
Til all of the tears are all dried
Because you know deep down inside

That all of the prophets lied

Sometimes stars align, gravity waves reinforce and the groove establishes itself. Everything is tuned but there's a tension too. It makes for excitement. Edge. This is such a time. The crowd up for it. They sway and look heavenward. No-one wants to be nowhere else. Lucy smiles across at Bob. They play a blues now and his raw edged Yamaha notes rise to the ceiling, they survey the crowd and burst like sonic fireworks shimmering and showering the audience. Bob's low notes rasp with even harmonics. Mike Remo smiles at him now. His sound sets women on fire. Mike Remo knows it; he has channelled that saxophone energy himself. He glances over the audience to the back of the room and sees light bounce from dark hair that draws him in, weaving around his optical senses. He thinks it's Felicia. His body conducts electricity back and forth like tides speeded up. It's definitely her disturbance in the crowd ocean? Got to be. There is no other theory that fits his observations. He watches as the disturbance moves around the perimeter where a raised floor contour provides for a coign of vantage over the mosh. She-ite, it's not Felicia. His first emotion is disappointment – but not for long. The dark hair descends to her collar but there the sea of curlwaves ends chopped at a faded denim jacket over a well worn motorbike jacket over a loose black T. Her Levis a perfect fit before they terminate at her biker boots. Mike Remo's fingers on autopilot as they form chord strikes in groovetime with TheGnome. He's never seen her before? Or has he? He would've remembered? She climbs on the groove swaying her hips. Too cool for this room.

The fates gather as shadows in the distance. James English bounces over the crowd. He soundchecks. He couldn't adjust it any better. He senses fate energy. Something building. Fates converging. A confluence. He can't work it out. All too complicated. He too sees the hair as she arrives and he sneaks glances at her almost forgetting that no-one could see him anyway. He swoops over and looks closer she looks familiar?

Speedy Copp has never been to The Coochie Lounge before but she has decided to check out The Dirtkickers. Although she is now "off the case" she is still obsessed by the case. Business and pleasure. She loves live music and she needs to know the band that James Smith, the suicidal Dog Driver, had played in. This is all part of the jigsaw puzzle she had been assembling before she had to kick Lathan's dumb ass. The buzz hits as she walks in. This sound is different to other bands. Very different. The groove grabs her, invades her mind and sways her body. The Dirtkickers play a sparse ballad now and her eyes are drawn to the girl singer who takes the vocal. This is cool. The song speaks of beauty and sadness, resistance and inevitability. Gravity; why fight it? Speedy looks around the crowd. A lot of motorcycle angels. Then she sees Marv at the other side of the bar. He's looking at her. She fires a vision torpedoe back. She is not intimidated. She turns her attention back to the band. The girl sings "Gravity pulls us all down." True enough! The song ends.

"You like this band?"
Speedy turns around to face none other than Felicia. No-one on stage had noticed Felicia enter this time. Maybe because they'd all noticed Speedy? She smiles,
"I do!"
"First time you seen them?"
"Yeh"
"Welcome to Skulk Rock."
"What?"
"Skulk Rock! That's the groove here!", Felicia smiles.
Speedy smiles back as Felicia offers her a bottle.
"Oh I was just gonna get one."
"Bar was crowded so I got two. Good plan eh?"
Speedy smiles and takes the beer. They clink the bottles as the band starts the next song. She could do with a friend.

From the stage, Mike Remo thanks Lucy Smith and Speedy takes note,
"Same surname as James Smith deceased?" Her mind concentrates.
Mike Remo now introduces,

"On the Tenor Saxophone tonight – Mr English Bob!"
She looks at Felicia and asks,

"You like this band?"

"I love them. Skulk Rock grows on you!"

"He's English?"

"Dunno, not seen him with them before?"

"They used to have another English guy?"

"Jimmy English."

Speedy sees a sadness drain into Felicia's eyes as the song begins. Skulk Rock begins to grow on Speedy too.

The band kick into "Tempted" and English Bob rules the venue. He's older but the Skulk Rock audience don't fuck with any thoughts about that. Just the groove, the sound, the words, the rollercoaster ride that it all provides. English Bob sends forth ocean wave packets of Yamaha magic. All the saxophone gods align, His mind, his fingers, his lungs, his breath, his "embrouchure", his "Texas Growl" (at least that what he called it back in Manchester), years of working on a "big sound", his "23" (how often he toyed with a grand idea of getting a "62" or a "Mark VI" or a "Big Bell Super 20") and now he was so glad he was on his 23 and channelling the "English Bob Sound" on the blank canvas it lays out for him. The best horn ever! English Bob is happy.

As the song finishes Speedy waves her now empty bottle and asks Felicia if she wants another. Felicia smiles and nods and Speeds makes her way across to the bar. As she waits in the queue the band finish the next song and take a break. A crowd floods the bar as Speedy makes her way back with four bottles (she figures it will save a wait further on down the line). She walks around a pillar to where she left Felicia and finds her chatting to one of the band. Felicia takes a beer offered and Speedy offers one to Mike Remo,

"It's ok. I get my beers for playing."

"It's well earned."

"Are you a friend of Felicia's?"

Speedy looks at Felicia; embarrassed as she doesn't actually know her name.

"We just met. Everyone calls me Speedy."
Mike smiles, nodding at Speedy's beers,
"You thirsty?"
Speedy smiles,
"Fuckin band brings in too many people! Tough to get served. Gotta think ahead!"
Mike's smile widens,
"Skulk Rock is thirsty work. Long may it continue."
Felicia touches Speedy's shoulder,
"Thanks for the beer........Speedy."
"Got another one in the bank for you. Saves time!"
Felicia smiles,
"My saviour!"

English Bob places "23" on its stand and finds his way off stage. His heart pumps. His veins wide open. His blood is like a flash flood. He needs beer. He looks for Lucy but she is busy chatting to TheGnome and TMan and he wanders over to Mike Remo, taps him on the shoulder,
"Thanks for the gig Mike. Best one of my life."
Mike smiles. Bob is a fellow traveller. Mike can recognise them. Bob looks over at Felicia and Speedy, almost as if he is not entitled to look. Mike speaks,
"Hey Bob. Thanks not necessary. Meet Felicia and Speedy."
The two women smile and Bob's heart whacks a pint pump into his arteries. However much finds it's way to his brain, his brain can't come up with anything cool enough to say to these two women. Women? These are heaven sent angels from the highest echelon and he is just a mortal. Bob tries to avoid looking like he is in shock as he smiles,
"Nice to meet you."
Speedy responds,
"Wanna beer?"
"I'd love a beer."
She passes him a bottle.
Felicia looks at him for a few seconds now before speaking,
"Where are you from Bob?"
"Lincoln City Washington State."
"They all talk like that up there?"

"Ah no, I'm from England."

"Near Manchester?"

Bob looks shocked.

"Yeh. A place called Bredbury."

Felicia's eyes widen,

"I knew it. Jimmy used to talk about Bredbury."

"Who is Jimmy?"

"Jimmy – who used to play in the band!"

Bob realises now who they are referring to. His memories of Bredbury flicker.

"What'd he say about Bredbury?"

Felicia thinks. Speedy looks at her face. Mike looks at her face. Everyone is happy looking at her face.

"He said it had a steelworks................."

She continues,

"...............where he used to watch the guys pulling red hot metal bars across a floor....."

Bob listens intently,

"...........like they were red hot snakes being born out hell!"

Felicia lays on the melodrama and they all fall silent as she finishes. Mike is first tp break the silence,

"The Limey sure had a way with words – ""snakes born out of hell!""" – will probably pop up in one of the songs he left."

Everyone silent now until Bob speaks as if in a bad dream now,

"No – he was right. I did that job. They were Snakes from Hell!"

Everyone in the small group now wrestling with unwanted mental image memory. Jake Snake looms into Mike's memory. Felicia remembers Jake Snake too and leading him and his sons into Jimmy's trap. She shivers and puts her mind to moving the conversation elsewhere. Bob carries on though,

"Nearly ten years I did that stuff. No life. The kids used to watch us from the railway embankment."

As Bob speaks some part of his memories explode into view. Keeeerrrrrrisssst – the kid who liked his saxophone playing was called James! He puts two and two together, he completes a definite integral, his Euler Series is convergent. This James they talk about could be the same kid who once stayed back to listen to him playing the saxophone. His mental maths says it's possible. He has the necessary but not the sufficient.

"Sufficient" was actually stood next to him now. Sufficient was looking at English Bob, looking at Mike Remo, looking at Speedy, looking at their bottles of beer but most of all he was looking at Felicia. If only they knew?

James' and English Bob's reminiscenses are interrupted now. Marv appears around the pillar and parks himself in the group. Mike slaps his shoulder but Marv just fixes on Speedy. A tension erupts. Eventually he speaks,
"What's the bitch wanna know this time?"
Everyone slightly shocked at Marv's demeanour. Mike speaks,
"Hey Marv – keep it cool?"
Marv glares at Speedy,
"Says she's a friend of young Jimmy?"
Mike Remo puts an arm around Marv now and, looking across at Speedy, he laughs,
"Well, that's possible!"
Marv is undeterred,
"Don't like bullshit bitches coming around my yard askin' bullshit questions Mikey."
The underlying menace in Marv's voice is obvious to all. All too obvious to Speedy and she struggles to rebut him. Mike has seen Marv like this before and begins to lead him away,
"Hey Marv – you need a beer? And – will you do a song with the band next set?"

Mike moves the aggressive angel slowly back to the bar. Felicia comforts and reassures,
"Hey Speedy……………….never seen him like that before!"
Speedy takes a deep breath to compose herself, Felicia's arm around her shoulders. English Bob excuses himself and follows Mike and Marv. Speedy is no shrinking violet for sure but Marv's aggression was like the minutes before a tsunami wave and was sucking everything into the distance. It has shaken her badly. Felicia asks,
"Were you a friend of Jimmy's?"

"Well I met him once."

Felicia looks at her quizzically,

"Let's finish these beers and then go somewhere quiet?"

Speedy looks at Felicia for a drawn out legato moment, her eyes taking in Felicia's face. That's an invitation no mortal could ever refuse. Speedy nods acceptance with the reappearance of a smile. Long time since she's felt this way and Motormouth Marv melts to the back of her mind as Felicia takes over front and centre.

The band takes the stage again, kicking through the Skulk gears now. TMan and TheGnome control the room. The vocals, the bass, the guitars and English Bob's tone adorn the groove. Felicia and Speedy take to the dance floor and somehow take the eyes of everyone else whilst they only have eyes for each other. As Mike Remo introduces the next song he looks out over the crowd and sees Felicia and Speedy leaving together. A Skulk Blues numbers sees Michael J Remo with the blues now. He is not going to be the one going home with Felicia. He sighs and looks down at the fretboard of his Stratotone. He wonders what trails Jimmy English has left here for them to trip over?

Chapter 11
Fate Friends

As Speedy and Felicia depart the Coochie Bar into the cool breeze between the buildings they don't speak. They do smile. They make their way to Felicia's Porsche. As Felicia unlocks it Speedy has to convince herself she is not a hypocrite for getting into such a car. She has spent years persecuting drivers of these. She giggles to herself. She looks at Felicia and concerns of hypocrisy melt and evaporate to nothing under the onslaught of Felicia's attraction force. Tonight is tonight and the two of them have it enslaved. The moon itself appears between clouds. Speedy smiles across the car at her companion. All time slows. As the Porsche exits the side street and cruises past The Coochie Bar Speedy glances at the entrance as two unlikely clientele are entering.

******

"This is the bar?", WanglyDangly speaks to BorisTheCranium as the two men enter the bar. Wangly lopes and Boris, as always, looking deep in thought,
"This is where Bob said he'd be?"

The two men enter and pause in amazement at the scene. Their conservative dress sense and general awkwardness make them a little obvious. The groove prevails though and Wangly cannot disguise his enthusiasm for the rhythmic sounds. He gyrates as he walks and leads Boris towards the bar as they scan for English Bob. The tone of the Yamaha once more dances on the atmosphere, Wangly immediately recognises the sound and turns to see his friend English Bob, appearing from behind a PA stack on the stage. The trademark bulging veins on Bob's neck and on his forehead appear as he fills the crowded bar with sweet but tense overdriven saxophone tones. Wangly smiles to Boris as he orders two IPAs from a friendly barmaid. Some of the regulars assess them for coolness but the atmosphere is relaxed and everyone is happy smiles. Mike Remo's stratotone cuts in and sends packets of harmonically edged chords dancing over the crowd. They reverb from the ceiling and shower the audience. The band takes it down now but no loss of groove. Now they hear Lucy's vocal. Wangly turns to Boris and happiness reigns.

From stage, Lucy spots Wangly and Boris as they gravitate to the bar. In truth Wangly is not hard to spot. Her mind replays the open mics up in Oregon. She tries to catch their eye but they are intent on beer. She smiles but memories of her nightmare trip in The Dog begin to return to boundary of her conscious thought. Vividly. English Bob, Wangly and Boris were amongst her first new friends. Funny how it helped at the time. As her Dad always used to say; "one door closes another one opens". She winces as she feels a wave of guilt from the past. Maybe she closed the door on Seth Snake a little too decisively and she deserves all that followed and all that will follow?. She's got Little Joan to worry about now though. She shivers and turns her mind back to the gig.

*****

Speedy sings to herself as the spring air over the windscreen of the Porsche toys with her hair. Felicia doesn't speak as she accelerates across intersections. The houses pass by. Speedy tunes to the sound of the engine. She's heard these enough times from the street. She would be reaching for her speed gun by now. She giggles to herself. Intoxicated! Why? She hasn't drunk that much? She looks at Felicia. Felicia turns and smiles. Both women relaxed and at ease. Speedy is sad to admit that the car thrills her. Felicia drives well too. She watches Felicia's fingers and wrists as she steers; her legs as she operates the pedals. She feels her own blood carry excitement around her body. She needs a change in her life after the bad experience with Lathan. What a prick!

She flips her mind and wonders where they are headed? Felicia's legs dance under her short pleated leather skirt. Expensive. She looks so casual even though the skirt is high end. Ankle boots and denim jacket and T-shirt complete her look. A heavy silver chain too. She would look cool in anything. Felicia's legs dance on the pedals as they cross The Panhandle and then the late night traffic left and speed towards the park. Speedy is glad she set out tonight. It's a tough life being an obsessive and she can't forget the "Snakes Case" and, in the back of her mind she still moves the character pieces around trying to fit them together. She liked the band; that is for sure. Felicia looks across at her as they pass the Botanical Gardens. Moonshadows from tall trees dance on the breeze.

"I figured we could go to my place in Sausalito?"

"Sure!"

Speedy relaxes back into the seat. Now they turn north. Cross the park. The Presidio underpass and now the great towers come into view. Who would live anywhere else? The Golden Gate thrill never diminishes. Tonight it's amplified by the moon, the car and, most of all, Felicia, most of all Felicia, most of all Felicia.

****

Mike Remo locks TheGnome's groove with his Stratotone bark. His mind wanders but his eyes don't. He looks to the door. In despair. He saw Felicia leaving. But still hope. He burns to see her enter again. To talk to her again. These feelings sneak up on you. He remembers a gig in Susanville, years ago now, when Jimmy English first set eyes on Felicia. "That was the start of all of this!" He remembers the long drive to the next gig and trying to tell Jimmy that such women can eat your heart, crush your heart, piss on your heart. He figured he was immune to all that and was in the business of the impossible task of putting the old head on young shoulders. Probably it's a good thing that such a project is not possible. He was swimming against the tide for sure on that one from the moment Jimmy set eyes upon her. Now here he was, a victim of the same blitzkrieg. Over two years later and she's eating his mind and heading for his heart. "Don't plead with fate Michael Remo!", as his Mum used to say. He decides to ignore his Mother's advice and hope that fate will make Felicia walk back through the door. No sign. His mind wanders to Jimmy. He misses the little limey. Maybe Jimmy would warn him now and the old head would be on the young shoulders and his own head has suddenly turned back time. He would settle for that. He barks some bad tempered chords from the stratotone at a turnaround and sacrifices himself to the gig now. Some things are not meant to be – but this is – Skulk Rock,

Catch Your Eye
https://badpeoplethemusical.bandcamp.com/track/catch-your-eye

This has got nothing to do with the truth
My girl likes baseball and she's a babe called Ruth
I saw her ghost in the mirror of the past
But I knew that I'd never see her again – this side of the glass

I should never have changed my routine
Circumstances caught me at a crime scene
I should've used petrol – not paraffin
The jury's still out – I heard them laughin'

Never believe what you see in mirrors
Everything is on the other side
You might even see an ill-spirit
Be careful they don't catch your eye

I been feeling lowdown strung out and blue
The doctor told me to go away cos she don't know what to do
I got a long time curse and it hurts
It just gets – worse and worse and worse and worse

Never believe what you see in mirrors
Everything is on the other side
You might even see an ill-spirit
Be careful they don't catch your eye

I'm working as a lawyer - I got an office and a sign
I got a business lunch with a client of mine
I make air move while I'm waiting for the wine

I got lots to prove but I'm taking my time
I got lots to prove but I'm taking my time

*****

Felicia and Speedy are quiet as they cross the bridge. The moon and stars watch them. The waters still between them and the island. They glance at each other and smile. Words are never necessary on The Bridge. Felicia swings the vehicle into the observation area on the north side. Late night and not so busy so they can park facing the island and the towering city of high rise and hills. The moon hovers maintaining its surveillance, the stars as its security like snakes eyes in the darkness. The two women are safe, untouchable, immortal – at least for now. The lights of Oakland sparkle in the clear distance. They gaze on the view and an eternity passes. Maybe three fifths of a millisecond? Before they kiss.

Now, as they smile and watch clouds pass under the moon, Felicia speaks,
"I just got this apartment in Sausalito. No-one knows yet?"
"No-one?"
"My husband."
Speedy smiles and looks away. Not knowing how to react.
"I'll take you back over The Bridge if you want?"
"No I'd love to see the apartment."

*****

The band break from the second set now. The crowd loving it. Mike Remo is happy again. Skulk rock kicks ass and trumps everything. His disappointment of Felicia's early departure has evaporated into the night air and been blown away on the groove breeze. He smiles at English Bob. Slaps him on the back.
"Beer time EB!"
"Sounds good Mike. And……..thanks for the gig."
"Hey, no problem. You're on the groove, don't overplay, big sound……and the women love it!"

English Bob smiles from ear to ear. They move to the band table where jugs of beer have appeared. Lucy is already chatting to a very excited Wangly and Boris. Mike smiles at the group. Lucy's friends are not the usual clientele of The Coochie but that is good. Widen the sphere of influence of Skulk. Lucy introduces the two guys giving them their full titles

"Mr WanglyDangly and Professor BorisTheCranium".

Mike smiles. Where would the world be without eccentrics?

Now Marv appears in the group and helps himself to a beer. Lucy smiles but she is always slightly nervous in Marv's presence. Especially since James told her of the events on the beach. She knows what Marv is capable of. Mike Remo looks at him,

"You're a tetchy fucker tonight Marvo?"

Marv stares back through the silence of the group, he holds their attentions before smiling,

"Ohhhhh – Did I scare your supermodel friend off Mikey?"

"You'd scare the Devil off! Marv Fuckin Motormouth!"

Marv laughs out loud. He turns to Wangly and Boris and makes an aggressive face,

"Do I scare you fuckers?"

Wangly looks worried but Boris never has much handle on normal human behaviour and smiles at Marv,

"Boris Kranum – at your service!"

Marv looks puzzled but then smiles,

"Marv Motormouth – at YOUR service! Goddam, you gotta be a mad scientist with a name like that? Professor Von Kranum?"

The group all laugh. Mike thinks "wtf has come over him?", as Marv continues,

"……..well top scientists are always Von Something?"

The communal laughter brings Wangly's confidence back,

"I'm Professor Von Wangle!"

Marv offers a hand,

"Pleased to meet you Von Wangle!"

He shakes hands with Wangly and Boris and looks across at English Bob,

"I already know this limey fucker!"

They clink glasses.

Felicia guides the Porsche down the hill into Sausalito. She hangs a left before the bayfront and winds up narrow roads to a small detached building crammed onto a small footprint. They park in a small bay the other side of the road and once again look out over the water to SF.

Felicia seems strangely unconfident as she opens the door and they climb stairs to an open plan room with an even better view.

"Oh wow!"

"Yeh"

The room sparsely decorated but a couch sits in from of the vista window. Felicia pours wine and they sit. Quiet at first.

"I needed a place of my own."

"I know that feeling."

"I've not got around to all furnishing of this place but I come here from time to time and, if anything ever goes wrong, it's my place. I got a legal friend and she has made sure of that. None of hubby's money here."

"You don't sound too happy?"

"Sorry, don't mean to sound that way. I'm lucky. Only me to ever blame."

"How long married?"

"Over two years now."

"Is it ok?"

"Thought it would be but it's evaporated."

"How so?"

"Not sure. Ever since Jimmy went really?"

"Who's Jimmy?"

"An old friend...", Felicia seems to drift off in memory, "...he used to play in The Dirtkickers."

Speedy suddenly realises who she is talking about. Her "investigation" obsession suddenly leaps back into her mind. She could find out more information here? The thought lasts for a whole instant before her liking for Felicia crushes any thought of deception. She tells Felicia of her traffic cop career. How she once met Jimmy in the street. Then her chance at being a detective and then how and why she upset Marv...

Felicia listens with thoughts jangling as Speedy relates her story. She thinks of her own part in it all. She considers how her involvement might incriminate her. Guilt shivers run down her body and tingle in her fingers. She considers lies she could now use but her liking for Speedy reciprocally crushes any thought of deception. She tells of The Snakes and their, then, evil intent towards Lucy, Jimmy's illness and his last acts to save Lucy and her new life? She leaves out the bit about leading The Snakes to their demise.

They move closer together on the couch in front of the window in front of the town in front of the bay in front of the city in front of the moon as it begins to turn red.

Felicia turns to Speedy, her eyes clouded
    "I'm a bad person."
    "Heyyyyy......"
    "Always taken the easy way. Life put so many chances my way."
    "We're all bad people!"
    "Not as bad as me!"
    "Maybe not!", Speedy strokes her hair.
    "I miss Jimmy. I miss his music."
    "Some things not meant to be?"
    "Or it WAS meant to be and I fucked up?"
    "You can never know that?"
    "First time I saw him was nowhere. Nowhere, Northern California."
Speedy lets her talk,
    "A wedding – crazy. The Dirtkickers had a gig in the bar of the hotel where the wedding was. Why is it you can like somebody so soon? We could've had time together. We did have time together. But not good time. Just time. Stolen time. He was a kid really. So far from home. Like me..............."

Speedy's finger falls from her hair gently on to her neck. She takes a blanket from the back of the couch and throws it over them both. Felicia carries on as if in confession,

"I always loved music but modelling was easy. Easier to get started. You gotta survive though. You're on your own. No band to be part of. I had a few scares. Learned how to take care of myself. I got some good friends and we look after each other. He so nearly talked me out of my marriage. He never knew but I would've given up on my marriage for him. He looked so unwell though and I knew he had a thing with Lucy by then. Or maybe it was my own selfish greed? I tried to help. I did help. I hope I did?"

"Sounds like you did!"

Felicia lifts her head. She looks at Speedy. She smiles and holds her hand. Speedy feels like she is holding someone hanging from a precipice. She grips tight. Felicia whispers,

"If you fall in love you got to mean it!"

Crooks Don't Know

https://badpeoplethemusical.bandcamp.com/track/crooks-dont-know

Well I know it's easy
To hurt the one you love
Crooks don't know
It's responsibility
You gotta be careful of
Crooks don't know - crooks don't know

So when you hold another's heart
Don't bruise it or lose it or tear it...
If you ever fall in love - you got to mean it
If you steal a heart - you gotta keep it

Well you're callin' down a curse
You're singin a hymn with a backwards verse
Crooks don't know – they don't even suspect
You're drivin' too fast in a hearse
It'll only ever make things worse
But crooks don't know –and what will they think of next ?

So when you hold another heart
Don't bruise it or lose it or tear it....
If you ever fall in love - you got to mean it
If you steal a heart - you gotta keep it

Well I didn't make the rules
And you can't change 'em
Crooks don't know – but it's true
God will give away your souls
To his nasty angels
Crooks don't know – They will kick the shit out of you

So when you hold another heart
Don't bruise it or lose it or tear it....
If you ever fall in love - you got to mean it
If you steal a heart - you gotta keep it

Be careful of your lover's heart
If you're messing around
The Devil can fire a cupid dart
If he wants to drag you down

So that's the chance you take
With all the love you make
Crooks don't know- that love can mean hard work
Even a vampire's heart can break
There's so much at stake
Crooks don't know – Holy Water will really hurt

So when you hold another's heart
Don't bruise it or lose it or tear it .... apart
If you ever fall in love - you got to mean it
If you steal a heart - you gotta keep it

****

Marv puts his arm around Boris. Mike Remo and Lucy look at
each other in amazement. SF's Senior Angel and Professor Boris

Von Cranium! They smile. Marv asks, in only slightly drunken tone,

"What brings a top scientist to SF Prof?"

"Giving a paper at The Institute tomorrow."

Marv actually sounds interested,

"What's the subject?"

"Kind of unification theory?"

"You mean like unifying relativity and quantum theory?"

Boris looks pleasantly surprised to be asked a sensible question – from a most unlikely source.

"Well yes…"

Marv continues,

"As I see it, gravity is the bending of Space-Time and that is what causes the attractive force?"

Boris nods. Marv is on a roll,

"And…its so called Mass that distorts Space-Time?"

"That's right! Einstein's General Theory!"

"But Mass is the same thing as Energy?"

"E equals MC squared! Irrefutable!"

"So that means there's no need for any fuckin bullshit exchange-particles?"

Boris smiles now,

"Sure – so called Gravitons are a complete bullshit concept!"

Marv beams, his tone getting more and more confident,

"I knew it! Fuckin complete fuckin bullshit that there has to some fuckin exchange particle to go with any force. It's never gonna fuckin sit. There's no fuckin maths that can explain how swapping particles gives rise to an attractive force? No fuckin gravitons! And then we get to magnetism! How the fuck does that work? The fuckin bullshitters will tell you that particles are exchanged? What fuckin particles? Photons? Like fuck they are? No maths to explain it man! Then they bullshit you bout fuckin virtual particles? Do they think I'm fuckin stupid or what?"

"You don't sound stupid to me Von Marv! This is what I been saying for years!", Boris smiles.

Marv slaps him on the back and leans back smiling,

"I knew it! Fuckin Professors know fuck all!", he smiles looking at the ceiling but suddenly looks back to Boris, "…apart from you Professor Von Kranum!"

"Well – I am not really a Professor Von Marv!"

The two men laugh and smile at each other before Marv carries on,

"What it is Von Kranum is…we need to show that electrical fuckin charge is equivalent to energy is equivalent to mass. Then…we can show that electromagnetic forces work by warping Space-Time too?"

Boris responds, adopting Marv's delivery to some extent,

"Fucking right Von Marv! I have been developing that for years. Tricky though because you got the repulsive force as well as the attractive one to explain?"

"Trust the maths Von Kranum. The correct theory will explain attraction and repulsion. That's the fuckin beauty with maths. No fucker can say it's lying! They can say it's wrong. Like you made a fuckin mistake but if the maths says something is right then it fuckin is fuckin right. Look how Dirac predicted anti-matter? You'd have to say ""that's gotta be bollocks Paul"" but you wouldn't be able to show no mistakes and – fuck my crazy ass – now we found anti-matter! Scientists these days all got chicken brains. They fuck with computers and smash up atoms trying to make sense of the wreckage like fuckin CSI detectives. They need some maths. They're fuckin chickenheads Von Kranum!"

Boris holds his high-five palm in the air and Marv slaps it as he exclaims,

"That's fuckin right the fuckin Mascara fuckin Snake!"

Boris looks a little puzzled at this.

Mike and Lucy and Wangly and English Bob erupt in laughter

Happiness reigns.

Mike Remo looks at his two bandmates,

"We'd better get this third set rockin."

They return the Skulk Rock salute and make their way back to the stage.

Mike Remo introduces the song,

"This is for chicken headed professors everywhere…",

Chicken Time

https://badpeoplethemusical.bandcamp.com/track/chicken-time-2

I got a chicken eye – in my head
I got a chicken eye – in my head
I got voodoo vision – I can see the dead

I got a chicken head – on my neck
I got a chicken head - on my neck
I got a foul mouth – what the hell do you expect

I got chicken feet in my shoes
I got chicken feet inside my shoes
I don't know how it got there – I guess it just grew

I got chicken legs in my jeans
I got chicken legs inside my jeans
It's a lickin' chicken – if you know what I mean

I got a chicken feather on my chest
I got a chicken feather on my chest
If I take off my shirt – you will be impressed

I got a chicken liver – in my gut
I got a chicken liver – in my gut
The more I drink – the more it gets my pecker up

I got chicken thoughts – in my brain
I got chicken thoughts – in my brain
I told the army – they said I wus insane

You gotta fight – when you get the blues
You gotta fight back – when you get the blues
If you turn chicken – I'll eat you too

****

"The thing about Jimmy English is…was…complicated",
Felicia grips Speedy's hand as she speaks,

"He knew he was dying and he loved Lucy from the band. He did know he loved her. He thought he loved me but I'm not sure. It's difficult to trust men when you are in my business. I mostly trusted him cos he was so young and naïve. But....then....Lucy got pregnant and they had to do something about the bad people after them."

"Was that The Snakes?"

"Yes. They were pure evil!"

"No-one is pure evil?"

"Well no-one could save them!"

"Apparently not. They ended up dead on a beach?"

"Yup. Jimmy came up with a plan to push them into the next world."

"Good way of putting it."

"Well I don't think it went according to plan...and...it took Marv and his merry men to finish the job."

Speedy goes quiet as all the pieces now fall into place. The shotgun cause of death. Yes indeed! Shotguns sure can be deadly. The motorbike tracks. Felicia talks on auto-pilot now,

"They would've killed Lucy?"

Speedy is quiet. She measures all she has learnt. It all fits. This IS the truth of it. It's still murder though? She runs fingers through Felicia's hair. Drugs and money? Murder is awful and unlawful? She is beholden to uphold the law? It's an oath and she has sworn it? Her finger strays along Felicias shoulder now. Hell, uphold the law? She is only a traffic cop and likely to remain so now she has rearranged Lathan's nose? She feels Felicia's hand tighten on hers. Tonight seems so different? She's only known Felicia for hours? How can she be sure of anything? Hell, she's a married woman! What good would it do to try and build a case on this though? It would ruin Lucy's life and her young daughter's? It would also ruin Felicia's life? She holds her close now. So many thoughts. Duty or not she can't do it. Fuck it. Case closed. At least she solved it. Lathan couldn't find his way to the bathroom! She looks down at Felicia and kisses her. Felicia looks up at her, she shivers, she needs company, she needs help, she needs a companion, she needs protection, she needs love, she needs what everyone needs,

"Stay? Stay forever?"

Stay

https://badpeoplethemusical.bandcamp.com/track/stay

Is God ever there when you pray ?
So you and I may as well face this day
This is no time to run away
A frozen heart is gonna turn you grey
So stay – why don't you stay ?

Just consider all the facts
Time is never turnin' back
This mirror's is only cracked
Not as if the rain is turning black
So stay – why don't you stay ?

Let's fly into the sky a mile and
Float in clear moonlight
Take it easy for a while and
See what life is like when we get high

We may as well face the tide
This is no time to run and hide
Why don't we stay inside
Forget all the tears you cried
And stay – why don't you stay ?

Is it down to gravity
Pulling us apart
Of all the places to send me
Don't send me out of your heart

Tears will never dry at night
Let's wait for the morning light
I like a cup of tea

At about ½ past 3
And stay – why don't you stay ?

Let's soar into the sky once more
And follow angels round
Check the score on heaven's door
Until it's time – to go back down

Tonight is the night for bad dreams
But nothing is as bad as it seems
Why don't we stay up all night
Switch on all the lights
And stay – why don't you stay

When you got the devil on your trail
He's gonna make you cry and wail
He don't have any mercy
And he wants you to hurt me
So stay – why don't you stay

Come back from distant darkness islands
By frozen heart street light
Where ticking clocks are nearly silent
Since all the stars fell from the sky
And stay – why don't you stay

I know how fast life goes by
They always say time flies
So why don't we share tonight
Be like we did it twice
Stay – why don't yer stay

Bad beer before you sleep
Can make you wake up and weep
But bad dreams or reality
Will never last eternity
So stay – why don't you stay

Old and cold and rainy wind

Cuts and seeps beneath the skin
Of souls who never ever win
Or never even have a friend
So stay – why don't you stay

There's love above a crowded island
Away from city lights
Where you can hold my hand a while and
Every star is in the sky – tonight

When the devil in disguise
Comes flying out of clear blue skies
We know that we are wise
We know which lies are lies
So stay – why don't you stay

Is this the 7 year itch
Life can be such a bitch
7 years of bad luck
7 years to tell me that "love sucks"

I know that a stone won't bleed
I know nothing is garaunteed
In fact it is my holy creed
And that is all I need
So stay – why don't you stay

Every stupid step I've taken
Every second I wasted waiting
Every time I've been mistaken
Every dawn the world awakens
So stay – why don't you stay

I stalk the silent cities
With humble thoughts alone
Dragging ancient bones so weary
Over worn out cobble stones

Time can provide a strange reward

The opening and the closing doors
But I can hear the strangest chords
A future fate to drift towards

I'm on a distant darkness island
In cold and clear moonlight
Where ticking clocks are nearly silent
And every star is in the sky – tonight

I got all the time in the world
But there's not enough time in the world
You make me so alive
But there's not enough time alive
So stay – why don't you stay

The answer - if you look it up
Is cancer - that will fuck you up
Everything becomes so grey
Before it's ever taken away
So stay – why don't you stay ?

Sun streams through a crack in the curtains. Speedy Copp watches the circle of light it makes track across the blank wall. The blank wall is her life. Is this her fate being traced out by the laws of the universe? It's certainly the start of something. She feels certain. Felicia is still and as Speedy turns her head to look at Felicia's face she sees her eyes open wide. They both smile. Felicia speaks,

"Coffee time?"

"Maybe in 30 minutes or so?"

They both giggle as they slip under the blanket again.

Morning now and a bulk cargo ship moves slowly across Felicia's window. They finally get around to that coffee. They watch the ship. It's a big world out there. No need to speak. When one of them does it's Felicia,

"What will SFPD do about the Snakes case?"

"Nothing……if I was Case Officer…..but I'm just a lowly traffic cop…………….again."

"Time will tell I suppose?"

"Well, the guy in charge is an airhead for sure. I doubt he'll get anywhere. I'll try and keep a watch on any developments though."

Chapter 12
The Sidewinder

A flat sun feeds watery Saturday morning light through net curtains ot Ooljee's house in Halchita. Weekends are quiet, particularly in wintertime. Ooljee has a shift at a diner in Mexican Hat later. Ajei works whatever jobs she can find. Sometimes, outside of winter, she gets to take hiking tours around Navajo Mountain and around the San Juan River. Sometimes, she gets work in schools and academies teaching music. Life is ok and as settled as could be expected. Seven seasons have passed since they left Montana. No bad news from The Chief and the shadows of the past are receding. Nevertheless, apart from the distant relatives from whom they rent the house, the two of them keep low profiles. Shadow thoughts of the past grope into both of their minds. They know it but they don't readily talk about it. Ooljee knows that, however evil The Snakes were, the band was a creative force, particularly for Ajei. She was so proud of what her daughter brought to it all. She glued the groove together with bass lines that were understated, subtle individual, edgy. These days though, Ooljee saw the bass guitar more often than not propped in the corner of the room. Untouched. Ajei would sit and watch TV into the evenings and, sometimes, even during the day. It made her uneasy. Life in the territory can be hard and sparse. It is always good to create but once that fire dwindles it can be hard to re-kindle.

Sleeping Beauty

https://badpeoplethemusical.bandcamp.com/track/sleeping-beauty

Hey...ain't yer got no time for me today ?
You're just sitting and watching the same old shit on TV
Hey...wake up today

Why...don't we try maybe a walk on the beach ?
We can watch all the surfers – freezing in the sea
Hey...wake up today

Are...you going to the pub tonight ?
Is it the Champions League or is it just the quiz machine ?
Hey...wake up today

Well – it ain't like it was
And it ain't like it could be
We're just hanging around
Half asleep

Why...don't we go to a singer's night ?
You can take the melody and I'll try the harmony
Hey...wake up today

This very Saturday morning, Ajei leans over the faucet looking out over the snow covered mesa in the distance. At a speed almost too fast for her eyes to register a grey shape descends from the sky and there is an eruption of powder snow. Then she sees a white tail bird with feathered feet manifest from the cloud of snow thrown up with rodent in its talons. "Caska!" The last thing Ajei expects, as she watches and listens for the boiling water, is any visitors. A drum riff on the door is unexpected. The caska hears it at the same time as her and looks over, its prey now lifeless. She turns and looks through the window the other side of the small kitchen. She sees a figure in a long black coat with a long ponytail of hair stretching down his back from under a snakeskin banded Stetson hat. Ajei assumes it is one of the council men who visit from time to time to ask for views on some administrative matter. She moves wearily to the door.

A weathered face with a small tattoo on the cheek greets her gaze. The slim figure hops from foot to foot, each in dark snakeskin boots that appear from under a long black coat. He speaks English,
    "Howdy Sister."
    "Howdy Mister?"
    "You be Ajei?"
    "Yup."

"Can we talk?"

"Yup."

"Can I come in?"

Ajei runs out of conversation and stands back. He enters and she closes the door. His eyes penetrate as Ooljee appears from the bedroom.

"Hello ladies", his weathered face lights with a smile, "Looks like I'm just in time for coffee?"

Ooljee and Ajei exchange glances saying "cheeky bastard?". A pause and Ajei moves to the counter as he moves his weight from snakeskin boot to snakeskin boot whilst lightly clapping his hands in front of himself.

"I'm Sydney."

"OK Sydney. I'm Ooljee and this is Ajei."

"Mind if I sit?"

Without waiting for a response he makes a strange movement that seems to begin with his hips as he moves sideways to the small table. The two women blink as his movement is somehow strangely camoflauged by it's speed. He smiles as he sits,

"Sydney Wynder. My old man had a sense of humour!" his smile widens before he sits, "they call me The Sidewinder!"

Both women look at each other wide-eyed. Not more fuckin' snakes! Ajei puts a coffee in front of him. Ooljee speaks, half jokingly, half tactfully,

"We are both a little nervous of snakes."

"With good reason from what I hear."

"And what did you hear?"

"My friends in the north told me about Snake Rock!", he smiles, knowingly. A silence follows and he lets it mature before he follows on,

"......thing is......I play music too......and......we just lost our bass man to a woman. That's to say....he saddled up and moved on up to Denver."

The two women wait in silence. Ajei glances out of the window and sees the hawk feeding and scanning. The Sidewinder carries on,

"So.....we need a bass player."

"What lineup you got?"

"Me on geetar and verbals, sometimes harp and sometimes saxophone and my amigo The Fatback on the kit drums."

"You get much work?"

"Bars and sometimes Casino lounges. Small time gigs but it pays.....just!"

"What kinda groove?"

"Solid, spaced, LoFi. It just is!"

The two women smile. The Sidewinder has a charm. His eyes sparkle and dance. His face drawn handsome.

"Covers or originals?"

"We're in the Big Game ladies. Our own material. We ain't no karaoke singers doing sell out shit!"

Ajei answers,

"We're in!"

Ooljee looks at her sternly. The Sidewinder looks lost for a momentary moment,

"We?"

Ajei re-emphasises,

"Yes – we?"

"But I only need a bass player?"

"Well you got another geetar and vocals.......and a whole load more glamour!"

The Sidewinder sits back, he smiles and thinks before replying.

"Well girls......it could work. There are gigs around here. Me and The Fatback don't make too much but a touch of glamour won't hurt our chances. Let's wind it on up?"

The "girls" giggle now. There is "something" about The Sidewinder that is insistent. He smiles.

"Wednesday night in the Old Motel in Medicine Hat and we can cruise some songs?"

The girls look at each other and nod. The Sidewinder finishes his coffee and stands to leave. He puts on his black hat and fastens up his long black coat which has been thrown open as he sat. He smiles and seems to slide across the floor towards the door. Once again the two women blink. Halfway down the path he turns and smiles,

"See you Wednesday."

As they watch him turn and walk, he holds out an arm to the horizontal and the hawk Ajei had been watching swoops from the swirl snow of the air to land on it and the two of them walk up the windswept high plains street.

"You heard of him before Mother?"

"Nope!"

"What planet is he from?"

"There are many wanderers daughter! I liked him!"

Ajei laughs,

"You liked Jake Snake!...once?"

Ooljee, the ex Mrs Snake, lowers her gaze to the floor and holds the counter for support. Ajei moves to her and they embrace. Ajei tidys her mother's hair,

"New times. Things will be better?"

Ooljee nods, smiling sadly. Ajei adds,

"Could do without the snake shit again though! The Sidewinder? What's that about?"

The two women giggle. A giggle tinged with nervousness?

****

The same wisp snow that dances in the air of Utah also swirls in Montana as a long convoy of black vehicles moves slowly from the city northwards towards the cemetery. At the head of the convoy, a long Mercedes hearse followed by a longer black limousine. Inside sits Lincoln Xylo or LynkX and his aging mother, his wife and two children. In a vehicle behind is "Skinny" and four other "securities". Behind follow various business contacts, some dignitaries and other families. The long courtege slowly turns right into the windswept cemetery. The indifferent hills in the northern distance.

As Boston Xylo, or BossX, is lowered into the cold ground, his gold encrusted casket reflects what weak sunlight there is. The LynX (as he now likes to be known) looks around the assembled people. Some he owns, some are enemies, some are the women he has bought and some are the women he covets. Most people avoid his gaze. Hats removed now and the assembled begin to feel the ice touch of the mean spirited wind. No-one looks at The LynX, his disfigured scalp and hair on display. The eagle scars could not be hidden by failed cosmetic surgery and his hair, and possibly his sanity, had never recovered. The assembled are relieved as The LynX walks forward and throws a handful of frozen earth onto the casket. His look would freeze the earth harder. Skinny silently suveys the assembled. He thinks of the years passed and tries to cast his mind to the future. Whichever way he casts it things look worse. He studies The Lynx.

At a downtown hotel the courtege cars progress to the red-carpet entrance of a downtown hotel. Dark haired hursuit men attend the doors and Mrs Xylo is helped from the limousine. The Lynx supports her along the carpet. A lone reporter gets pictures. Skinny's eyes take in everything.

An uneasy conversation rumbles throughout the meal as people struggle to think of suitable words. Women nervously cut their food their pale faces, framed in black, nodding wide eyes in fake interest at the inhibited chatter of their companions around them.

After the meal, and as the guests trickle away, The LynX takes Skinny to one side,
    "Times have changed Skinny. Things is gonna be different. Fuck yes!"
Skinny's eyes momentarily look to the ceiling. This is unlikely to be a "good different".

****

Ajei hangs right onto Highway 163 for the short drive into Medicine Hat. Snow swirls around on the surface of the carriageways. She follows The Sidewinder's directions and find what was once part of a Motel but is now semi-derelict. She sees lights on in the building and parks the truck at the entrance. She grabs her bass from the rear seat and knocks the door. It opens immediately, almost shocking her. The Sidewinder stood smiling,

"Welcome to ChiricahuaRock HQ!"

Ajei smiles. He's a Mescalero but, there is something about The Sidewinder which is irresistible? She has her doubts as she notes his snakeskin boots, lace tie with snake motif though. It all looks so "snaky". She can do without that. He even seems to move like a snake, his tall slim wiriness winding as he walks. She is almost hypnotised.

"The Fatback is on his way", The Sidewinder gestures to the small footprint drumkit sat in a corner. A log burner heats the space, glowing red. Ajei smiles,

"Ooljee is here after her shift. Lets me hear some Chiricahua sounds then Mr Sidewinder?"

"Call me Sid!", he picks up a little old parlour guitar which whacks out a sound way above its worn out look. The Sidewinder seems to move in bursts, Ajei can't work him out.

Faith

https://badpeoplethemusical.bandcamp.com/track/faith

I see a grey angel at night
His eyes pierce into mine
He marks my life and my time
Puts his hand on my shoulder if he hears me lyin

And if there are demons in the trees
He clears the holy path for me
Dead demons are history
They better not mess with me

Only my faith keeps me sane
Only the faithful will remain
The devil is on my trail
But my belief will never fail

He knows the demons' disguise
Checks the light inside my eyes
He's a heavy heaven sent sentry
No demons can ever get entry

There are times when I fail
The flesh can be weak and frail
I got a pistol that fires nails
Crucified demons mark my trail

Only my faith keeps me sane
Only the faithful will remain
The devil is on my trail
But my belief won't ever fail

These days last a lifetime
Death comes in the night time

Ajei smiles at his intensity. The Sidewinder don't care. His ordinances are his own. She realises that no-one can dent The Sidewinder. No-one could land a blow. His mind is made up. Made up strong. Like a fortress with a hightower and surveillance sentries. Looking. He has ideas. She can tell. Lot's of them. The Sidewinder is cool. He's scary but she isn't diminished. Working for Jake Snake has given her all the confidence she needs.

The Sidewinder points her to a large bass rig in one corner. Ajei unpacks her bass and begins to tune. The door opens and now frames a small mountain of a man. Workboots, coveralls and a leather shouldered work jacket, woven helmet hat in black with a long black pony tail. His build is an opposite to the long wiry power of The Sidewinder, but just as quirky an apparition,
     "Ya'ateh compadre!", he stamps his feet to shake off snow.
     "The Fatback......meet Ajei....", The Sidewinder gestures to Ajei.
Fatback walks to her and raises his palm. Ajei so slight next to him. She raises her palm, detects no negativity and smiles. The Fatback smiles,
     "A big axe for a small Navajo!"
     "I'm Assiniboine!"
     "That's ok then. The Fatback has no enemies except the virus."

Ajei knows exactly what he means and she smiles.

The Fatback removes his hat, coat and coveralls. He is all power. His solid legs in tight jeans, work shirt over a T. As he turns to walk behind the kit, Ajei realises why he is so named. His back and shoulders a solid sheet of rock like muscle. He is a superhero with a cape. He sits and spins sticks that look like toys in his hands. He looks at The Sidewinder who is now holding a lil' old Harmony Bobkat and begins to riff the same tune as before, Ajei waits, she looks at The Fatback, he telepathises the 1-2-3-4 and they drop in together. Ajei keeps it simple and adds tension as well as gluing a groove that imposes itself on the atmosphere.

Keep The Demons Down
https://badpeoplethemusical.bandcamp.com/track/keep-the-demons-down

I got a six gun in my hand
Are you saved or are you damned ?
You don't understand - Nobody understands
But I got the future planned

And I got a licence too
I proved all I got to prove
I'm as sane as him and I'm as sane as you
Do you know what a six gun can do ?

An angel spoke to me
In a dream but unmistakably
He said keep your six gun close at hand
You never know what the Devil has got planned

The Devil's work is all around
There's demons crawling out of the ground
We got to take those demons down
We got to take those demons down
We got to take those demons down

This land was built with the gun

And I ain't scared of no demon
We don't surrender to no-one
Not until my gold bullets are all gone

Golden bullets in my gun
6 gold bullets for 6 demons
I am the chosen one
I am the chosen one
Six gold bullets in my six gun

As she walks the frozen dirt path from the diner towards the old motel, Ooljee hears the bass and kick drum first. Ajei is back! This is EXACTLY what they need.

****

The Chief is tired. Life itself is so so complicated. He has become double weary since Ooljee and Ajei had left. He knows BossX had passed and he knows it is bad medicine for himself. His worries though, have been for the rest of the Reservation and for Ooljee and Ajei. If BossX was ten years younger and in good body health then the money issue from The Snake demise would gradually be forgotten. His years of business with BossX had generated some trust in the enemy. Some things are not meant to be though and he knew that Lincoln Xylo would not let it lie now. TheLynX is stinkshit from a bat's ass and he knows what is one day coming. He has summoned the spirits and asked for a "Guardian" for Ooljee and Ajei. His own departure would be enough protection for The Reservation. He would not have long to wait.

When the time came, Skinny had taken his instructions from LynX. He'd tried to persuade him otherwise but LynX has a small mind, easily overloaded and prone to malicious obsession. Skinny had decided, out of respect for The Chief, to carry out the instruction in person. He could've sent soldiers but he did not want the Chief to suffer. So, heavy hearted, he had driven from Helena to Wolf Point during the daytime hours. At dusk he stopped for a steak dinner. His car was non-descript with fake plates and skinny wore a businessman disguise. At dusk he drove on to The Reservation and rolled his car to a silent halt half a mile or so from The Chief's trailer. He checked his weapons, put on a deep pocketted black hunters jacket and a black balaclava cap. He wouldn't bother hiding his face unless there were others about. He walked the last half mile. All was silent.

Skinny tries the trailer door handle and finds it open. He enters silently, his silenced pistol in hand. As he scans the trailer he nearly misses The Chief sat in his armchair, the full moon framed in the window behind him. The Chief speaks,

"I knew you'd come."

"Didn't want to Chief."

"The young boss is an impetuous cunt."

"He is!"

"BostanX and I had old business arrangements."

"I know."

"All that is over now!"

"I will ask."

"No Mr Skinny. It IS over!"

"If you say so Chief?"

"If BostanX is gone and I am gone any arrangements and debts cease to exist."

"I will tell him what you say."

"He will have to negotiate with my successor."

"He will."

The Chief pauses. Sighs. Looks out of the window. He looks back at Skinny,

"You are white man's brave warrior?"

"I was trained as such."

"Are the white man's warriors shit brained greedy fuck-heads like them?"

Skinny smiles,

"Yup."

The Chief sighs,

"I used to be brave warrior too. Way back."

Skinny pauses,

"He wanted me to cause you pain Chief but I have respect for other warriors............"

Before Skinny's sentence is finished, The Chief reaches down to grab a tomahawk and launches it at Skinny's head. A lesser warrior may have been caught but Skinny is trained and manages to avoid the tomahawk. It clatters against a shelf and sinks harmlessly to the mat below.

**

Skinny sighs now. Moves to the window and looks for any movement. Nothing. He takes a last look at The Chief, peaceful in his chair. He silently exits and wipes the door lever both sides. As he steps backwards from the trailer step, he is aware of a movement above him. Looking up he sees The Eagle atop the trailer roof, stood still and staring at him with one piercing eye. Skinny stumbles backwards from the step fumbling for his weapon. His memory replays the eagle attaching to The LynX's head at this very spot. Skinny rolls sideways, as trained, and stands now, weapon in hand. He looks back to the trailer roof and the eagle is gone. He scans now and picks up the eagle circling above as it crosses the disc of the moon. Skinny can't make the shot and begins the walk back to the car. The eagle silently circles above. Skinny keeps his weapon in hand. Nervous now. His heart rate up. He is disappointed in himself. His walk almost breaking into a run. At the car he fumbles for the key and is relieved to close the door. He calms himself and looks around before starting the engine and accelerating away.

Hitman

https://badpeoplethemusical.bandcamp.com/track/hitman

Well you won't hear me comin
In the darkness of the night
You won't even see nothing
Not even a flash of light
You might be laughing
With a woman on each arm
But you must've done something

Because someone wants you gone

Hitman – yes it's true
I could be after you
Hitman
Let Mr Jones
Take care of your bones

One minute you're there
Next second you're gone
Maybe a paid for witness
Who just got it all wrong
Maybe a judge who didn't
Do as he was told
If you don't listen
You might not grow old

I never hit no-one
Under 21
But if you haven't learnt by then
You won't get another lesson

I don't do torture
I got my pride
I just do quick departure
You won't even know you died
I can work from distance
I can work up close
I can work in silence
Nobody ever knows...

Hitman
I don't advertise
Hitman
A word to the wise
I didn't make the world
And I won't make heaven
But nobody says nothing
I avoid suspicion

Hitman
Let Mr Jones
Take care of your bones

I'm a hitman – listen to me
I got a hundred identities
Let Mr Wyatt
Keep your enemies quiet
Let Mr Johnson
Take care of your problems
Let Mr Evans
Show them into heaven
Let Mr Gold
Free their souls
Let Mr Brown
Take them all down
Let Mr Jones
Take care of your bones
Mr Jones

The Chief soars with The Eagle now. His spirit on The Eagle's back. He rides like a young brave once again. He looks down on the white man warrior below with pity and with disdain.

"White man warrior is like all white men. Arrogant and greedy and no respect for their planet. Their time is ending. Soon!".

As the car below drives away, The Eagle shits over it before wheeling upwards. The Chief laughs. Things are simpler now. The Chief is not tired any more.

****

Time has passed in Halchita. Life has returned to Ajei and Ooljee. Winter turns to spring turns to summer now. The Sidewinder and The Fatback have been saviours. The music rocks and Ajei and Ooljee are key parts of it. The band gigs around The Navajo Nation. Sometimes outside The Nation, as far south as Sedona in the red rocks. Sometimes as far west as

Nevada. The Sidewinder seems to organise gigs and payments but they don't find out much else about him. Or the Fatback for that matter. Apache.

The gold sun hovers above distant mesas one evening as they sip coffee after their meal. Ooljee is quiet and Ajei senses it too. Ajei sees her mother lift her eyes to the sky and slowly tilt her head back with eyes closed. Ajei's young eyes look up to the same sky and they see the eagle. High and circling. Her mother sings in a low wail now as the eagle begins to lose height. Ajei too understands now. Both their tears run as the eagle glides over them, wheels and lands on the red sand in front of them.

All things pass. All times come to an end.
The eagle looks at them both in turn as it turns to gold under flat sun rays of evening.

Chapter 13
Unification Theory

As the next day dawns, Wangly's head throbs like a bad record on a good HiFi. He groans. Too much IPA. His mind registers where he is. A cheap hotel in Lower Haight. What a night though? He smiles through the clamour of his mental kick drum. "I need coffee!"

Breakfast now. Boris is beaming. Wangly smiles,

"Professor Von Kranum! Is the world ready for your thesis?"

"It better be! Or they better be able to show me my errors?" Wangly smiles. He certainly could not do that. His knowledge and facility with Mathematics, or Physics for that matter, is not at Boris's level. He sometimes wonders if Boris is a bullshitter? Everybody is sometimes? But, if Boris is one then he has to be a really good one and he is on the case all the time. Anyway, Wangly loves his company and his bullshit. Boris can actually explain his reasoning (on his many subjects; he's unifying absolutely everything) very well to the scientifically illiterate. Or maybe Wangly has just tuned in to him over the years?

Boris is buzzing this morning though. He talks about his presentation later today with enthusiasm. He talks about Marv and what an understanding he seemed to have of Boris's theories. Wangly smiles. Such unlikely compadres. It was a great night though. Wangly loved the band. Boris seems genuinely excited at the prospect of putting his theories in front of some "real professors". Boris is always enthusiastic. Wangly sometimes worries that he could be hurt by uncaring people. He was even slightly worried when Boris was talking so much to Marv, The Hell's Angel. It seems such an unlikely friendship. Nevertheless, they had talked (and drank) away all night and ended on good "sentimental drunk" terms.

Boris retreats to his room after breakfast to work on some possible questions he might get. Wangly takes in a walk and gets as far as Pacific Heights. Didn't the Dirtkickers do a song called "Pacific Heights" last night? His brain clearing now. These are nice houses, he walks around looking at the houses, transposing his life to that of a "rich sonoffabitch". Who could ever afford something like this? He laughs to himself and reassures his greed that he is ok up in Lincoln City. He's not a greedy man and friends are more important and he has Boris, English Bob and Adrian. He also has the possibility of a new girlfriend he met on a trip down to Crescent City the other weekend. He has nothing to complain about. After late morning coffee they take a cab across to the institute in the park. They find the lecture and reception room on the 1st floor. A nice well mannered administrator is helpful to Boris and helps him organise his papers and projections. Boris loves it and seems eager to get started.

Wangly leaves his friend to his concentrations and takes a seat. A mixed crowd of academics, students and various eccentrics begin to assemble. Boris smiles from a seat next to the lectern. Boris never seems to get nervous. His brain is so overloaded with theories, or so Wangly supposes. English Bob and Lucy appear at the entrance and Wangly stands and waves; his name totally describing his movement. Lucy spots him straightaway and giggles. She lucked out meeting these guys. They join Wangly and talk in hushed tones as the auditorium fills with people and all their similarly subdued conversations. The claustrophobia is suddenly scythed by a raised voice at the entrance,

"What the fuck do you mean? We're in the wrong place?! The fuck we are!"
They turn to look at the entrance and see Marv and Don Estrada arguing with a suit at the door.

"We're here for Von Kranum's Lecture. It IS open to the public? Right?

"Yes sir."

"Well we are The Public my friend! Wanna make something of it?"

Wangly laughs to himself at this exchange. He has to admit, Marv and Don do look a little out of place in the refined respectability of the lecture theatre. Boris spots them from the stage and gives them a wave.

Some Professor or other takes to the stage now, tapping the lectern mic,
  "...as part of the open science forum...getting some amateur views on aspects of science...we are pleased to welcome a frequent contributor to our journal's letters page...Mr Boris Kranum..."

Boris stands to light applause.
He summarises the standard results of Special Relativity as resulting from The Lorentz Transformation. He asks the audience if they are prepared to accept this. He is greeted by silence until Marv acknowledges affirmatively,
  "Agreed!"
Wangly imagines there is something of an uncomfortable shuffling from the assembled academics. He's not sure why.

Boris moves on with the concept of the momentum of bodies moving through space, or as he puts it, moving through Space-Time. He considers Conservation of Energy with two bodies colliding and soon shows the variation of mass with relative velocity. At key stages he asks for audience ratification. Marv responds, with a growing number of other attendees. This is going well. Boris has real style and gets into his "zone". Wangly smiles for his friend.
Next, by the deft use of some algebra of functions, Boris develops the famous relation between mass and energy and light speed. E equals M C squared! Marv punches the air and affirms the landmark,
  "Yes Sir!"
The audience laugh. This is quite lively. Wangly does notice a subtle unease in the ranks of the assembled academics.
Next The Cranium summarises General Relativity pointing out the "general" means the inclusion of 3-dimensional space plus

1-dimensional time leading to a 4-dimensional Matrix formulation. He jokes,

"Let's try and act like show off smart-ass mathematicians and call them Tensors?"

Marv leads the sniggering. The academics are stern faced.

Boris then points out that the General Theory also involves acceleration and makes the terms in the Matrices complex functions.

"It gets tricky......but it's just maths........and computations prove it quite correct at most limits......except for the moment of The Big Bang, a so-called singularity or the sub-atomic mess of particles, many of which are virtual? However, as far as General Relativity goes it does show the Force of Gravity for what it is. A so-called warping of Space-Time."

The audience silent now awaiting the next development. Boris has them.

"But.....it's not a ""warping"", this is how Space-Time is and Gravity is just part of how we and all units of Mass and Energy moves along it or within it! Let's say within its constraints."

Wangly feels a buzz. He understands and he feels the general audience riding the wave too.

Next Boris switches to electromagnetism and summarises Maxwell's Equations.

In a plot twist now, Boris delivers a cornerstone of his presentation,

"It is easy to conclude we know everything there is to know about electromagnetism because these four equations precisely describe electromagnetic manifestations. Everything from guitar pickups through to radio waves and beyond."

He pauses, and adds, with drama,

"BUT WE DON'T!!"

The audience silent now.

"We do not know how electromagnetic forces operate!"

Total silence,

"There must be a mechanism!"

"There is talk of ""exchange particles"". Well, what are they? And we can ""see"" some of these if we engage in the business of smashing things up. Things like poor unsuspecting atoms, doing their best to survive in this world!"

The audience laugh. Boris turn serious,

"But there is NO MATHS!"

"No maths to explain how exchanging particles can or could give rise to forces! Especially attractive forces, AND THEN, we also have repulsive forces to contend with?"

"People will tell you ""There is maths but it is too complicated to be written down here!""!"

"Well that is bullshit! Where are the papers?"

"Einstein wrote down his theories for scrutiny!"

"So did Maxwell!"

"They stand up to scrutiny!"

"But there is no scrutiny of particle exchange forces because there is no maths!!"

"Any such maths can never work either! Not if we are to conserve energy!"

Boris reaches an intermediate conclusion,

"So - we need the maths to describe electromagnetic ""mechanisms""?"

"As with Special Relativity, we need a relation between the much overlooked concept of charge and energy. Something similar to E equals M C squared but with charge replacing mass?"

"Then we should be able to demonstrate the charge and associated electromagnetic forces also ""warp"" Space-Time. In a similar manner to gravity!"

Boris asks for audience agreement. There is a buzz of yes. Marv exclaims,

"OH YESSSSS!"

The general audience are with Boris, but the academics are silent. After a suitable pause, Boris resumes,

"I believe this paper provides that mathematics!"

Boris puts up a slide of the title page of his paper and continues,

"It provides the following relationship for Charge and Energy, somewhat analogous to Mass and Energy!"

An overhead shows his equation now and he continues,

"Moreover, the paper shows how charge ""warps"" Space-Time and thus explains the mechanisms of electromagnetism! The magical magnets that mystify all children!"

Boris concludes his presentation with his equation on screen and a bullet point list of things his "unifications" have provided.

- It explains electromagnetic forces.
- No need to consider the existence or mechanical involvement of "exchange particles".
- As a corollary, it shows the existence of possible parallel "universes". These may be time shifted.

Boris briefly discusses the allowable (under his theories) existence of parallel universes which drop out of the theory as algebraic series which may be divergent or convergent. Convergent series could almost be construed as "fate lines". These connect certain existences and could even be considered to encompass energy in certain configurations – or even life forms. This is possibly a mathematical indication of the manifestation of fate or at least some kind of resonant existences that may be drawn together over time.

He explains that his paper lays out all the mathematics and he is "placing it on the altar of scrutiny". He invites questions. The audience applaud is good, very good. Wangly smiles, happy for his friend.

As the applause subsides the audience hums in a vibrant silence. Boris beams as he stalks the stage. Waiting for questions. There is an inevitable pause as attendees try to formulate any questions. Nobody wants to ask a dumb question. As the tension mounts, a smart suit walks on to stage to to the lectern microphone. He introduces himself as Professor Wang Hing. He thanks Mr Kranum for the "contribution" to this years "Citizen Contribution Science:Open Forum". He immediately begins to summarise contributions scheduled for the second afternoon session…………………..until Marv's hand goes up,

"Hold your horses there Prof Wang Hing…..I got a question."

"Ah – ok – errrrrm Mr…….?"

"Marv – of Marv's Motors: Truck and motorbike expertise!"

"Thank you ….. errrrm Marv. You have a question for Mr Kranum?"

"I do. It strikes me this is a quite monumental contribution if it all checks out? Do I take it that a lot of the time and money spent smashing up atoms and trying to explain the fragments will be time and money wasted?"

Wang Hing looks a little edgy as he invites Boris back to the microphone. Boris answers,

"Well Marv…..many of the particle theories that are unfounded in mathematics may well be considered to be "drifting anchorless observations". Having said that, the blunt force collision Physics is still useful in demonstrating the existence of entities predicted by solid mathematical reasoning. Anti-matter for instance. My formulations do include for some of the statistical variations of quantum physics but the need for exchange particles should be very much eliminated if these developments cannot be refuted."

Marv responds,

"So I am right in concluding that you have shown that electromagnetic forces are actually similar to gravitational force and explicable totally as Space-Time warps, man!"

"That would be correct Marv."

At this juncture an academic stands up and Wang Hing introduces him as Professor Kerr,

"I think at this point we ought to curtail this discussion as the theories expressed have not been fully reviewed……and…….with the best will in the world the mathematics provided is somewhat naïve?"

Boris responds,

"I did submit the paper and all mathematical reasoning some six months ago."

Marv jumps in again,

"Seems to me that mathematics is our only true window on the world. Without a mathematical law anything is nothing. You are left with blackjack science. Always a gamble. At least this provides some exact mathematical models?"

The academic fires back, condescendingly,

"QED my good man. Statistics and approximations are all we can have at the sub-atomic level!"

He looks around at the assembled academics for support. Marv is straight back,

"Weren't you listening? My man Von Cranium here has shown the exact mathematics for the electromagnetic force. This might kick your QUANTUM ELECTRODYNAMICS right on out of the window. If I was you I would have read it by now?"

The academic responds, sounding a little annoyed now,

"We do have on going research and teaching commitments and we can't look at every cockamamie paper that arrives...."

Wang Hing steps in,

"Thank you Professor Kerr and thanks to all attendees. Perhaps we should leave this here?"

Before he can fully bring the "discussion" to a halt Marv, on his feet now, addresses the auditorium,

"Well, well, well! Professor Wang Hing and Professor Wang Kerr! Looks like the days of atomic atom smashing vandalism could be coming to an end. No more plate smashing physics parties. The equivalent of rock bands throwing TVs out of hotel room window parties, and hoping to learn how they work by looking at the smashed parts. Hell I could do that if I had billions of bucks to waste! I think Professor Von Cranium's story should be checked over in due haste..........there's some good investigators at the SFPD I could recommend..............but in the meantime, and on behalf of the San Francisco and Oakland HAMC I'd like to thank the real Prof here. It has been an honour to be at one of the most important science gigs since 1921!!"

Marv turns to the audience and spontaneous applause erupts once more. He turns his arms to Boris and directs the applause.

**

"Thanks for your support Von Marv", Boris greets his friend in the hospitality area.

"That's ok Von Cranium!"

Lucy, Wangly and English Bob stand watching. Lucy is amazed at the common ground Boris and Marv have established. Who would've thought it? Attendees approach Boris and nervously ask questions. He tries to explain in a very patient manner, giving copies of his paper to interested people. It is noticeable that none of the assembled academics approach him. They stand in a group to one side. Lucy is aware that Boris occasionally glances their way, expectantly. She takes it upon herself to walk across the room to the academics and suggest that one of them might give some feedback to Boris. They look at her as though she has just appeared from another planet? So much so that Lucy even checks what she is wearing today? Wang Hing is actually quite dismissive as he tactfully explains that the institute has given Boris "quite enough time and facility". She notices him glance at "Wang" Kerr as he speaks. Kerr gives a discrete nod. As Lucy walks back to her group she is red in the face with rage, trying to keep some sort of control. She doesn't want to spoil Boris's moment in any way. Marv has watched her and his look makes it obvious he realises what has just happened. Marv slaps Boris on the shoulder and finishes a strand of their conversation before he peels off as Boris chats to an attendee.

Lucy watches Marv now as he crosses the floor towards the academics. As he breaks into their circle she is struck by the surreal nature of the scene. Such conventional academics and Marv, the uncrowned King of the Angels complete with his trademark red bandana. Marv speaks calmly but his voice audible across the room,

"You fuckers have no idea."

They fall silent. Open mouthed.

"None of you have even approached Von Cranium to discuss the paper?"

Wang Hing attempts to calm things. A suit backs off and then breaks to a trot across the carpeted hall towards a wall mounted telephone. Marv carries on,

"If his fucking theories are fucking wrong fucking tell him fucking why! If they are not fucking wrong you should fucking cong-fucking-ratulate him!?"

At this point Professor Kerr loses it and a strange voice escapes via his rage tensioned larynx,

"Of course it's wrong. We get hundreds of papers from unqualified amateurs...."

"Fucking Einstein was a fucking unqualified amateur! Better than a fucking arrogant fucking overpaid fucking snobwit pro-fuckin-fessor!"

Lucy giggles at Marv's delivery. The suits have never seen this situation before. Security guards approach now. Two from each end of the gallery room. Don Estrada walks across. He places a hand on Marv's shoulder. He holds a palm to the first security guard to arrive. Don speaks now,

"Don't!"

The four guards pause, motionless

"Don't do it!"

He slowly backs Marv away. Marv speaks once more,

"I can't see any mistakes in it............but then my maths is a bit rusty and I only had this morning to read it."

Security guards looking relieved now as Don and Marv turn to walk away. A few more paces and Marv turns once more,

"You guys wanna get someone to explain it all to yer!"

Back with Boris now, Marv apologises. Wangly and English Bob smile, smile broadly and then laugh. Boris slowly joins the laughter now. Marv too,

"See you guys at Deirdre's Bar tonight? Drinks on me!"

Marv and Don walk slowly from the room now. The security men follow them like timid cowboys guiding two steers back to the herd. Marv speaks to Don as if nothing had happened and nothing was ever going to happen,

"Hey Don? Interesting shit about fate popping out of Boris's equations there? Whaddya reckon about fate? Could be it ties

us all together? Obsessives like Boris are the ones that take the big steps Don Boy. Take Einstein for one!"
Marv rambles now,

"You ever hear of Heinrich Schliemann the archaeologist? He wouldn't let it drop man! No-one believed him but he found the city of Troy. For damn sure he fuckin did. Made his own money and did it his way. Easy job fuckers on the payroll never find fuck all! Heinrich made his own fate."

Fate

https://badpeoplethemusical.bandcamp.com/track/fate

Do you believe in a fate - Everything comes to him who waits
Chance will bring you all you need - Ambition is a form of greed
The wind that takes the autumn leaves
The tides within the silent sea
These things decide your destiny

But **you** - are the one - with a childish - obsession
The future has'nt happened yet - and there's a past you can't forget
Do you know where you want to be
Do you believe what you can see
or do you see what you believe

Shovels - in the hands of men
Makes a time machine - once again
Now it's dusty - where there was dirt
The windy city - beneath the earth

So Turkey is out of bounds - Secret agents chase you around
They all want what you have found - Stolen secrets from the ground,
A jewellery cache and a face from the past
Is Helen's necklace and Hector's mask
Fate displays its winning ways at last

Now where - can that treasure be - Somewhere in Adolf's
legacy
But Sophie looked so fine - an image of the time - (was this?)
The face that launched 1000 ships
And caused the earth to move for you
And you to move the earth for it

Archaeology is somethin new
Homer laid a trail for you
A magic tale of golden days
Can seize your mind and change your ways

****

"Where is Gnomio today?", Mike Remo asks The Thunderman as he pours two coffees. Thunderman smiles,

"We had a Saturday night off so Dierdre probably planned a Saturday night ON! He could be lying in a coma somewhere Mikey? His heart couldn't handle it?"

Mike Remo looks down at the coffee cups, as if in another world momentarily, or permanently. TMan detects he has something on his mind? Normally you can bet your bass guitar that Mike Remo will find positivity but today black waves of "pissedoffness" are emanating. TMan picks up his coffee,

"Hey Mike. You're the High Priest, The Pope, The Archbishop and The Ayatollah of The Dirtrock Wave, The Dalai Skulker!! Whassa matter man?"

"Women TMan!", Mike stares into his coffee.

"They eat your heart Mikey boy. Then leave you face down in the dirt with high heeled footprints all along your back. Lovesick scars. Your "lovesnake" in cold hibernation for what appears likely to be a never ending ice age………."

"Thanks TMan. You got a way of making things better!"

"Well, Michael J Remo, most people would've employed tact and commiseration at that juncture but I always tell it like it is! You gotta push on through, soldier on, KEEP ON FUCKIN ROCKIN. Get yourself a beer man!"

"No bullshit TMan! So – do me a lifesaver – and lay off the self-help shit!"

The TMan suppresses a laugh and thumbs a music mag as he sips his coffee. Mike stares through the window on to the yard, sometimes looking down to write in his notepad. The Gnome enters quietly and smiles at his two bandmates as he rubs his hands together in front of himself,

"Oh what a night!"

"Keep Deirdre happy did we?"

"We? No way TMan TheGnome can handle it alone!", he gives a half-hearted hop and adds, "well I am a little whakeroonied today though! Helluva night in Deirdre's last night. Marv and Don were in with that mad scientist friend of Lucy's. Man.......they were all wasted. Apparently the scientist guy is gonna change the world? Well......according to Marv he is!"

The Thunderman smiles as Gnomio sits next to him. TheGnome nods over to Mike with a question mark above his head. TMan half-whispers a reply,

"Lervsick! Down on the killing floor! His head in a lervnoose. Strapped into the electric chair of despair!"

Mike Remo suddenly stands and faces them. He smiles,

"Time to go to work shitkickers!"

TMan smiles,

"Michael J Remo has returned from The Fucked Planet!"

They move to their battle stations and Mike declares,

"Got a new song..............."

Hypersleep

https://badpeoplethemusical.bandcamp.com/track/hypersleep

Little girl put a spell on me
Some kinda curse from history
Now I can't sleep and I can't wake
Walk around in a dreamlike state

She's a singularity
A turning point of gravity

How did all this come to be?
It's been a long century

In Hypersleep for light years now
All of this dreaming it wears me out

But space travel don't ever do you no good
Never turned out like you think it would
Poison your mind, it poisons your blood
All of my dreams misunderstood

But I've seen my death and this ain't it
I use my last breath begging for more
I die in bed with seven whores
Then they lead me to where the devil sits...

Six supermodels wait in their Cadillac
But they prefer my V8 Pontiac
So we ride all night and we don't look back
We don't even stop for a heart attack

In Hypersleep for light years now
All of this dreaming it wears me out
In Hypersleep for light years now
All of this dreaming it's worn me out

Thunderman and The Gnome smile to each other. Mike Remo gazes into space. His mind somewhere else, TMan is first to speak,
    "Mike Remo has the blues for sure! But out of adversity comes creation!! Nice one Mikey!"
Mike turns and smiles,
    "Nothing keeps The Remo Man down for long. Skulk it out boys!"
Sunlight strikes a beam through the Dirtkickers HQ now. TMan looks puzzled, as if in doubt about whether to ask, but he does ask,

"That song's about our supermodel friend Felicia?...Eh?...Mikey? Eh?...Eh?"

Mike's face turns serious,

"TMan...you should know better than anyone...being a Skulk Initiator...that song lyrics are not really about anything. Only your listeners think they are ""about"" anything. We just deal in imagery and try and make it as weird as possible? Scientists are the ones who are put on earth to simplify – poets are here to disguise and complicate?"

TMan looks at TheGnome,

"Sure thing Mikey!"

Mike Remo changes the subject now,

"Our illustrious agent has secured us some work out of state"

TMan and The Gnome face him inquisitively,

"You buttbrains fancy a mini-tour in Utah?"

"Where the fuck is Utah Mike?"

Silence reigns. Eventually Mike Remo laughs,

"Down south a bit....couple of states away...didn't you ever go to school TMan?"

"School is for losers...I had shit to get on with!"

"Thing is, according to our agent..."

The Dirtkickers interrupt,

"Mr TwnetyPerCent!"

Mike continues,

"...well...there is a bit of a music scene down there and, just coming into summer, they are looking for bands to play a few bars and maybe casinos."

"Casinos?"

"Right! The native americans run the casinos generally and there can be bars attached where they might like a bit of Skulk?"

"Will we have to bust out our tuxedos then Mikey?" (mockingly)

"Casual smart should do TMan. Be the best you could manage anyway?!"

"It's a deal. I'll play anywhere."

"How about you Gnomio? Can Deirdre survive without you?"

"Sure! What about Lucy though? She got Little Joan to deal with?"

"She says she's ok with it? She says Ronee has two weeks work leave and is happy to look after LJ."

The Dirtkickers smile. Another adventure. Is Utah ready for Skulk Rock? They all give the salute.

****

Marv groans as his eyes open. Light streams through the skylight of His and Don's residential premises at MarvMotorsHQ. His eyes come into focus on a seagull's ass as it perches at the side of the skylight glass. Marv's thoughts begin to roll,

"If that fucker shits I'm getting my Winchester."

He turns over as he smells bacon and coffee.

Don has laid out a table and pours Marv a coffee as he appears,

"Some night Von Marv!", the two angels giggle, "Couldn't stop old Von Cranium talking to you!"

"He's an interesting guy Don. Gets my vote!"

Don smiles as he brings breakfast over,

"You sure it was wise to introduce him and his compadre The Wangle to Dolores and Danielle?"

"Sure! They can handle it!"

"The Cranium will have entered Dolores's wormhole to her alternative universe by now? Probably looking for a way out as we speak."

"The Prof can handle it?", Marv smiles hopefully

They begin to eat,

"Hey Don...............when I need out.......don't make me beg? You're good at departures?"

Don looks up, still, he stares at Marv's face. Along long long long second elapses before Marv continues,

"I don't wanna not be me? If you know what I mean?"

"Why wouldn't you be you Marv? You crazy old turdhead."

Marv smiles, looks around,

"We built quite a business Don!"

Don looks quizzical,

"We sure did El Marvo. And it is still rockin!"

"I'm forgetting stuff Don boy."
"What the hell you forgetting? Your shitbox song lyrics?"
"Yeh! Amongst other stuff."
"Like you forgot my birthday?"
"Did I?"
"You sure did! You take me for granted you selfish prick!"
The two angels laugh until it subsides to serious silence. Don looks quietly across the table to his friend. Marv slowly repeats his previous,
"I don't EVER wanna not be me?"
Don looks at him. No reply is necessary. Trust is everything.

Once Upon A Time

https://badpeoplethemusical.bandcamp.com/track/once-upon-a-time

The night is tricky
Ghost dreams like rattlesnakes
Daylight don't restrict me
They're still here when I'm awake

The past can be a difficult book
All the pictures time has took
But I love to take another look
I just can't get enough

So leave me intact
It was my life give it back
I don't want to forget
Nothing that happened yet

Please leave them for me
They are my property
Please leave something for me...
Memories

A black star where I fell
Is this the depths of hell?
Bad JuJu
Evil Voodoo

Is there a contract I can sign?
I need memories to defy all time
A conductor stuck on the line
I'll keep it with mine

So leave me intact
It was my life give it back
I don't want to forget
Nothing that happened yet

Please don't take them away
Please don't take them away
Please leave something for me...
Memories

A lamp post in the tired rain
Oh no not memory lane pain again,
I don't want to use it right now
But I don't want to lose it no how

Once upon a time
Once upon a time
Once upon a time...

Chapter 14
Travels

The bruised pride of Lieutenant Lathan begins to obsess. He's worked hard to get where he is. Never compromised any of his principles. SFPD needs integrity like that. He has followed every principle of good police work that he picked up on at the academy. Everything he has ever achieved has been done through adherence to an undeniable and single minded defiance of every urge to depart from his gospel. It is his faith. He's kept it for so long it can never be left behind. Not even for a moment.

He has to endure those moments regularly now since the debacle with Officer Coppola. He gave her a chance and she was unable to rise to the occasion. She should've checked in with him for guidance instead of some naïve, immature, amateur, misguided and potentially dangerous unsolicited investigations. Initiative? Lathan does not think so. Modern police work is built on teamwork. Coppola has been watching too many movies. He had even tried to explain that. Take her under his protective wing but she had kicked back against it. Literally. Sad bitch. Now he has to pick up all the pieces. He's informed her line superiors and hopefully a review will emerge soon. Meantime, he has to face the outer office and he is sure they snigger. He could've subdued her easily but he didn't want to risk her injury. That's the only reason he let her get the better of him in the "heated discussion". Oh well, for now he will have to keep his head high and regain the respect of the outer office in time. Particularly Jane, his administrator. She always seems busy when he tries to engage her in conversation. Some people are just not sociable. She will see him for what he is when he sorts out the tangle left by Officer Coppola. Unbelievable!

He plucks up courage to face Jane once more as he asks if there are any letters for his department today? He has written to lawyers in Helena Montana who seemed to be acting for the victims in The Snake Beach murders informing them of developments. Good policework these days is following paper trails like money, insurance claims and business connections. Not Coppola's gung-ho driving around interviewing potential perpetrators. You had to build a case silently in the background and then you will know the exact lines of enquiry to follow. It needs patience and application. He will not let the embarrassment of the Coppola incident change his methods. They will all see in the end how his methods will lead to closure on this case.

Jane hands him his daily bundle of communications relating to all his current enquiries and, at last, a response from Firkov and Dikov Attorneys at Law. He opens the letter with anticipation. As he reads he smiles mentally. At last someone appreciates his painstaking work. They seem very impressed that he has re-opened the investigation here and are suggesting he travel to Montana to liaise with them and Helena PD to share information and potentially sift out criminal connections in Montana. They are offering to fund his travel. At last. Progress.

Lathan feels like a modern detective now as he exits his office and politely asks Jane to book him flights to Helena Montana. When she asks who is paying he proudly gives her the billing address of Firkov Lawyers and how they have extended first class travel to him. State Police co-operation. This has opened up new lines of inquiry for them now. At last some progress Jane. Jane looks dis-interested but efficiently books his flights. It's six hours with a stop at Denver so she books a stopover motel for his evening arrival in Helena Montana. He asks her to confirm with Firkov Lawyers that he will be picked up the following morning. Jane is smilingly efficient and tells him it should be a nice trip. She loves The Rockies in spring. Lathan has a spring in his step.

The Rockies are amazing as he sips his morning coffee and looks from his high window first class seat. The hostess tops him up as she serves breakfast.He thinks how lucky he is to serve this great nation. The peaks below are crystal clear with snow lines so well defined and spring greenery beginning to appear. He sees traffic snaking along highways and interstates and wonders of the hopes and aspirations of all these people. Someone has to protect them from criminals.

The plane loses altitude to a flat land with distant hills. Lathan is sad the flight ends. He enjoys the attentiveness of the hostesses and the chance to marshall his thoughts. He disembarks and takes a taxi to his downtown hotel. He takes a steak dinner. Next morning, a driver awaits him in the lobby and he finds himself in the plush offices of Firkov Lawyers. A receptionist furnishes him with coffee. Finally she ushers him into an office and Mr Yuri Firkov graciously thanks him for his visit and introduces a Mr S.K. Inyov who handles all their liaisons with Montana State Police. Skinny smiles and greets Lathan asking about progress with drug cases in the bay area.

Miss Trulove enters the room to sit in and take notes. Her heels click-clack across the floor. She sits, crosses her nyloned legs, dangles a shoe and fires a smile and eye laser beams at Lathan. Soon Lathan has told them all details of his investigation. The connection with James Smith who appears to have driven a vehicle that has rammed The Snakes prior to their shooting. How he was a musician in a band called The Lowdown Dirtkickers and how there seems to be some sort of connection to a Hell's Angel Motorcycle Club. As he talks, he has a nagging realisation that this is all information Coppola has given him. Nevertheless, he reasons he is now using the information in a responsible police investigation through proper channels.

As the meeting finishes Firkov and Inyov thank him for his cooperation. They tell him they have appointments the rest of the day but that Miss Trulove will take him for lunch.

****

"Where's the gig tonight Mikey?"
"That will be Carson City TMan. You know where that is?"
TMan is stung by the sarcastic question,
"I know it is where Mark Twain was born!"

The Dirtkicker van turns silent in awe of TMan's knowledge. Lucy speaks up,

"I thought he was from Missouri?"

TMan looks over to her, his chest full of pride,

"Well Samuel Langhorne Clemens was, but Mark Twain first beamed down to earth in Carson City man!"

TMan settles back, pleased with himself. TheGnome now breaks the silence,

"Kit Carson!"

"What about him?"

"Named after him – Carson City man."

"Who was Kit Carson?"

"Frontiersman. You wouldn't wanna cross him!"

"Fast on the draw?"

"And a sonoffabitch!"

"How so?"

"Massacred Indians."

The van falls quiet for a while. They pass Sacramento and now on Highway 50. They are in silent awe of one of America's great highways. The Lonely Highway itself. Would it bring them loneliness? The dirtkickers stared it down. TMan breaks the silence now,

"Kirk Douglas could take him."

"Take who?"

"Kit fuckin' Carson"

"Thunderman – Kirk Douglas is a film star."

"I know – one of the best!"

TheGnome thinks for a while,

"OK – well Spartacus could kick the shit out of Kit Carson and Kirk is Spartacus, but then, did you ever see "Lonely Are The Brave"?"

"Nah – was Kirk in it?"

"He sure was and he gets his lights punched out by a man with no arms – so he's not so tough is he? Great movie though!"

Lucy sits back and lets it flow over her, "What ARE they on today?" She smiles to herself.

"Kirk would never lose out to a no-armed man!"

TheGnome giggles. TMan quiet now but thinking. Mike Remo enters the conversation,

"Big Jake could take 'em?"

"Who the firk is Big Jake?"

"John Wayne in the movie of the same name. Jacob McCandles!"

Mike Remo continues,

"See The Duke has the power. He's a mountain of a man. He could take a bullet and still strangle you one handed?"

"Sure Mike!"

They go quiet but TMan is eventually having none of it,

"Charlton Heston! He could take The Duke. Charlton was fit see – in shape! The Duke carries too much weight? He cant even find his gun for his overhanging beer gut!"

Mike Remo splutters over the steering wheel now,

"No, no, no....The Duke is THE man!"

TMan seeths. Lucy suppresses a giggle. Eventually TMan formulates a resolution,

"OK Lucy...Do you reckon Charlton could take The Duke?"

Lucy glances at Mike Remo and feigns thinking, but eventually speaks,

"James Bond!"

TMan's turn to splutter now. It initiates him having a coughing fit. Mike and Lucy swap smiles. Eventually TMan gets control of his speech powers once more although his voice is risen a clear octave,

"James Bond. He's fucking limey playboy!"

They sit waiting, knowing TMan is thinking before his next outburst. Sure enough, he carries on,

"Only reason he's alive is because the so-called bad guys in his movies never bother to kill him when they get the chance. He's too inconsequential to them. They always try to laser his testicles or lock him in an underwater car or drop him from an aeroplane......instead of just killing the fucker!"

They all giggle now as TMan carries on oblivious,

"They ought to cast me as a villain. Answer is....don't give the fucker chance to escape.......pop him straight away!"

Lucy and Mike red now with suppressed laughter. TMan's voice further on up through the registers now. He's playing "lead bass". Mike and Lucy break into laughter, but TMan carries on, now in a "bad" german accent before breaking into the James Bond theme,

"A quick bullet in ze head! How do you like zat Herr Bond? Ding diddle-ing-ding-Ding, Ding, Ding - Ding diddle-ing-ding-Ding, Ding, Ding - Ding diddle-ing-ding-Ding, Ding, Ding - Ding diddle-ing-ding-Ding, Ding, Ding – De Ding – ding-a-dong!"

The Dirtkicker van erupts to laughter as they all sing the James Bond theme with the sierra scenery of Highway 50 all around them.

Now the blue waters of Lake Tahoe. Cross the state line to Nevada.

"YeeHaa – Kit Carson Cowboy Country!"

"Can you get stratocasters in Lake Tahoe blue?"

"Where's the gig Mikey – let's rock these gun totin cow-pokes?"

The Skulk Rock Salute.

Killing Time

https://badpeoplethemusical.bandcamp.com/track/killing-time

Hey Baby - give me some wine
Hey Baby - let's kill time
It was draggin me down – but I'm fighting back
I'm on the fast track
I just gotta keep moving on
I been hit by a speed gun

I want to step out of these hurried streets
Where the people are talking like parakeets
Is this really a capital city?
They huddle in corners with their conspiracies
Preachers and prostitutes and football teams
Fantasy figures in reality dreams

I like the privacy of attic heights
The lonely star is my leading light
I am the saviour of the city

I tried the police but they don't listen to me
John McClane is my hero
Die Hard five point zero

Big business
Big heat
Big chill
Big sleep
Gotta keep moving I'm a wanted Man
The law can never understand

This world is a burned up mess
Typically Tarantinoesque

I'm crossing North Bridge but I'm heading south
I'm watching my back and I'm watching my mouth
I'm looking for the dark side of the city
And the authorities - are looking for me
I gotta keep moving - don't put me in jail
I got a cruise missile on my trail

Big business
Big heat
Big chill
Big sleep
Gotta keep moving I'm a wanted Man
The law can never understand

This world is a burned up mess
Typically Tarantinoesque

I finished my unfinished symphony
Sacrificed my legitimacy
When copied some lines from a hymn I knew
Hey pretty girl I'm talkin to you
Hey pretty girl give me some wine
Hey pretty girl let's kill time
Hey pretty girl let's kill time
Hey pretty girl let's kill time

Motel breakfast now. Mike Remo looking at the map book as
TMan and TheGnome sit and stare. Lucy boots up her cell to
call Little Joan and Ronee. She comes back to the table smiling.
TMan asks after Ronee. Lucy replies,

"She loves kids – you should have one!"

"Don Estrada would pull my balls off!"

"That wouldn't be painful enough for Don's vengeance!"

They giggle. TMan effects a nervous voice,

"Can we perhaps try a paternity test first Don?"

Then he effects his "Don Estrada voice",

"You suggesting my Ronee might have various partners
Bassman? I'm gonna tear your knob off too for that!"

Mike Remo looks up from his map book,

"She-ite – I thought Don Estrada had arrived!"

TMan garruphs, but looks around nervously as his imagination
takes hold once again.

They finish breakfast in silence and head to the van,

"Where we going today Mike?"

"Reno."

TheGnome rudimentises a drum lick on the back of Lucy's seat
and sings,

"I shot a fucker in Reno just to watch the fucker die….."

"Oh very good Gnomio. How long you been dabbling in
lyrics?"

"Can only provide the groove for your shitpile lyrics for so
long Mikey Remo. Bout time I kicked this band up a gear."

"Maybe you should consider joining a poetry and deafmetal
band then boy?"

TMan asks about tonight's venue.

"According to our most conscientious and thoughtful
agent…………", Mike Remo pauses.

The Dirtkickers chant in unison,

"Mr TwentyPerFuckinCent!"

Mike continues,

"It's a biggish bar near the university!"

"They got a university in Reno?"

"Sure thing TMan."

"They run courses in watching people die?"

"It's Reno – innit?"

"You still bring that gun to gigs Mike?"

"Wellllllll – you never know what might happen at a gig!"

"Way to go – MIKE RENO!"

They cruise past Washoe Lake now. Easy drive to Reno and there's time to kill in the afternoon.

At the soundcheck Mike announces a new song and they soundcheck it.

The gig is packed,

"I'm Mike Reno and these are my Dirtkickers.............Here's a new song for y'all!"

Gun Laws

https://badpeoplethemusical.bandcamp.com/track/gun-laws

I shot every man in Reno
But I got bored watching them die
Then I shot every woman so
They didn't keep askin me why

Well we all need to defend ourselves
And this world is full of pricks
It's better to be tried by twelve
Than carried by six

I keep saying to myself
It makes no sense
Attack is the
best form of defence
And I got this right to bear arms
Like our ancestors before
It never did nobody no harm
Gun Laws

No we don't need, we don't need - Gun Laws

I got a 45, 22 - 9 millimetre
If you're a criminal – I can't wait to meet yer

I'll put an end to knife crime
What you gonna do? Stab my bullets?
I'm serious this time
I got a zero tolerance

I keep saying to myself
It makes no sense
Attack is the
best form of defence
Did we kill too many ?
Well what the fuck are guns for ?
And we don't need any more
Gun Laws

Gun Laws we don't need - Gun Laws

The next morning already. Mike kicks the van to life.
"Where to today Mike Reno?"
"Fallon Nevada – Highway 50 boy."
"What happens in Fallon?"
"Skulk Rock happens TMan!"
"Bring it right on in!"

****

"What ya got for me Yuri?", The LynX addresses his attorney over a mesa sized desk. Skinny sits to one side.

"SFPD officer gave us some new info about The Snakes incident?"

"Can we get our money?"

"Doubtful still – but – there seems to be a connection to some beat group in San Francisco and some Hell's Angel Motorcycle Club. That's all we got."

"What's the connection?"

"Seems that some guy rammed Jake Snake's van off the road before they were killed and the money and the product went missing."

"Do we know the guy's name?"

"James Smith."

"Can we get to him?"

"No"

"We can get to anyone?"

"Not him. He's dead!"

TheLynX bangs the desk. Yuri continues,

"Want my advice?"

"I'm paying you!"

"My advice is let it go – it's three years ago now Lincoln! Boston had written it off. He cut a property deal with TheChief."

"Chief is history now", The Lynx looks at Skinny.

"It's all gone Lincoln. Ancient history. Let's move on?"

TheLynX removes his baseball cap. Yuri averts his eyes from the scarred head. He tries not to but he does. Momentarily. TheLynX notices and it seems to inwardly enrage him. Skinny turns and looks from the 4th floor window. The LynX speaks,

"I don't run things like my father. Rest in peace. Fuckin stoners are not going to fuck us over. Thanks for your help Yuri."

Yuri stands and, leaving his coffee untouched, he picks up his briefcase and leaves.

TheLynX turns to Skinny,

"Find this pain in the butt beat group. Kill them all 'cept one. Bring that one back here and we'll see what we can find out?" That way we send a message and keep hopes of retrieving our money and drugs ticking?"

Skinny sighs,

"I did some checking Boss. They are on tour in Utah."

"Utah – what the.......Didn't you tell me The Chief's whore daughter went down that way?"

Skinny nods,

"Might just be a coincidental Boss?"

"Nothing happens by coincidence Skinny. That's what my old pop used to say. Kill 'em all."

TheLynx turns and looks out of his window to the city in the distance. Skinny looks at the eagle scars under his wispy hair,

"I'll send some men down."

"Do it quick!"

****

Speedy Copp sits at her desk processing speeding tickets. She thinks about life in general. Her career is certainly on hold now since the incident with Lathan. She giggles as she remembers him staggering backwards in shock holding his nose. Her and Felicia are inseparable these days. Speedy is in the process of renting her own flat and moving in at Sausalito. She smiles. The prospect is exciting. Felicia is exciting; like spring all year around.

Felicia has told her all about Jimmy English and Lucy and Little Joan. Felicia stays away from Lucy Smith although they are on speaking terms at Dirtkicker gigs. Partly for her own peace of mind and partly out of concern for The Dirtkickers, Felicia has asked Speedy to check on any progress of the investigation into The Snakes Case. Problem is, it means contacting Lieutenant Lathan once again. She doesn't fancy that prospect much. This day though, as she sips her afternoon coffee, she decides to give Lathan's administrator a call.

"Hey Jane!"

Pause,

"Speedy Copp!", she laughs, "You gonna come around and kick his pious butt once again?"

Speedy laughs,

"Could be fun!"

"What you after?"

"Wondered if he'd chased up any of the leads I gave him?"

"Well, the only development I know of is he wrote to a lawyer acting for The Snake people in Helena Montana. Then they paid for him to fly off up there."

"Really?"

"First class travel no less. He was full of it."

"What did he find out?"

"Dunno, he's on his way back today."

"What was the name of the lawyers?"

"Firkovs!"

- 189 -

"OK! Hey thanks Jane."

"S'ok Speedy – you take care."

Speedy sits quietly with her coffee now. Her instincts tell her this could be bad karma for Lucy and The Dirtkickers. What to do? She looks up the lawyer details and wonders about ringing them. That wouldn't work; it would get back to Lathan. She decides to ring the Attorney General's office in Montana.

"Officer Coppola SFPD"

"Can I help?"

"We are processing evidence a Helena Lawyer has been asking about."

The operator disinterested,

"Civil or criminal?"

"Criminal"

The phone clicks and rings through, a female voice answers,

"Assistant Attorney Peters"

"Hi Peters, Officer Coppola SFPD..............................."

"How can I help?"

"You know anything about Firkov Lawyers?"

Peters goes quiet and then,

"You need watertight case. They represent some badass clients?"

"How bad?"

"Bad as they get round here if it's drugs, gambling or whores?"

"That bad eh?"

Peters carries on,

"Most organised crime round here was controlled by a big name called Bostan Xylo, known as BossX. Or it was, until he died a few months or so ago. Now his son runs it. His son is a bigger asshole than Bostan was. He's Lincoln Xylo, known as LynX or The Lynx."

"Thanks Peters."

"S'ok. Your name and number – just for the record."

"Officer Coppola SFPD Traffic. Sounds like stuff a bit above my level."

"Handle with care Coppola. These assholes are as nasty as assholes get!"

"Thanks again."

Speedy puts the phone down and mutters,
  "Oh fuck."

****

Fallon is a good gig for a Sunday. Monday morning and Mike Remo points the van east on Highway 50. The Lonely Highway. The plain out of Fallon runs to distant foreboding hills.
  "Who lives up here Mikey?"
  "You don't wanna know Gnomio."
TMan embellishes,
  "They gonna boil your tender drummer ass Gnome. They like it with a few potato fries. It ain't called The Loneliest Highway for no good reason!"
  "Give it a rest TMan!"
TMan continues, the "give it a rest" suggestion having served only to spur him on. He speaks in a horror movie type voice,
  "MMmmmmm it's a while since we had musician's ass Momma! – But this ain't any musicians ass little Homer this is a drummer's ass!"
TheGnome quietly looking from the window now as the van climbs the first wave if hills. TMan still continues,
  "Tenderised and fattened by years sat on a specially softened drum stool. Sliced wafer thin and lightly fried. It's your Poppa's favourite. He heard there was a gig Fallon last night and he's got the Highway staked out with Uncle Cyrus…"
Lucy enters his monologue now,
  "This is civilised compared to Montana. They'd just eat you alive and fight over the warm bones."
  "How did you escape Lucy?"
  "I fought my way out with daggers and pistols. Sleeping in snow holes and laying false trails to lead my trackers into the quicksand mires of the snake."
(TheGnome in a resigned tone now),
  "I need a new band. I got a hankering to play some cool school jazz. This Skulk Rock shit is going nowhere. Wasted

years. How did I get hypnotised and kidnapped by such a bunch of FUCKIN LOSERS!"

The van erupts into laughter now. They ride the basins and ranges of Nevada. Skulk Rock is going nowhere but it's coming. Monday night they play Ely; a small town. Mike Remo gasses the van ready for tomorrow before they cruise past a casino and bars on the main street. They check in their motel and find the venue; a large bar mopping up clientele from the casino.

"Won't it all be quiet on a Monday Mike?"

"Casinos never quiet TMan. Always people wanting to strike it rich."

"They should get into Skulk Rock then!"

"Oh yeh – with an agent who books you out on The Lonely Highway?!!"

The Ely gig is organised by a muso called Mark. He's seen The Dirtkickers on a vacation to San Francisco a couple of years ago,

"Best gig I ever saw...then you shot the snake guy's Les Paul....nice one! Goddammmmmm what a gig!"

"Hope gigs in Ely are not like that though Mark? Not on a Monday?"

"Hell no – never any trouble in Ely – everyone carries a gun see!"

Lucy, TMan and TheGnome exchange glances as they eavesdrop Mike talking to the guy!

The gig is actually well attended and goes well. The next day Mark checks by their motel as the have breakfast. They thank him and become lifelong buddies. They tell him their next gig is in Cedar City.

"Mormon country man! You's all take care."

"Carry a gun?"

"And git yourselves a few wives!"

"How long to get there?"

"About 4 hours."

"Easy day then. Great."

"Hey – if'n you got time to spare have a look around our railway museum. This used to be a rail depot. Check it out!"

The Dirtkickers are up for that and soon find themselves loving a morning's sightseeing. "Iron Horses" of all types. Train history of iron and copper mines. They mine for songs. America is rich in all these things. Not everyone is aware of it. Mark is though. As they leave the railway museum and hit The Lonely Highway once more, they turn momentarily to Ely and give Mark the skulk rock salute. KOFR Mark!

Cedar City turns out to be a rockin little place. It rocks a little more as skulk hits town. The gig is a bar near the university. They convert many groove-susceptibles. The Dirtkickers hit the last encore at midnight and drift back to their motel. There is a free evening the next day before a scheduled gig in Holbrook Arizona. Mike suggests they go see Monument Valley as they need a night off from bars and beer. There is slight resistance at first but as the wind and time worn rock mesas come into view they are all spellbound. Twenty bucks gets them all into Monument Valley itself and Mike takes the Dirtkicker van around the park road. They pile out fire off endless ammunition in fake gunfights which might seem childish to the mature mind. Not many mature minds in The Lowdown Dirtkickers though. Maturity is a precursor to death and may there be lots more immaturity before the passing years take their inevitable toll. They take in the Navajo run visitor centre and get to stand at a place which a placard informs them was the favourite place of John Wayne. Mike Remo smiles as he stands there,
    "The Duke! A giant amongst men!"
The Duke gets the skulk rock salute before they motor off to a motel in Kayente. Evening meal in a diner,
    "Hey Mikey – I don't see no bars around here?"
    "Navajo Nation TMan – no alcohol."
    "No shit man?"
    "Nope."
    "Well where can I get an IPA?"
    "Bar in Holbrook."
TMan looks at his watch,
    "Eat up! Let's get down there!"
Mike looks at him smiling,
    "Four hour drive TMan. We're there tomorrow."

TMan looks at the other two,

"You mean to tell me we're lost in a desert with no means of re-hydration. It's a fuck-up man!"

"You'll survive. We are back to normality tomorrow."

"Where's tomorrow Mikey?"

"Holbrook Arizona – On Route 66."

TMan sings sarcastically,

"Git your kicks on Route 66!"

Next day sees them hit the road south. Highway 191 now. The desert scenery makes them sleepy. Minds and imaginations take over. The road begins to weary them. Lucy misses Little Joan. TheGnome misses Deirdre. TMan misses Ronee. Mike Remo thinks of Felicia. He thinks of Felicia. He thinks of Felicia. Then he tries to claw his mind back. He thinks of Felicia. His mind grabs a lifeline and he sings,

"I'm riding time down to Texas."

Lucy looks across and smiles at him, she adds

"Highway white line guiding me. Nobody will suspect us."

"Nothing ever better stop me tonight – the future all at stake."

"Nothing ever stops us – we never make mistakes."

The Gnome adds a Texas shuffle on the back of Lucy's seat before TMan contributes,

"Ran outta luck in Tijuana – had to run across the border...."

And so The Lowdown Dirtkicker van rolls on its merry way. The happiest humans you could imagine. You couldn't not like these guys (unless you are a mature person hanging around being mature and surrounded by boring maturity. SKULK ROCK rules here..

****

"Kill 'em all! – 'cept one, and bring that one back here!"

Skinny looks across at The LynX and the other four men stood in the office with them,

"Is that really necessary boss?"

"If I say it is it is! Do I sound like I don't mean it? We need to make an example here or our competitors will think we are weak now Pops is gone. This'll send a message. The world won't miss another rock and fuckin roll band. We'll be doin the world a favour!"

Skinny looks across at the four hoods and sighs,

"Take a works van. Fake plates. They got a ""Gig"" in Flagstaff Arizona on Friday. It's a shit-end bar. Do it there. Make it quick make it public. Bring one of them back. Can you do it?"

HoodOne nods, smiling, tapping his heat,

"Sure thing Boss!"

"No fuck-ups! Straight back here and disappear the van."

HoodOne nods.

****

Thursday morning and the Dirtkickers head east then south.

"What do we know about Holbrook Mike?"

"Its reputation is - Too tough for women and churches!"

"Caramba! – no women?"

"Not ones you would like Gnomio."

Desert scrub scenery now with flat top mesas watching them from the distance and middle distance. They hit Highway 191. Lucy Smith tenses up at the highway sign. Her mind is teleported back to Malta Montana. Vivid. Too vivid. Her memory sits nervously in the diner there. The Dog parked outside. Would it keep going? She was gonna take this very same Highway 191 south and west. Her only hope. It turned out ok though? Just! Or was all that a dream? A bad dream. A nightmare dream. A snake dream of death. Road dreams. Looking in the driving mirror for evil spirits on her trail. Alone in the vastness of America. She now sees those distant nightmares at the edges of her memory universe. She works to push them completely out of sight. Into memory mists. She knows they will always be there but she doesn't have to replay them. She can push her fingers in her ears and chatter loudly. *"Mountains: there was a heaven of sunrise, cool purple airs, red mountainsides, emerald pastures in valleys, dew, and transmuting clouds of gold; It is time to drive on".* Here she is now in the "Badlands". The terrain worries her. It's a moonscape. She needs to escape its gravity downpull. What did Boris The Cranium say? Her mind whirls. She runs the Bruce Song. ""Ding diddle ing ding a ding – ding ding ding ....I'm caught in a crossfire that I don't understand....." She thinks of Little Joan and, suddenly, longs to be back home with Joan and Ronee. She pushes the feelings down. She owes so much to Mike and The Dirtkickers. This is no time for weakness. She idly manifests the skulk rock salute as she sits staring into the distance. Mike Remo notices. Mike notices everything.

Talk of Holbrook being a tough town sits in all their minds as they get closer. The town looks fine and normal and quiet though as they drive in on a Thursday afternoon. They check in at the motel and go find the gig bar. A big red painted bar. Hank the manager has already moved three pool tables to the side of the room. The stage not big but big enough for The Dirtkickers. A few daytime drinkers at the bar look at them with interest or suspicion. Hank is friendly though,
"Thursday is the new Friday around here man. There should be a few in for our live music night."
The sound check is good. Hank suggests three sets start about 8pm. They find a corner seat and Hank lays on food. Mike Remo gets a good feeling. He's played enough gigs to know. The first jugs of IPA appear and The Dirtkickers sit and watch the clientele arrive. Mike knows they are slightly apprehensive that this might be a tough town but all the people through the door radiate positivity. Singles, couples, groups, even families. Hank welcomes them all with a smile.

"Good evenin Holbrook! They told us this town is ""Too tough for women and churches?"" Looks ok to me so far! Not sure about the churches though.........."

Deal The Cards

I'm riding time – Down to Texas
Highway white line guiding me – No body will suspect
Nothing better stop me tonight – The future is all at stake
I can see by starlight – I don't make no mistakes

Deal the cards again
No 2 days are the same
Can't go back to yesterday
Make the same mistakes again

Deal the cards - Roll the dice
That's how to look at life
Nothing ventured nothing gained
Lost a few - never complained

Tried my luck in Tijuana – Had to run across the border
Slow in San Diego – Tried San Francisco
Didn't work out – What do I know?
Time is now – And now it's time to go

Turn the record over
B-sides can be good
Always be a chancer
You never know your luck
Deal the cards - Roll the dice
That's how to look at life (That's my advice)
Nothing ventured nothing gained
Lost a few - never complained

Desert wind in my window
Stars strung on the sky
All the thoughts inside my mind now
Make me wonder why
I'm on the run
All that I done
That time is gone

So sometimes you got to get – mad dog low down mean
A cruel guerrilla fighter – fiercest you ever seen
Fate don't fight so fair – So why should you?
Fight like you don't care – In everything you do

Roll the dice again
No 2 people are the same
Can't take back what you say
Regret is all in vain
Deal the cards - Roll the dice
That's how to look at life
Nothing ventured nothing gained
Lost a few - never complained

Deal the cards again
Give me one more chance to win
Give it one more spin
Roll the dice again
Give it one more try
True love don't die
While I'm alive

The Holbrook gig turns into a great one. Dancers, listeners, hecklers, drunks, stoners. Jugs of beer appear. Hank smiles from behind the bar. The audience swells as the three sets progress
    "Best bar we played this tour!"
    "Yeeeee-haaaaaa!"
Mike even hears a few shouts of "thank you!"
Makes it all worthwhile.

As they relax after the last set people thank them personally. A few guys even help them pack the van. Turns out quite a military presence in and around Holbrook. The guys are eager to talk and be helpful,
    "Where are you guys playing tomorrow?"
    "We're down in Flagstaff."
TheGnome does his little dance, singing,

"Flagstaff Arizona don't forget Winona..........."
Mike smiles and whispers,
"Drummers!..."
The locals share the joke but a couple of the guys look serious,
"You take care down there!"
"We always do!"
"Flagstaff can be rough. Where you playing?"
"Ilkasin Bar."
The guys look at each other, one speaks,
"You know Navajo Nation is dry?"
"Oh yeh. We discovered that last night."
"Well........flagstaff is just outside the boundary of the na-
tion and some bars at the edge can get wild."
"OK – thanks man!"
"Ilkasin is Apache – means Witch – I think!"
"Thanks a lot man – see you next time we are down here!"
The Dirtkickers give the guys The Salute before staggering off
back to the motel. They will pick the van up in the morning.

****

As close as it is possible to get to simultaneity (and you'd
have to ask BorisTheCranium about that), Speedy and Felicia sit
on their couch watching moonlight flicker across the waters of
the bay as The Dirtkickers trudge across Holbrook Arizona.
"You know how you asked me to look into The Snakes Case
and see if it was dead in the water?"
"Yeh?"
"Well.......turns out the airhead 'tective running it has only
gone and gone to Montana to see the lawyers acting for The
Snakes....."
"Yeh?"
"Well......turns out that the lawyer only works for one ma-
jor client and he is a big bad crim!"
The two women stare at each other. Felicia asks,
"Is that bad?"
"Well......new information to them might be the connection
to James English!"
Felicia looks down and thence out across the bay. She grips
Speedy's hand tighter,

"They can't touch Jimmy now?"

"No but it might draw their attention to The Dirtkickers. They tend not to forget money!"

They move closer together on the couch, as if to keep out of darkness.

"Better give Mike Remo a ring tomorrow?"

****

The Dirtkickers roll along Interstate 40 heading west. They pass the sign for Meteor Crater Road. TMan suggests a stopover but Mike says he wants to check over tonight's venue so they fast forward it to Flagstaff. The snowcap mountain in the distance slowly moving closer.

In Flagstaff Mike Remo's directions fall short and they stop and ask a local. He gives them directions to a road running north from the east side of town. Countryside is greener with pine trees now. The town seems a long way behind as the trees open up for a large parking area in front of a wooden built collection of buildings. The roadside sign says "Night Spot" with a series of bars and casino and motel listed under. The "Ilkasin Bar" is listed and Mike turns the van in. They cruise past verandas of the various establishments until they find the bar. Buddy Weiser neons, Liquor neons and a grotesque face sketched in neon just coming into light as dusk approaches. Mike Remo is quiet and leaves The Dirtkickers to go find the contact. TMan is first to speak,

"This place looks different?"

"Good different?"

"Well – Holbrook turned out good? So why not?"

They sit in subdued tones until Mike returns with a power-house of a man. All muscle and leather, his dark hair tied back in a long pony-tail,

"This is Nduco."

They exit the van. Nduco seems friendly enough but vacant, as though it's a little early in the day. He helps them in with equipment. Posters are all around. TMan looks at the listings,

"Hey Mike – we are support band tonight."

"Who with?"

TMan peers at the listing,

"Klis Diyin? Hey Nduco what is Klis Diyin?"

Nduco looks down at TMan,

"Snake Power man! They sometimes work as The Snakekings."

TMan jumps back in feign alarm,

"Hey – we're not into snakes!"

NDuco smiles,

"Just The Sidewinder – he won't bite!"

TMan looks across to his bandmates as they stand staring. TMan knows they are running the same memories as him. The Snake Band at Ho's Bar. They all got thought bubbles hanging over them now saying one thing,

"OH FUCK!"

****

Chapter 15
Ilkasin Bar

The Ilkasin is a large bar. Roughly circular in shape. The "stage" at one side (if a circular shape can have sides) and a perimeter bar along three other sides. Five or six steps lead up from the large dance area to the elevated bar area. Mike Remo is reminded of The Coochie Bar back in SF. This is bigger though. A raised atrium over the dance area is full of structural wooden beams supporting a planked roof in turn supporting roofing slabs visible in places. From the timbers hang a variety of native american objects. Spears, bows, tomahawks, rifles, headdresses, (what looks to be a full sized) bison but the centrepiece is a warrior brave, leaning back, supported by hooks through his nipples, elongating his chest into stretched tapered breasts, his hands out to the side holding a tomahawk and a dagger.

It's still early but The Dirtkickers decide to get soundchecked. Mike Remo suggests they get it out of the way so they can relax before "showtime". Nduco is hardly enthusiastic but he is efficiently helpful. No bullshit, or the native American equivalent, would be his prime directive. Mike Remo expects problematic acoustics but is surprised how good the PA system is and how good the room is. The complexity of roof trusses and angled roofing boards, not to mention the hanging exhibits, seems to help. There is an unassuming drum kit already on stage and Nduco says, "That's Fatback's kit, it's ok to use it though". They soundcheck TheGnome and TMan. The drum sound is amazingly huge from such a small footprint kit and shocks Mike and Lucy initially. However, the all important bass and drum groove from TMan and TheGnome fills the extended space with power and headroom to spare. Early attendees at the bar turn and face them. The Dirtkickers can't work out whether they get "interested" looks or "we are gonna enjoy beating y'all to pulp" looks. Mike turns around and can't fault the sound. He sends Lucy up and they check her acoustic, her telecaster/amp and her voice. Mike smiles. "At least the sound is gonna be good. We can die kicking out high quality skulk!". He's happy with his own sounds and he thanks Nduco who walks off behind the bar. Mike thinks "he's done this a thousand times before. That's good!"

The Dirtkickers find a table at stageside and sit surveying the bar. TMan finds words first,

"'kin she-ite Mike. This is a new one?", he is noticeably uneasy.

"Holbrook turned out ok?"

"This seems edgier?"

TheGnome adds in,

"Play the gig. When it's your gig!"

TMan stares at him. Mike smiles,

"Gnomio is right. We never been beaten yet!"

TMan delves deep and comes back with his courage refreshed,

"Better not try nothin with me or they get a P-Bass sandwich!"

Mike looks across at Lucy now,

"Get the beers in Lucy."

She looks back in silence. They all sit in silence. Mike let's the tension build until he smiles,

"Only jokin'. I'm on my way!"

He walks over and catches Nduco's attention. He returns with a jug of beer and glasses.

"Burgers on the way and no charge! Nduco is THE man!"

They nod, unconvinced. Mike adds,

"Bit of a miserable fucker - but he's ok!"

The Dirtkickers sit and peoplewatch now. The bar getting steadily busier with a high content of native americans. At perimeter areas where there is no bar there are some stools and drinks counters. They notice the appearance of elegantly dressed women who stand or sit in these areas. Some of them in subdued chatter, some read, some study cell phones. TMan looks at them and turns to the others,

"Hey – it must be film star night?"

"Femme fatale night?"

"Right!"

"What a way to go though?"

Lucy looks at the TMan with impatient disgust.

Nduco arrives now with a tray of burgers and fries. TheGnome ventures a question,

"Hey Nduco. What's with the power dressed women?"

Nduco looks around before replying,

"Godistso!"

They look at him quizzically, he looks back sternly,

"Love magic women! Too much for you!"

TheGnome opens his mouth but no words exit. They all look at him before laughter arrives. TheGnome shrugs and picks up a burger. Mike Remo summarises,

"Love Magic Women – there is a song if ever I heard one!"

Mike Remo reaches for his cell as they all eat burgers with growing relish,

"Hey Felicia……………..?"

The Dirtkickers feign disinterest and concentrate on their burgers. They swap "raised eyebrow" looks as TMan mimics Mike's phone characteristics. Mike notices and gives him the finger before walking away, phone at his ear.

Mike Remo crosses the dance floor idly looking at the Love Magic Women and listening to Felicia. It's too much for a man to bear! His mind wanders. He wonders what he's doing out here on tour? Are they making money? Not a lot! Is it worth it all? He puts these thoughts to the back of his mind. Like he always does. Negative thoughts, or otherwise, he submits to her voice. His expression slowly changes as what she is saying begins to sink into his conscious mind,

"Speeds says the SFPD have moved on their investigation of the snake deaths."

Mike has never heard her tone like this before,

"What's that gotta do with me?", he kicks himself for sounding slightly bad tempered. Felicia is the last person on this earth he would want to sound bad tempered to. He apologises.

"I'm sorry Flea. Pressure gig here!"

"Well Mike – it's just that they may have connected Jimmy English to the death of The Snakes."

Mike thinks. Felicia carries on,

"Speeds says that might mean they might be connecting The Dirtkickers too."

"I can see that – but it all went down a long time ago?"

"Yeh – but – Speeds says the officer in charge went up to see a lawyer acting for The Snakes and that the lawyer basically works for a crime boss. We were worried and we just wanted to warn you?"

Mike Remo notes her language. The news worries him. Her tone, as she talks about "Speeds" and "we", worries him more.

"OK – hey thanks Flea."

"Where are you anyway?"

"We're down in Arizona. The weirdest roughest bar you ever saw. Showtime in about an hour."

"Break your guitar Mike Remo! Come and see us when you get back. We can keep an eye on this situation?"

"Sure thing. I wanted to see you anyway?"

"Looking forward to it Mikey."

And she is gone. Mike looks down at his cell. Fucking technology. She's helping and she's a friend. He wants her more than a friend. He doesn't want hassle. She'd just given him other shit to deal with and he has a tricky gig to front before then. When you got a gig to carry you need space before. You need other problems from the "boredom universe" like you need a guitar that won't stay in tune. He pushes all the thoughts of SFPD and criminals from his mind. He only has a small mind and Skulk Rock is all he can concentrate on right now.

Mike Remo decides he needs some "time". He wanders out of the bar and through the scruffy lobby. Keeeeerrrrriisssssst some of the people coming in now are unlike anything he has seen before. Even the meanest Hell's Angels they have played to would look like fine upstanding citizens compared to these guys. He wishes that Marv and Don were here now for security. But they are not. He's got to handle this. He avoids all eye contacts as he moves through people in the lobby and out to the parking area. He sees a shelter with some benches overlooking a childrens play area some distance away. The play area and shelter deserted, he walks over to think things over. The set list for one. His life for another. Felicia for another. He tells himself to pull it all together.

As Mike Remo sits, the moon rises over treetops. He looks at the stars appearing. The wind rattles the trees and a branch falls loudly onto the shelter. He looks vacantly into the distance mentally rifling through Dirtkicker songs for tonight's set. A shadow falls across the moon now and his eyes move focus to the playground fence twenty feet in front of him. A bird has landed. FUCK it's a BIG bird? His mind overloads and he freezes. Is that an eagle? It IS and eagle! He sits and stares not moving, his thoughts suspended. The eagles head moves side to side. Its eyes like lasers scanning him. Everything suspended now as if he is in some slow motion universe. He has no idea how much time has elapsed as he now watches the eagle launch into the air. It flies a tight circle in front of him. He expects it to soar at any moment but it hovers ungainly over haphazardly parked vehicles. It lands on a black van with tinted windows. It walks front to back before jumping once more into the air. Mike's eyes are glued. He has to laugh as he sees the eagle take a dump on the van. He falls back to silence as it lifts its massive wings and grabs the air before gliding back to the ground in front of him. Mike speaks,

"Whaddya want buddy?"

He laughs at himself as he speaks,

"Are you trying to tell me something?"

He's talking to a bird? Mike Remo tells himself not to lose it now. There is a gig to play.

"He's trying to tell you the four guys who arrived in that van are planning to kill you!"

The voice from nowhere shocks Mike Remo. He stands and turns. His hand already strayed to his gun, but he is still again as he sees the long dark hair of a woman curtaining her face at each side. She wears a snakeskin tailored dress and looks shockingly out of place against the shady trees behind her. Mike's radar working perfectly as he takes in her appearance and starts to run programs to work out her angle here. He moves his hand from his gun. The result of his computations tells him she is a "godistso – love magic woman" from the bar. Keerrriiisssst she is an attractive one! She continues,

"They are from Montana. Sent by TheLynX!"

His voice is no longer his own, it is raised in pitch,

"Who the fuck is TheLynX?"

"Boss of crime in Montana."

He no longer thinks she is a love magic woman and his "who is she" algorithms begin to run out of ideas,

"Who are YOU?"

"I'm Ooljee. I used to belong to Jake Snake."

Mike's mental mists begin to clear now, although a cloud of anxiety comes sweeping in, wondering if she is one that wants to kill him? His hand moves slowly back towards his gun. The eagle furls and unfurls its wings. Mike is way out of chartered territory here,

"Belong?"

"Well. I was his wife. That is a story too long for now."

"What are you doing here?"

"I'm in The Sidewinder's band. We are the other band playing tonight?"

"What is it with you guys and snakes?"

Ooljee smiles. This parasite man has strength of character.

"Klis Biyi – Apache for Snake Power!"

"You are Apache?"

"No - I am Assiniboine."

Mike wonders to himself why he is asking these questions? His mind is not functioning. He gets back into the present,

"Four guys?"

"Four pieces of parasite shit!"

Mike is not quite sure of what she means but he figures the four guys are not very nice and mean them harm. It fits with what Felicia said.

"What do I do?"

"Do what you think best Michael Remo. My daughter has told me about you. How you shot Jake's guitar. That made her laugh."

"Your daughter?"

"Ajei played bass in Jake's band."

Mike remembers Ajei now and some jigsaw thoughts fall into place. Mike re-asks his question,

"What do I do?"

"Play your gig Michael Remo. If you leave now you will make it easy for them. The Sidewinder is here and he will help!"

"Who's the fuckin' Sidewinder?"

"*Klis Biyi* – he is *gan*. You might say from another world? White man cannot think correctly. Trust me Michael Remo!"

She turns and walks away. Mike Remo finds himself studying her slender shape, her calves and her ankles above the heeled shoes she wears. He looks back and the eagle still stares at him. It slowly shakes its head before grabbing the air and taking to the sky. Michael Remo shakes his own head now. Gathers his jigsaw thoughts and makes his way back inside. He detours past the van and checks that it does indeed have Montana plates.

His mind fizzes and pops as he walks back into the venue. He's anxious to see The Dirtkickers again. He has no idea how long he's been away. The lobby not at all busy but he can tell the venue has filled up mightily, by virtue of the noise breaking out of the doors. Mike begins to order his mental legionaires. He is slightly phased as what he thinks must be some kind of shade passes over him. He blinks and stops. Suddenly facing him is a slim weathered face under a large hat. The eyes are dark pools with dancing reflections of the lobby lights in them. Mike doesn't need another conversation and he tries to walk past. The voice commands attention though,

"Are you the band?"

"I'm part of the band sir", Mike's mind runs the procedure for reaching for his gun should it be required. Now is not the time though. Not yet anyways. They could be from Montana though. Keeerrrrrisssst he is spooked.

"I'm The Sidewinder and this is The Fatback", he gestures to a guy now stood to Mike's side and slightly behind him. Mike holds still and The Sidewinder speaks again,

"You must be Michael Remo. We're the other band sir. Pleasure to meet you", he holds out his hand.

Mike is relieved to take the wiry handshake. He then gets a bone crush handshake from The Fatback. Mike thinks to himself, "A bullet would bounce offof this dude!"

"Pleased to meet you guys too and thanks for use of your drum kit Mr Fatback."

The Fatback smiles,

"No problem. We just met your drummer. He is happy."

Mike smiles,

"Great! I just met someone from your band."

"Ooljee, she said you were outside."

"I lost track of time out there."

"Ooljee can have that effect!"

Mike laughs,

"I bet! How long to showtime?"

TheSidewinder stops and listens,

"Ten minutes or so? Best play a long set Michael Remo – keep them rockin!"

The Fatback smiles at Mike. Mike responds,

"One long set it is. If they let us live?"

"Your gig Michael Remo! We got your back"

Mike blinks and somehow he's now watching The Sidewinders back as he disappears into the venue, yet he never saw him turn and walk.

Mike walks back into the bar and is shocked at how the crowd has grown now. He scans for the four guys from Montana. It's futile because everyone in there looks capable of murder, or at least that's what Mike thinks now. His mind in overload again. He looks across the expanse of dance floor in front of the stage and groups of people stand. Some chatter, some scan for others. There's tension here. There are way more Love-Magic-Women now. Some sit on stools, some lean over the balcony rail to the dance floor. He looks across at The Dirkicker's table and sees TMan, TheGnome and Lucy sat talking. He makes his way quickly back,

"Fuckin hell Mikey – Where you been?", TMan sounds nervous.

"Got a call and met some of the other band", he doesn't tell of the eagle or the four guys from Montana. He doesn't want to spook them. TheGnome speaks,

"Hey we met The Sidewinder and The Fatback. They seem ok? Fuckin weird – but ok!"

"You probably seem weird but ok to them too Gnomio!"

"That Nduco topped up our jug too."

The Dirtkickers manage a nervous laugh. Mike pours himself a drink from the jug as his mind begins to clear, as it always does at showtime. Mike speaks,

"This is another gig for us. I not seen this gig before. So - remember the rule – the groove is everything, the groove is everything, THE GROOVE IS EVERYTHING! We play what we play. It's our gig. We own it. These fuckers have not heard skulk rock before. They might be ready for it, they might not be. We just play it. Play it like we played it a million times. It's what we do! We don't owe nobody nothin'.He gives the skulk salute."

They nod.

As an afterthought Mike tells them,

"Stay alert tonight though. We're doing one long set. If anything happens do what I say!"

The Dirtkickers know Mike Remo. They believe him. They believe in their music. They believe in their groove. They believe in Mike Remo. They would take a bullet for Mike Remo. They might fuckin' have to tonight?

They take their places on stage as Mike walks over and finds Nduco. "Make it loud Nduco – make it fuckin' loud!" NDuco moves to the sound desk and nods. Mike walks back to the stage. They all nod they are all ready. It begins,

Loving Limit
https://badpeoplethemusical.bandcamp.com/track/loving-limit

Apologies
It's down to me
But I can see

You lost the spirit
Well all along
I was so wrong
It all fits You've hit
The loving limit

These things can happen
All too often...it's so sad

You've reached your loving limit
We built this house but now there's nothing in it
Tears in my eyes long since dried...but I'm still sorry

The stars don't stay
They move away
With every day
It's a law of physics
This universe
Is a big hearse
Heaven's curse
Is somewhere in it

Eternity
Is not for me...is that so bad ?

You've reached your loving limit
We built this house but now there's nothing in it
Tears in my eyes long since dried...but I'm still sorry

These days I hear the Highway Ghost asking if she's leaving
On the dark roads outside of town his tyres squealing
It is night - she is awake - she don't speak I know she's still day
dreaming
If I could turn
If I could turn the stars
If I could turn the stars around she'd be returning

Beautiful trick angel
Love is contagion

I'm only saying
Look in your rear view mirror
Behind is gone
We all move on
Run run run run
Right now it's all too clear

These memories took a lifetime
And it's all gone in no time

You've reached your loving limit
We built this house but now there's nothing in it
Tears in my eyes long since dried...but I'm still sorry

Everybody's got – a loving limit

Mike Remo's prayers are answered and Nduco is a fine sound man. The Stratotone splits the air with the opening riff and when the groove kicks, he sees faces turn around. TMan's bass wobbles their bellies and Gnomio's kick drum slaps their asses. The Snare and Lucy's Telecaster marks down time and synchronises everyone. Mike Remo watches the audience. He's been here so many times before and he sees them tune in. He looks across at his band mateş. They feel the surge of confidence Mike and a good sound can always give. Lucy remembers the first time she ever met Mike, her first open min in SF. He looked after her and he's looked after her ever since.

Mike knows the band is now on trial though. The audience-jury, however hard, cool, sophisticated (maybe not here though!), cynical, judgmental, negative, positive, explosive, are now nibbling at the groove bait. He looks at the Love-Magic women around the raised perimeter. Some have turned and look at the band, their hips swaying. Mike smiles to himself. This is the first battle we need to win. He is confident though. His troops are well-drilled and know their ordinances. If they can achieve any dancers it will be the equivalent of sending in the first wave of cavalry. If that happens he knows TheGnome will have them on his orbit. Trapped forever in groove gravity. They will be hooked in and on the line. Then the TMan will give them the rollercoaster bass lines and drag them into the addiction phase. They will fall. They will be ours. Easy! This audience is as easy as all the others – as long as you have the moves, the personnel, the belief and, MAINLY, as long as you have the songs. They have the songs for sure, The Lowdown Dirtkickers don't owe anything to anybody. We play our own stuff we ain't no Karaoke dudes......his mind wanders........like it always does on stage. This is the drug.

The crowd sways at the edge of the lower dance floor, like it's a pool and they are unsure of the temperature. There's no ladder into this pool – if you're going in you dive in. Mike waits. But. Even he is surprised by the sudden appearance of a dancer propelling himself into the middle of the floor as if from a high river bank into rapid waters. A mighty leap. Mike's eyes open unblinkingly. The figure is a warrior-brave. Just back from a raid somewhere up on the plains. No doubt about it. Centre-parted jet black hair with bright red but desert-dusty headband completed with 3 feathers. Tan leather embroidered waistcoat and banded adornments to the long hair hanging down his chest. The waistcoat open over a scarred body of total power. Where had this dude come from? Not Montana, he hopes. Mike had been scanning the audience for Montana macho-men and he had not picked up on this guy at all. So much for looking after his band if he hadn't even noticed this guy. The Brave dances like nobody Mike has ever seen. Tension rises in the audience. The band on autopilot extend the groove. TheGnome and TMan have him on the line for sure but this one fights. He pulls the line tight as he moves across the dance floor lake. They give him line and then reel him in. The audience silent now. These events are not quite in Mike Remo's playbook. This guy is different. His muscles like a middleweight boxer. Native americal jewelry and adornments to his arms. His face cheek-bones and paint. Would you say war-paint? Mike Remo strug-gles for tactical guidance. As the dancer spins Mike notices, for the first time, tomahawks on a diagonal leather belt from a shoulder and downwards across his torso. Are they real or ornamental? She-ite this guy is as real as you get. TheGnome plays him out to the back of the floor and then pulls him in with a series of crescendos even Mike has never heard TheGnome release. The dancer moves to the middle now in a limbo dancer type backwards lean. His muscles tense, his body almost horizontal, his hair adornments now hanging down behind his head and dragging on the dance floor. The dancer howls at the ceiling now, his notes cutting across the music and, as he raises his body, his sinews tight and glistening his arm flashes and he releases a tomahawk. It flashes through the stage lights. Spinning. It passes between Mike Remo and Lucy Smith, over TheGnome's ride cymbal and whacks into an oak post at the rear of the stage with a dull but audible thud.

Mike Remo's mind in temporary overload now. WTF? This is well outside the norm of San Francisco fringe gigs. He's played rough bars before but not like this! Lucy looks at him, scared. TMan moves in front of Lucy as if to protect her. The band almost falter but TheGnome explodes the rhythm for one last flourish to a big crescendo and the number ends in fading crash cymbal to total silence. The dancer tense in the middle of the floor, his muscles defined and moist with sweat under the house lights. He stares at Mike Remo, walking slowly forward. Mike doesn't flinch though. His Stratotone hangs around his neck and in his right hand is his 38, pointed at the ground. For now.

The whole bar watching now. The Brave fixes Mike Remo's gaze. The silence holds like a black star blanket on the whole bar. Mike's right hand twitches. His gaze never falters. They are eye to eye.

The Brave walks slowly forward until he almost reaches the edge of the stage. He stops and grins. His white teeth catching the house lights. He slowly slowly slowly raises his hands and claps. Single clap. Double clap……..then he claps and turns to the audience. Tension is resolved. The tension runs out of fuel, it's membrane fissures and turns to harmless droplets that rain down to be trampled underfeet. Mike Remo relaxes and turns to face his band. The audience now applaud. Mike walks to the rear of the stage and takes a hold of the tomahawk. He extends the moment with pretence of not being able to release it. Eventually, he works it loose and walks to the front of the stage and gives it back to The Brave who puts it back into its place. Mike imagines that he'd need more than a 38 to stop this guy anyway as they smile at each other. As The Brave walks slowly away now Mike notices The Sidewinder stood watching from the edge of the dance floor.

Mike turns and calls the next number. The gig is theirs now. The dance floor fills, the tension droplets under stampede, with the Dirtkickers holding groove for a long long set that is over way way too soon.

As the Dirtkickers vacate the stage Mike realises his mind has been zoned and he had forgotten to scan for the dangerous dudes Ooljee and The Eagle had warned of. He admonishes himself. "Warned by an eagle? Am I crazy?" He wonders if it really happened. Christ, he has been on the road too long! They sit at their table and breath slowly. Nduco has left two jugs for them. Things are settling down. TMan leans over, they all lean in,

"I was worried there Mikey! No bullshit!"

"Me too T"

They four way handshake, suddenly noticing The Sidewinder is stood next to them. They blink. No-one had noticed him approach. Mike pushes out a chair to invite him to sit. He smiles at them all,

"Fuckin Rock and fuckin Roll The Lowdown Dirtkickers! – love it!"

"Thank you Mr Sidewinder sir. Have a drink."

The Sidewinder pours himself a beer. Mike asks,

"The dancer guy was a tense moment?"

The Sidewinder smiles,

"He is ""gan"" Michael Remo! It's a power you would not understand. Your bullets would not have worked but he could sense your inner power too."

The Sidewinder says it in a tone that is large part "matter-of-fact" such that the listening Dirtkickers are slow to comprehend. They look at each other as the words fall into the past. The Fatback sits with them now,

"Nduco will send beer over. No need to move."

The Sidewinder fixes them all in his gaze,

"Best not to leave here during our set. Bad spirits around."

They look at him for a sign he is winding them up. No such sign. He continues,

"We are going on now. Please stay and listen?"

TMan replies full of his enthusiasm,

"Sure thing Mr Sidewinder. Beer to drink and I am the man!"

The Sidewinder and The Fatback offer them fist-bumps and walk slowly to the stage. Lucy leans across to Mike,

"What did he mean? Not to leave during their set?"

Lucy stares at Mike now. Suddenly worried. Mike leans in and takes a breath,

"This has been some week!"

"Sure has Mike."

"I love it. Wouldn't be anywhere else."

Mike sees Lucy's worried look arrive. What can he do? He can't not tell them but he doesn't want to worry them. Not after such a "memorable" gig. Should be a time to relax and enjoy. Seems improbable that there would be bad guys on their trail. But, there was all that business with Jimmy. He knew Jimmy didn't tell him everything but he also knew that Jimmy and Lucy had made money out of all that. With the help of Marv and Don for sure. Marv had donated some cash to The Dirtkickers. Other than that, Mike hadn't asked too many questions. Marv and Don are not the type to answer questions. Lucy had used her money towards a nice property in SF. A place for her and Little Joan. Mike didn't want to know any more details. But hell, if The Sidewinder and Ooljee were bullshitting him - why? And what about the eagle. She-ite! That was too much? He can't take risks. He needs to tell them.

Mike leans over to all The Dirtkickers. He looks down and then looks each of them in the eye. He tells them what Felicia had told him. He leaves out the bit about The Eagle and Ooljee in case they think he is struggling for sanity. He actually wonders if he did dream that bit? Lucy feels a chill descend over her. The nightmare thoughts flood back. Mike leans over and holds her hands.

"We will sort this out Lucy Smith. I'll pull the rest of this tour and we will head back – fast – tomorrow."
Lucy nods trying to smile.

Now they hear a bass note check out the air. It seeks out corners of the room and notifies the audience. They look across at the stage as a slim athletic figure with her back to the audience adjusts the tone on the bass stack. Another note, this time airy and light riding on a lowdown power wave. The Fatback slowly swells a press roll from a meagre hiss to a tension that no-one in the room can ignore. TheGnome locks on. This has his total attention. The Sidewinder is now onstage with a Tenor Saxophone. His tone manifests and it is an outrageous combination of depth, tremolo and distortion. His notes bend and swirl. As the rhythm kicks now the audience are hooked in. Even The Dirtkickers, with all their current worries cannot resist the allure of this music. The dance floor heaves and ripples under the control of this force of nature. As Boris The Cranium would tell you, every force is actually a "field" and all ripples on that field are "particles". In this case the field is"groove" and the ripples are packets of sound. A kick drum pulse like you never heard before; the largest cannon amongst other artillery fire, the snare a variety of gunfire, bass glues everything together on a cliff edge road. Ajei veers it close to edge so the audience can look into an abyss but then she drags them back. This spatial symphony even beats back Lucy's current nightmare recurrences.

Three of the four hoods enter the venue at the rear. Confident. Hood One repeats orders, "We pop the three guys and take the woman back!" They move to the bar and stand watching. The

Sidewinder Band take the groove to quieter seas. The Sidewinder himself sets off the song.

Snakebit

https://badpeoplethemusical.bandcamp.com/track/snakebit

They say it will be fine
All in good time
But it's your time but they take it

It'll happen one day
That's what they say
They call it advice but but it's bullshit

Because you can't find love
You can't find love
You can't find love – You got to make it

Sometimes it goes like this
Hear the love snake hiss
The venom that it spits
You been hit – You been Snake-bit

And if it's not right
You fight and fight and fight
Trying too hard is to fake it

All this time trying
But all along they were lying
And now you're dying – Snake-bit

Because you can't find love
You can't find love
You can't find love – You got to make it

Sometimes it goes like this
Hear the love snake hiss
The venom that it spits
You been hit – You been Snake-bit

Now you're fading fast
Just thinking of the past
How long can you last – when you're snake-bit

Sometimes it goes like this
Hear the love snake hiss
The venom that it spits
You been hit – You been Snake-bit
You been hit – You been Snake-bit

Godistso women keep watch on the hoods as they make their way to the bar. The hoods smile. Confident, but out of their depth, although they don't know it yet. These Love Magic women begin a low wail, just audible above the groove. The Sidewinder hears it though and glances to the back of the room. He nods to TheFatback and they take the groove quieter and quieter. The tension winds. The Love Magic women in a kind of dialogue now, wailing to the Sidewinder. The musical effect is so so different. Lucy leans across to Mike,

"Christ Mike I need to piss?"
Mike looks back, smiling,

"OK Lulu, I'll ride shotgun."
Mike nods to TMan and TheGnome as he and Lucy depart. They walk around the edge of the room at the opposite side to where the hoods stand. As Mike and Lucy reach the door to the lobby and rest rooms Mike clocks the four hoods. They stand out like turds on tiles. He tenses but he doesn't alarm Lucy.

As Mike and Lucy enter the lobby The Sidewinder leaves Ooljee fronting the song. She answers the Love Magic chorus in a continuation of the dialog. The hoods don't know it but their every move is being broadcast.

HoodOne directs his forces and HoodThree and HoodFour make their way around the room perimeter towards where TMan and TheGnome are sat. Their weapons in deep pockets inside their jackets, silencer devices fitted.

Lucy Smith disappears into the Ladies Room and Mike Remo waits at the door. HoodOne and HoodTwo enter the lobby and begin to walk towards Michael J Remo. As Mike sees them all time slows.

Inside the main bar, HoodThree in front of HoodFour slowly walk the perimeter and close in on the table where TMan and TheGnome sit. They think they are anonymous in the crowd. How wrong can you be? HoodThree begins to extract his weapon but at the same time he receives a kick from the pointed toe of a snakeskin high heel love magic shoe. All time slows here too.

In the lobby, HoodOne and HoodTwo now approach Mike Remo. Mike faces them reaching for his 38. As he does, HoodTwo seems to stumble and slowly fall. Visible behind him now is Nduco with a bow in hand. As HoodTwo falls on his face Mike sees there is an arrow in the middle of his back.

Back in the bar, HoodThree gets a shot off but his aim is deflected by the kick. He stumbles in front of HoodFour. The shot strikes TMan as TheGnome is already accelerating toward HoodThree. Attack is the best form of defence. The dance floor crowd are crouched, all except for The Brave stud upright in the middle. As HoodThree regains his composure, moving his weapon to point at TheGnome, a tomahawk spins through the lights. As it flies it is audible due to its speed and spin. It embeds in the side of HoodThree's head with a dull wet thud. HoodFour turns to look across at the dance floor in shock and sees his tomahawk already on its way.

In the lobby, Mike is slower than HoodOne and is now almost looking "down the barrel". His thoughts race. He is amazed how many thoughts he can have as he tries to raise his 38 in what Lucinda Williams might call his "long last moments". He asks himself, "Does the body rule the mind or the mind rule the body?". In this case the thoughts rule, but the body is not fast enough.

In the bar, HoodThree and HoodFour are now laid on the floor, tomahawks firmly embedded in their dead heads. TheGnome looking down at them turns to check on TMan. Blood pumps from his shoulder. TheGnome, in panic, is moved aside by Love Magic women. One appears with a towel and they compress his wound. The band carries on. TheGnome, in a daze, looks down at two bodies each with tomahawks firmly embedded in their heads.

At the same time in the lobby, Mike Remo is vaguely aware of some kind of blackout. At least, that is what he initially thinks. It moves across his eyeline. Momentarily. But, then, it lifts again and HoodOne is still in the same position. His weapon never quite pointing at Mike. Mike focusses on the gunman's face now and clearly sees two closely spaced puncture wounds in the middle of his forehead. His eyes now frozen and hollow but they seem to stare at Mike. Mike is suddenly aware that The Sidewinder is stood next to the gunman.

In the bar, Three or four Love Magic women support TMan as they take him away. TheGnome follows. They lead him to a private room to the side of the bar. TMan is in shock, pale and incoherent.

In the lobby Mike Remo speaks to The Sidewinder,
    "Is he dead?"
    "Not yet but he will be by morning Michael Remo."
Lucy appears from the ladies room now. She staggers in shock. Mike grabs her,
    "Hey, it's ok it's ok!"
The Sidewinder is calm,
    "I got to get back to the gig. See you soon!", he smiles and seems to disappear.
Mike suddenly gasps,
    "TMan and Gnomio?"
They hurry past Nduco and two other barmen as they begin to move the "bodies".

They enter the main bar and the music rules. The Sidewinder is back on stage and firing his saxophone. Mike and Lucy walk quickly around to their table. It's overturned and Mike sees blood spatter,

"Oh fuck, oh fuck, oh fuck!", he turns to Lucy.

Love Magic women put arms around their shoulders and comfort. They slowly guide them away to the room where they took TMan. As they lead Lucy and Mike away the gig is carrying on.

Sidewinder

https://badpeoplethemusical.bandcamp.com/track/the-sidewinder

The Sidewinder
You can't move
Whichever way you look
He's looking at you
Hypnotised
By his eyes
He sees through
Your disguise

He's just like eyes
In the night
Crazy evil
Points of light
He can easy
Easy hide
He just shuts
Shuts his eyes

The Sidewinder
He's gonna bite
Then you die
But it takes all night
You might not see
The morning light
It's never gonna be
Alright

Sidewinder
Sidewinder
The Sidewinder

The Copperhead
He is gay
The Black Mamba
Is an ocean away
The Rattler sound
Is his giveaway
But the Sidewinder
He just waits

Well maybe
You been bit
This is your last night
You don't know yet
You gonna wake
In a cold sweat
Heaven or Hell
Is all you get

The Sidewinder
He's gonna bite
Then you die
But it takes all night
You won't know
If you're dead or alive
Through the dark hours
Of your last night
Sidewinder
Sidewinder
The Sidewinder

I'm the sidewinder
You're in my mind   (Ride on out)
You're in my eyes
You won't survive
Do you like to be alive?

Do you mind dyin'?

The Sidewinder
He's gonna bite
Then you die
But it takes all night
The Sidewinder
Don't make a sound
He's coming
To take you down
Sidewinder
Sidewinder
The Sidewinder

He don't back down
He don't lie
Moves to the side
And then he strikes
Only he
Only he knows why
He's so low
He can't see the stars in the sky

The Sidewinder
He's gonna bite
Then you die
But it takes all night
You might not see
The morning light
It's never gonna be
Alright
Sidewinder
Sidewinder
The Sidewinder

Chapter 16
Healings

In the room where they are led to TMan is laid out on a table.
Women tend his wound. They try and stop the blood. There is a lot of blood. Lucy looks away in panic. Mike Remo looks in over the women's shoulders. TMan sees him and tries to smile. Mike asks a woman,

"What's happening?"

"Ooljee will be here soon."

Mike is lost in thoughts. He has no idea what to do for the best now. His mind in panic whirls. He looks over at TheGnome comforting Lucy. She is in a tearflood.

"Oh Fuck, Oh Fuck, Oh Fuck!"

The door opens and Mike hears the gig going on. His mind still circles. He turns to see Ooljee again. She smiles and walks past to the women crowded around TMan. They part. She moves the towel and looks at the wound. Blood flows. Mike looks over and sees a mass of loose flesh. Ooljee speaks,

"Looks worse than it is!"

"That don't mean it ain't bad though?", Mike's voice doesn't sound like his own.

Ooljee turns and smiles,

"He be ok – I hope."

"You hope?"

"I can stop blood and set healing off. Bone chipped but not broken. I replaced chip."

She goes back to work. One woman teeters in on her heels with something like a first aid kit. Ooljee first takes out what looks like drugs paraphernalia. One of the women cooks up some powder and they inject TMan. Ooljee soothes him as he calms now. Almost a contented look. She concentrates now. Stainles steel clamps to vein or artery. Mike doesn't want to know which. Is this right course of action? Or should he be fast-forwarding the van to a hospital. Ooljee pauses, as if to answer his doubts,

"Bleeding stopped. Now I fix vein."

Mike sits next to TheGnome,

"Gotta go with this Gnomio?", seeking confirmation.

TheGnome nods and holds Mike's shoulder.

Ooljee concentrates with needles. Next they see her carefully replacing skin flaps. Big skin flaps. Ooljee informs them,

"White parasite shit used soft nosed bullets."

The Dirtkickers look away. Eventually she stitches the external wound. She turns to The Dirtkickers smiling,

"He is fixed!"

"Will he be ok?"

"No bass guitar for a while, but ok!"

"How long is a while?"

"Couple of moons? He will full recover!"

"Thank you!"

Ooljee turns to look at Lucy,

"Lucy Snake! Long time!"

Lucy looks down, ashamed. Ooljee speaks calmly,

"Jake Snake had it coming for many years. His boys had followed his footsteps too. You should not feel guilty about your escape. Not my place to judge."

Lucy looks up now. Tears flooding again. This time badly. Like a weight of conscience is being lifted or shared after all this time? Ooljee sits next to her and comforts.

Ooljee speaks,

"Seth Snake was as mean as the rest! Maybe more so? He was pretty and could be nice. But, he used his skills for bad. Jake used to be nice too. Believe it or not. I was a worse prisoner than you! You did Ajei and I a service!"

Lucy holds Ooljee now. Mike and TheGnome listen as they share stories. Lucy's emotions flood out now. Ooljee holds her.

The gig outside begins to end. The encores. A drunken audience. Wild gig! TMan begins to surface from his dreams. They sit him up and talk to him. Lucy sits thinking.

Suddenly The Sidewinder is there. He smiles,

"Man! That almost didn't work out?"

They look at him. He speaks again,

"Didn't go down as I planned!"

He looks at TMan,

"How you feelin Mr Bassman?"

"Sore!"
"You will recover!"

The door opens now and in walks The Brave. The atmosphere changes. TheGnome stands and thanks him. The Brave stares and then holds TheGnome's shoulders, speaking in a strange language. Mike Remo stands to face him, smiling. The Brave stares before his face transforms to a grin. He slaps Mike Remo on each shoulder simultaneously. Mike smiles and bows. Next he turns to TMan laid on the table. TMan grimaces in pain. The Brave looks at his wound and speaks at some length. He finishes speaking with a broad grin. TMan looks at The Sidewinder and asks,

"What's he say?"
The Sidewinder laughs,
"He says.....errrm....you are a soft white parasite pussy!"

The Sidewinder laughs. So too The Brave. The laughter is infectious and soon spreads around the group although TMan doesn't quite seem to be into the joke. The Brave moves to the middle of the room now. He stands tall, left arm across his mighty chest, his mighty voice emanates as his right arm forms the Skulk Rock salute,

"SKULK ROCK – FUCK!"
He turns and walks out leaving everyone in silence. Mike laughs,

"Well he's getting to grips with English!"
The Sidewinder laughs too,

"Better than your Apache Michael Remo!"
TheGnome is serious now,

"Who were those dead guys?"
Ooljee answers,

"Bad soldiers from Montana. Jake Snake dealt for their boss all around Montana. They also had land deals with Assiniboine and Sioux. My father had deals with the white man boss they all serve. This boss died and son has the devil in his heart and soul. It is he who sent them. He thinks you have money from The Snakes that should be theirs. These white parasites have stupid and evil misplaced pride if they think they have been cheated."

"Maybe they were?", Lucy Smith speaks.

"They took farm from Ajei and I but we were happy to be out of that."

Ajei and The Fatback have entered now. Ooljee continues, downhearted,

"They will be back."

Lucy's head sinks. Mike speaks,

"They have information from police in SanFrancisco."

"Then that is where they will come and look for you!"

Lucy thinks of Little Joan and asks, in panic,

"Do they know where I live?"

She doesn't wait for an answer. She looks at Mike,

"Mike – we got to get back – now!"

Mike thinks and nods,

"Let's get packed and rolling."

Mike and TheGnome go back to the bar to retrieve their instruments. Nduco goes to help. He also gives Mike the gig money in an envelope,

"Play here anytime Dirtkickers!"

"We will! Best sound we ever had!"

They step over sleeping bodies on the dance floor. Nduco explains,

"Weekends can be sleepovers. Long way back to The Nation!"

They load the Dirtkicker van with one trip. Mike asks Nduco,

"What happened to the dead guys?"

"In their van. Van will disappear."

Mike doesn't ask anymore.

Lucy remains with TMan. Ooljee looks at his wound again. She retrieves a leather pouch and opens to reveal some kind of powder. She shows Lucy. She dips a finger into it and inserts finger into TMans mouth. His grimaces slowly turn to serenity. Within a matter of minutes he is smiling content. Ooljee smiles,

"Enough here to get him home and healing. Don't give him too much though! It can poison the mind."

Lucy nods. She sits with Ooljee and Ajei either side of her. She speaks,

"Sorry I brought this upon you!"

Ajei answers,

"You gave us freedom Lucy Snake. No need to be sorry."

Lucy shakes her head,

"I could've handled it better!"

They look at her and she adds,

"He broke my guitar! I just lost it!"

Ooljee looks at her,

"All things are written Lucy Snake! We are all connected by…well…white man does not have words?…maybe ""fate-lines""? This world and other worlds. There are connections. White man thinks he understands but he is blind. Blind by his own greed. His fate is written!"

Lucy shudders. She suddenly remembers Boris's lecture and how he talked of just such a thing? Governed by his equations. How the other professors seemd blind to his ideas. Her mind fizzes. Now she smiles,

"I'm Lucy Smith – not Lucy Snake – I was never really married."

The Sidewinder was sat quietly and now he speaks,

"What is wrong with snakes?"

Lucy realises her lack of tact and tries to start an explanation,

"Nothing………..!"

They gently laugh at her. Ajei speaks,

"Your friend James was gentle."

Lucy looks at Ajei as her eyes fill with memory tears. Ajei holds her hand,

"You will meet him again!"

Lucy nods.

Mike and TheGnome are back now. Ooljee shows Mike the pouch and how to use the powder,

"Will keep you awake and help vision when driving Michael Remo! Not too much though. The TMan will need it for a week or so. Be careful, too much will bring shadows!"

Mike and Lucy nod. They stand to leave. The Sidewinder has been deep in thought but now he speaks,

"Can you get us gigs in white man city Michael Remo? We will help you deal with parasite soldiers when they come. We will know when they come. You will need help."
Mike thinks,

"We have gigs and we can share? Hell, we will need a bass player for a while", he nods to TMan sat there smiling in a dreamdaze.
The Sidewinder smiles,

"Good! We like ""Skulk Rock""!"

"Well Skulk Rock loves you!"
Mike gives the salute. The Sidewinder reciprocates.

"I'll write down our address for you."
The Sidewinder smiles.

"No need Michael Remo. We will find you. No danger for a while!"

**

Under darkness they leave. Lucy in the rear with TMan. TheGnome and Mike up front. Interstate 40. All lost in thought. Events replay in their minds. Not like the movies. Real people. Real dead people. Us or them? Thanks to others it was them though. Who was The Brave? Keeerrrrriisssst! Who is The Sidewinder come to all that? Powers here that we don't understand. Lucy longs for Little Joan. This tour was fate for sure? Ooljee had taken a lot of gravity from Lucy's conscience. So maybe it is all for the best? These guys are the best ever. The TMan dozes and she doses him whenever it seems that his pain is too much. Mike tries a burst of Ooljee's powder as sleep tries to creep up on him. He sees the road crystallize in front of him; his senses magnified, his concentration enhanced and his focus total. Lucy Smith shuts her mind and watches the stars. At dawn they hit Kingman and gas the van. Lucy gets coffees. Mike drives on and into The Mojave. Desert hours pass. The sun chasing them now. Relentless. Lucy shivers at the thought of pursuit once more. She starts to think she needs to end this one way or another. She can't think of a way though. Her only hope is her friends, Skulk Rock and The Sidewinder. She begins to doubt. Now the highway descends. Down, down and down until there it is, ahead and left and down below. Green California. She's seen enough desert in the last week or so. They fall into it. Orange groves spring up on their left. They pass Bakersfield. Mike Remo like a statue holding the wheel. Mike Remo gun toting musical saint of the west. Praise the day she ever met him. Now it's time to fight again. Ooljee had said there is a fate. Boris has said there is a fate and proved it with maths. Sure there's a fate but it can't be that you just let fate roll over you? That is shit-talk. It might be written. It might all be down to equations that Boris has written somewhere but fighting back has to be a term in that equation. An entry in the matrix. A butterfly in the universe. Little things can have big effects. She wasn't ever going to quit. **Use your last heartbeat chasing your first dream.**

They swing north on Interstate Five. Busy now. So many people. Why can't Montana leave her alone? Why do her mistakes chase her? Too many questions. In late afternoon they cross The Bay Bridge. Home. She can't wait to see Little Joan.

Worth More

https://badpeoplethemusical.bandcamp.com/track/worth-more

There's no (secret) information
No train standing in a station
There's no Katoosha Rocket
No cheque in my pocket
There's no Harley Davidson
Nothing you can buy in Debenhams
There's no superhero
No number greater than zero

Worth more than you are – worth more than you are
Worth more than you are - to me

There's no useful contact

No historic artefact
There's no Lone Ranger
No escape from danger
No silver bullets or
No prize from Pulitzer
And there ain't no diamond
No tropical island
There ain't no golden chain
No sacred remains

Worth more than you are - worth more than you are
Worth more than you are - to me

I was dead in a deep freeze
Suffering from a sleeping disease
A body hanging from the trees
And I never asked for you – I never said please

Life was just passing
Amounting to nothing
The fates must have been laughing
At such a happy ending

There's no antique furniture
There's no classic literature
There's no special delivery
No new discovery
There's no high technology
There's no unclaimed territory
No chip from Intel
No supermodel
There's no Ferrari cars
No movie stars
No gold bars
No life on mars
There's no exotic travel
No mystery unravelled
There's no silver spoon
No life on the moon

Worth more than you are - worth more than you are
Worth more than you are - to me

Back in San Francisco. Familiar territory. Familiar but different now. Different because The Dirtkickers have cancelled half their tour and have a week off. As well as which, their God of the Bass Guitar and Skulk Rock Originator THE Thunderman, is laid up at Ronee's house; gunshot. What a tour that was? Talk about "ups and downs". A few more stories to add to the rock and roll legends. Maybe better not tell the one about four guys getting killed at their Flagstaff gig. Altamont Two.

Mike sometimes wonders what happened to the hood-bodies and their van. Whatever it was he wouldn't ever argue with Nduco. Back in his own world now though, he sees no point in rushing around trying to fit in gigs. A week or so off will suit everyone best and in any case he needs to think. Think how they can deal these evil fuckers being after them? Can he rely on The Sidewinder in any way? And Ooljee? He finds himself thinking about Ooljee more and more. Her voice, her style, her looks, her skills, her voice, her looks, her guitar, her looks, her snakeskin dress, her looks and her looks. He wonders if they will actually come to SF as promised. That would be great because she and Ajei know these bad dudes and so it might be possible to persuade them that The Dirtkickers had nothing (as in "fuck all") to do with the loss of their funds. That much was true. Sort of. AND, Ajei could play bass for them while TMan was off the map. If that didn't work out, and he thinks it highly unlikely TO work out, he'd better have a contingency plan? He'd have to get help from Marv and Don. Mike can not see many ways out of this. First off, he better go see Felicia and find out what else she knows?

He rings and fixes to meet her in a bar on Columbus. She tells of her split with "Rich Guy" and how she's over here retrieving stuff from the apartment. She's moving out. It's about time! She's been married two years! Mike smiles inwardly, but then immediately cries inwardly as she tells of her situation with

Speedy. He surprises himself by being able to put all that stuff to the back of his mind (well mostly, he still thinks of Ooljee, like, how old is she?). Right now though, he needs a plan. He needs a big plan, a foolproof plan, a strategy, a campaign, a master plan and NO BULLSHIT!

He tells Felicia the the events of Flagstaff. Felicia says he can trust Speedy. She was the one who had realised they may be in danger and insisted they be warned. Mike asks that they try and get as much information as they can about what actions the SFPD are taking here.

Now he's walking up Taylor Street once again, and, once again his heart beating a fast double time. He's not sure if it's his fitness or his sense of responsibility. Anyway, he doesn't like it one bit. He is alive and wants to stay that way. He wants to keep Skulk Rock alive too. As he reaches Ina Coolbrith Park he stops and clenches his fists. He stops and turns thinking of Jimmy English. He senses Jimmy's presence again. Like he did the last time he was here. He hears Jimmy English's voice? He spins and looks down Taylor Street from where he has walked. He sees The Island again, with a Sausalito hill behind. He remembers Lucy's first gig with the band over in Sausalito, That was the night some of the music clicked for sure. Skulk. He detours into the park and turns his gaze to see city peaks to his right. He loves this city. He will die here. He smiles, "not yet though MotherFuckers!" as he remembers feeling Jimmy's presence and thinking these exact same thoughts last time he walked past here. This time though, for some reason his eyes are drawn to a tall building with what looks like a gargoyle on the high parapet. As he blinks, two ravens launch from a near-by tree and he watches as their flight path meanders towards the distant tall building. Michael J Remo sings to himself,

Tailspin

https://badpeoplethemusical.bandcamp.com/track/tailspin

Out here is lonely
And it ain't no fun

Texas ranger looking for me
With his loaded gun

Everybody got somewhere
Somewhere to run
But I got nowhere
I'm not like everyone

I got no discipline
I'm goin down with a foolish grin
I'm in a tailspin
I know I can't win

She told me I was a prick
With a mind like King Kong
Now I'm long gone but I'm homesick
I know she wasn't wrong

I'd pay the Devil's debt
If I only could
Some things they won't forget
But I wish they would

I fell into sin
Goin down with a foolish grin
I'm in a tailspin
I know I can't win

I curse the automobile
And its evil wheels
The getaway car
The Highway Star
Took me so far
Into the dark

Now I got the FBI
Looking into my mind
But I'm gonna deny
Whatever they might find

So I got a Kalashnikov
And I got a Glock
You better not piss me off
Or I can stop your clock

I'm goin down so slow
Nobody wants to know
I'm in a tailspin
I know I can't win
I'm in a tailspin
I gave way to sin
I'n a tailspin
Goin' out with a grin

What Mike Remo doesn't quite realise is that this is the beginning of a "fate-whirlpool" or "convergence", in full accordance with Boris The Cranium's theories of space-time and fate and how fate-strands can stretch over multiverses dependent upon whether their series solutions in his state-equations are convergent (although not many people have read and understood his paper). Fate-whirlpools, in Cranumonian maths (to come) are the advanced mathematical descriptions of "singularities" (as sought by lesser mathematicians over preceding centuries).

On the waterfront, just down the hill from where Mike now stands, Little Harriet is the only other person in the whole of San Francisco to have noticed the eagle. The rest are too busy in their pursuit of their greed-lives. This moment in space-time, as described at the very first chapter of this account, marks the start of this particular fate-whirlpool. Not as important as others that have occurred in history but, nevertheless, who could ever devalue the importance of Skulk Rock in the development of mankind and culture in general?

Chapter 17
Fate Whirlpool

Mike Remo walks cross town. He takes his time. He sees the bay bridge through tall buildings from hilltop intersections. The street cars whirr and clang. He loves old stuff that has stood the test of time. He makes a mental note of "test of time", that's a song for sure. He thinks of his Stratotone guitar. Made in 1962 and still kicks the shit out of other guitars. Sculpted bodies? Alder? Ash? Mahogany? Single coils? Humbuckers? The greed of man. Get a Stratotone and keep it.

He reaches the gates to The Dirtkicker's yard and looks down at the padlock to insert the key. He is suddenly aware of a movement behind him. He turns and there is The Sidewinder. Mike staggers back as The Sidewinder grins,

"Here we are Michael Remo!"

"Just like you said", he holds out a fist for a bump.
The Sidewinder looks confused, fist bumps are unknown to the Apache, and there is a pause so Mike affectionately fist bumps Sidewinders chest. Mike can't help smiling as he opens up. Somehow The Sidewinder's presence is reassuring. He makes coffee as Sidewinder looks around,

"Nice place Michael Remo!"

"Thanks. Glad you could come."

"We said we would. The Fatback, Ooljee and Ajei will be here later."

"Awwww – great!"
The Sidewinder picks up Mike's Stratotone,

"Can I?"

"Sure."
The Sidewinder explores its sounds through one of the small tweed amps littered around.

"Can't beat real technology Michael Remo!"
Mike smiles,

"Get those valves rockin."
The Sidewinder looks around,

"Is that a beer handle?"

"Sure is!"

"Does it work?"

"Sure does"

"I could sure use one!"

Mike pulls The Sidewinder a beer.

"Never too early Michael Remo!"

Mike smiles and get's himself one. The Sidewinder thinks before speaking,

"They will come Michael Remo! Evil fuckers."

"What do we do?"

"Well I was thinking........maybe we play some gigs?"

Mike laughs, The Sidewinder continues,

"The Snake-Kings?"

"Got a good ring to it Sidey. I got some gigs organised and I will get The Snake-Kings on the bill"

"Meantime…..I got the sentries over this city and up north."

Mike looks puzzled. Sidewinder smiles, nodding to emphasise the validity of his assertion,

"We will know when they come."

"Any idea when?"

"Time passes Mike Remo. We will know!"

Time does pass. Mike Remo, true to his word, as ever, organises gigs. Ajei deputises The Thunderman on Bass. They split sets between The Dirtkickers and The Snake-Kings. They play The Saloon, they play Ho's Bar, they play The Coochie Lounge…..they play and play. Audiences swell. This is a new groove and San Francisco gets "snakebit". The fever spreads like an epidemic. Well, those people at the cutting edge of culture get it. The rest still fuck about with overblown music, overproduced music, overfinanced music, overhyped music which is now beginning to be overrun by previously over-looked music. Not before time.

The Sidewinder and Ooljee are such a stage presence. Mike loves the moments he looks into Ooljee's eyes. She welcomes him in. Time continues. TMan heals well. His bounce returns. He has long bass guitar chats with Ajei. TheGnome and The

Fatback are inseparable. Lucy too can be seen smiling when she is there. She is not there as much as she used to be as they have moved Little Joan to Aunty Ronee's house as a precautionary measure. Life is so good...........apart from the evil lurking sonoffbitch parasite shadows somewhere at the edge of their Skulk Rock universe.

****

"**Kill the fuckers**...and this time take your best team down and go yourself. What do I pay you for? Our competition thinks I'm soft as well as stupid. What happened in Arizona? We still don't know. Christ Skinny, what are we running here?"

Skinny closes his mind. This is such a movie cliché. He knows it. His lieutenants listening know it. They listen in silence though because TheLynX pays them. Their false empire is controlled by people like TheLynX who, somehow, control the money and the money runs these parasites.

As they travel the long sparse Montana highways heading south for the rockies now, Skinny explains the plan. They will be "special forces" from Montana aiming to strike blows against criminal empires. At least that's what they will tell Lathan, their tame SFPD officer. Lawyer Firkov and "Miss Trulove" have been down to "brief" him. The four Lieutenants smile, confident in the talents of Miss Trulove, and confident in their own capabilities. Confident in their armoury and confident in Skinny as their Colonel. As the distant mountains get closer now the Lieutenants sit in confident silence. Each listens to whatever in isolation. Skinny thinks differently, he thinks of The Chief, he scans the distant horizons for eagles. A tiredness encroaches on him.

Gunslinger

https://badpeoplethemusical.bandcamp.com/track/gunslinger

I walk through the valley of the shadow of death
I could be suckin' on my last breath
The lord took me for somebody else

And I don't even have to be myself

The third beast of the fourth seal
From the fifth gate appeared to me
No man alive ever said I lied
Nothing like whisky for my appetite

Gunslinger ain't no life
If you want my advice
If I knew then what I knew when
My 2nd bullet hit his heart again
He fell into heaven as I fell into hell

Round here the law is a pistol shot
And from a standing draw I can hit a padlock
But I never told a bragging lie
The last time I saw my mother she was hanging high

I can't help it if I'm swift
In temper love and shot
Even quicker when I'm pissed
But even meaner when I'm not

A lifetime making up for lost ground
In this cheap whore, cheap beer town
I like drinkin' more than a moose pisses
All night women and loose kisses

Gunslinger ain't no life
If you want any of my advice
If I knew then what I knew when
My 2nd bullet hit his heart again
He fell, he fell into heaven as I fell into hell

****

One fine fresh San Francisco day, around midday, in Dirtkick-ersHQ. Skulk rules the air. The Fatback is on the kit, Ajei is bending Bass lows into a binding groove glue. Lucy has brought over some new songs and is running them down for the band. She is now so much more at ease with her Telecaster. She's found the right amp now. An old Fender Blackface Mike Remo had stored away in his junk room. The tinge of reverb opens up the even harmonic overtones and was the final seasoning to her own personal guitar sound. She is having big fun. Mike was blowing some sax tones. *James sits in a corner just happy to hear some new stuff happening.* Marv and Don have arrived with a bike The Sidewinder has asked for a trial of. Marv and Don love The Sidewinder. As they relax at Dirtkicker's HQ The Sidewinder cruises the hilly streets of Frisco checking out this new machine.

The Sidewinder is loving the slow-rev rhythm of the bike Marv and Don have brought. He opens his lungs to the sea air around Ocean Beach when his hawk swoops in front of him. He knows immediately what it is and swings the bike back towards DirtkickerHQ. Fast-forward. His hawk high above.

This is Lieutenant Lathan's big day. The Montana "Special Forces Agents" pick him up right on time. As he walks with Skinny to their vehicle, he notices an unusual amount of bird excrement on the van. As they drive away Skinny asks Lathan how often they have to clean vehicles around here.

"Ours has been covered in bird shit since we got here?"

The Sidewinder swings the Harley around corners and guns it up inclines.

Lathan directs Skinny to the street outside DirtkickerHQ and Agent Skinny's "team" disembark and move swiftly to the entry gate. Lathan marvels at how these "special forces" guys handle themselves as they quickly disable the lock and gain entry into the yard. They leave one agent in the yard and quickly proceed inside covering them selves. Lathan grips his 9mm. Tense, excited, alive.

The Sidewinder looks up at the roof of the building opposite as he stands the bike. He sees his hawk, two ravens and the eagle lined up along the ridge. He nods to them.

The Dirtkickers finish the song and smile as the sound dies away. Mike Remo declares it a "keeper" and bends to put his saxophone on its stand. As he looks up he finds himself looking down the barrel of a silenced 9mm. His focus moves from the gun to the face of a uniformed officer holding him covered. There are five other officers in the room by now. All falls silent. Don and Marv put down their beers and turn to face the agents. TheFatback sits staring behind the drumkit. Lucy is last to see the invaders as she is facing the others to play. She sees everyone freeze and turns around in shock.

As TheSidewinder enters the yard, the agent left there immediately has him covered with a silenced 9mm. The Sidewinder stares him down. The agent is tense and motions him inside. The Sidewinder moves slowly – for now. As The Sidewinder is ushered into the room Skinny speaks,
    "Welcome to the party Tonto!"
He motions him to stand over by Mike Remo. The Sidewinder looks at Mike and looks at The Fatback. The one officer in SFPD uniform speaks,
    "I'm Lieutenant Lathan SFPD and you headshits are under arrest pending the ongoing investigations relating to the murders of The Snake family."
It's obviously a well rehearsed speech and he carries on,
    "I would not advise any sudden movements. These agents are trained Special Forces officers!"

Lathan points his gun at Lucy and tells her to go and stand the other side of the room. She slowly removes her telecaster and leans it against her amplifier. A tense silence reigns.

James flys around the room. What can he do. So helpless? Thoughts rush his mind like a wave of barbarians attacking a helpless caravan of pilgrims. Oh fuck oh fuck oh fuck........

The skinny "agent" speaks now, interrupting Lathan,

"It would help your case if you were to tell us where any money or drugs you took from The Snakes might be?"

As he speaks, Lucy's guitar begins growing a low note as it leans against the amp. The musicians know whats happening but the agents look puzzled at first. Skinny's interrogation is interrupted and, as he realises what is happening, he asks Lathan,

"Can you shut that fucking thing down?"

Lathan bends to look at the amplifier. He has no idea. He turns the wrong control and the feedback worsens and assaults everyone's hearing. Lathan's "cool" totally lost now as he jumps back and somehow drops his gun. In desperation he stamps on the leaning guitar. The sound dies in a series of crackles. He then kicks the amplifier over to a series of crashes as the spring reverb unit complains. Lathan giggles, he doesn't notice Lucy Smith's eyes narrow and harden spitting laser beam bullets at him.

Marv turns to look at Don. They know each other so well they don't need to speak. Don shakes his head but Marv just smiles and slightly purses his lips, blowing a kiss to Don. Don subtly shakes his head but Marv turns away from Don to look at Skinny,

"One thing I know about Special Forces? They're dumb cunts who just really like messing with guns and thinking the girls like them for it. Their moms never let them play guitars and so they spent their time bending over for their gay pussy whipped fathers........."

Marv feints left and makes two rapid paces towards Skinny before Skinny snaps and efficiently puts a bullet in Marv's forehead. This happens in an instant but, as Marv knows from Boris The Cranium's theories, space-time can be different in different circumstances,

Bad Day

https://badpeoplethemusical.bandcamp.com/track/bad-day

I got a six gun pointing at me
In fact the bullet's on its way
I'm having a bad day – you might say

So I'm calling a time out
So many things I got to sort out
I don't want to leave you – in any doubt

Never saw you smile enough
Never heard you laugh enough
Never made you happy – for long enough

You are an angel of the first degree

Didn't have to be this way
Real life always got in the way
Of all the things I wish – I'd remembered to say

Never heard you sing too many songs
Never knew a time when you were ever wrong
No time with you was ever too long

It was always where I wanted to be - honestly

Now I wish I could turn back time
Be there for you all that time
Wish I'd turned my back on all of my crimes

Never saw you smile enough
Never heard you laugh enough
Never made you happy – for long enough
You are an angel of the first degree

Funny the way life turns out
But it's late for philosophy now
I see your face – as all the lights go out

Marv falls forward at Skinny's feet. As a shock wave emanates, it buffets everyone. Unexpected! Don reacts immediately and rolls forward. He seems to grab Skinny's thigh as he suddenly rises and now and has hold of Skinny's wrist. Skinny had been distracted by the strange blurred movement of The Sidewinder. Skinny's face drains pale as he manages to squeeze off only a single shot which thuds into a brick wall. It happens so fast that Mike Remo and Lucy have not moved. Skinny's right leg trouser material becomes wet with blood. Don has cut an artery in his upper thigh and his cowboy boot fills with blood as his life drains away. His eyes vacant and staring. He has no last thoughts like Marv.

The movement that had distracted Skinny, trained though he was, was The Sidewinder. He seemed to blur and disrupt Skinny's trained radar scanning to maintain the position of all personnel. Skinny's surveillance systems could not handle this final situation. Two of Skinny's Lieutenants are now stood paralysed with tell tale snakebite penetrations to their foreheads. Mike Remo has seen this before in the lobby of the Ilkasin Bar. One of these lieutenants now falls forward clattering to the ground in front of Lucy. His gun dropping at her feet.

The third lieutenant is now also motionless. Mike Remo looks across and sees the thick end of a drumstick protrudiung from the middle of his forehead like a strange diving board, his eyes vacant and staring as if waiting for the diver to appear on a downward arc into some swimming pool in front of him. No-one had seen The Fatback move, such was the speed with which he released the drumstick. The Lieutenant slowly sinks to the ground.

Lathan looks around in shock. His eyes staring. He finally manages to find A voice. It's not HIS voice. He looks around the floor for his weapon and slaps his pockets in hope. All he finds is his police badge and he holds it forth,

"I'm Lieutenant Lathan SFPD. I hereby arrest you all............"

Lucy Smith has now departed her own body. Oh my god! She holds her hands to her mouth as she sees her other self bend and pick the fallen Lieutenant's gun up from the floor. She has seen this happen once before in the Montana farm as she faced Seth Snake. She slowly points the gun and fires a bullet to Lathan's chest. He looks down in shock. Next she fires again and a bullet hole appears in Lathan's forehead. He stares and crumbles.

She sees herself stood, Mike Remo moving so so slowly towards her as if the whole world has slowed relative to her consciousness. She looks around the room. Memories whirling, fizzing and flashing. Her focus tightens and there, staring at her, his shock as great as hers she sees James Smith,
"Is it you?"
"It's me!"
"How? Where?, Why? What?..."
He rushes forward and holds her,
"I'm with you and Little Joan all day every day."
He cradles her head, strokes her hair. Tears.
"I had to do that. He could've taken Little Joan off me!"
"You did right!", he pauses, "and he smashed your guitar!"
Lucy looks at him and they cry their hands clamped, facing each other. James speaks,
"We don't have long but I am here. Always here. All the time!"
She smiles at him. His forehead creased as he tries to think of everything he wants to, has to, needs to, say,
"Look after Little Joan. Tell her about me. Buy her a guitar. Sing to her."
They feel the forces pulling them apart now,
"My Dad is here too. I'm not alone. You have a good life now Lucy Smith. Tell Little Joan her Dad thinks of her! All the time."

James begins to fade as Lucy is drawn back to her other self. Space-time zips up again. Now she is looking at Mike Remo who holds her shoulders and gently takes the gun from her hand. He speaks softly although she doesn't hear his words. She finds herself singing the James Bond theme,

"One bullet for your cold heart. One bullet for your evil mind. How do you like that Mr Bond? Ding diddle-ing-ding-Ding, Ding, Ding - Ding diddle-ing-ding-Ding, Ding, Ding - Ding diddle-ing-ding-Ding, Ding, Ding - Ding diddle-ing-ding-Ding, Ding, Ding – De Ding – ding-a-dong!"

Outside of DirtkickersHQ the 4th Lieutenant is alert. He assumes Skinny is interrogating their, by now, captives. He scans the surroundings cyclically like all trained combatants. Methodically scanning for movement or change. As he scans the skyline opposite, he sees two ravens, side by side. His gaze moves on. The next time around his scan cycle, he sees three birds side by side on the ridge. The new bird is slightly bigger. Again, he doesn't have time to dwell on it. His scan moves on. He's got the easy job here. He's not so keen on interrogations, especially if they need to use force to extract information. He just likes guns and messing with them. He thinks it impresses women. His Mom would never let him have a guitar and he has erased his father and his father's "private times" with him from his memory a long time ago. The next scan stops his scan procedure dead in it's tracks. A fourth bird is sat there now. This one three or four times the size of the other three. He thinks to himself, "Is that an eagle? Can't be?" He stares for a long time. Blinking. As he blinks, the two ravens take off and fly over and to each side of him. The third bird takes off now and flies off directly over him. His eyes still fixed on the eagle. His scan remains on the eagle and his training fails as he hasn't registered any movement above as the hawk is suddenly there holding his gun hand wrist in sharp talons which dig deep into his flesh gripping his bones. He struggles to free his weapon. Next, two ravens to his face. They peck at his eyes. Finally, he feels a stab pain to his chest in front of his shoulder and in his back to the rear of his shoulder. His senses, under pressure of panic, can't discern that it is three talons in the front of his shoulder and one behind. He still struggles to free his weapon as talons of the eagle's second foot pierce his neck. He hears his blood rush out as he feels himself weaken and crumple as darkness falls over him.

Inside the room Mike Remo holds Lucy. Cradling her head. Don Estrada kneels cradling Marv. His tears run like the Colorado River. Mike wonders if anyone has ever seen Don Estrada cry?

Mike Remo whispers to Lucy,
    "It's over, it's over, it's over!"
    "OK OK OK Roy Fucking Orbison!"

Chapter 18
Endings

Rocky Mountain passes, diverting and dispersing sound from uncompromising rock surfaces, desert highways-allowing sound to escape unhindered in all directions, forests, agricultural plains, city streets and wilderness forests hosted the sound of motorbikes as crusades of angels headed for San Francisco California. It was summer days. Haight Ashbury buzzed like the past. Some camped on Crissy Field. Some stayed up all night in the bars. The atmosphere was raucous but reverent, respectful but rebellious in most corners of the city. So many motorbikes arrived that the traffic department lost all control of some areas. Traffic locked down.

They launched the raft from one of the piers towed alongside a motor launch. It was dusk as they set the raft on its westerly course. On the raft was Marv's Fatboy with Marv seated. Majestic. His red bandana easily visible to those around the bay and lined along the shore and along the Golden Gate itself. Traffic on the bridge silenced. Don Estrada and Al silent at the bows of the launch as Marv was set on his last westward ride. His raft on auto-pilot striking an uncompromising course. The launch then moved swiftly alongside Torpedoe Wharf where Don and Al's bikes were waiting. They rode a lined and guarded route up and onto The Gate with escorts of Angels clearing the route. From the centre of the bridge they watched Marv's last departure from SF. Like El Cid passing through the gates of Valencia to vanquish all.

Marv passed under The Golden Gate where the hosts watched in a gathering dusk. Don Estrada's eyes fixed on his lifelong friend, golden light reverberating in his tearfloodeyes. Marv The Majestic reached a deep water channel as the sun disappeared beyond a distant horizon. Don remotely exploded the raft and a fireball painted the sky as the sonic boom dispersed across the Bay and the City.

****

City chief's are frustrated in their lack of control after the "angel invasion". The conventional TV channels and newspapers cannot handle it. They ask relentless questions of the Authorities. Their necks purple with rage at their loss of control. Fuck them.

Angels disperse over the next sad days. As the City returns to normal, Don Estrada and Al leave unnoticed on their bikes. They cross The Gate on 101. Then north to Portland. Across The Rockies. As they descend towards Helena their ranks have grown. Don and Al at the head of the Host. Other riders approaching from all sides of Helena.

Office staff at the renamed Lincoln Xylo building hear the growing thunder of Harley Davidson. Eventually they move from boredom desks to their upper floor windows and gasp to see a flood of Angels stream into and overlay their parking areas below. Don Estrada leads the group that forcibly enter the building. Security are of no consequence against this numerical advantage. The lead group moves to the top floor and smashes into The LynX's private offices.

The LynX sits behind his large desk basking in the security of his new Lieutenants. They are powerless as the tide enters. Disarmed and neutered. Don pauses and looks at The LynX. Emotionless. The LynX is enraged at the violation of his territory, at the heart of his empire and in front of his pathetic minions. He sits behind his desk, puce red, veins pumping with a rage orgasm,

"You cannot do this......You've gone too far.........we will make you pay........this is all on our CCTV systems........"

His veins bulge in his rageclimax as Don Estrada walks around his desk, grips TheLynX's neck and presses a 9mm to the top of the everpresent baseball cap. The barrel of the gun encloses the rivet at the top of the cap. The dull thud of the shot decays to silence as The LynX's eyes stare, lifeless now. Don Estrada unemotional and calm as he let's the limp body fall. As he walks away he sings,

"Ding diddle-ing-ding-Ding, Ding, Ding - Ding diddle-ing-ding-Ding, Ding, Ding - Ding diddle-ing-ding-Ding, Ding, Ding - Ding diddle-ing-ding-Ding, Ding, Ding – De Ding – ding-a-dong!"

He puts his pistol muzzle to Miss Trulove's head now and politely requests that the large safe is opened. The LynX's accountant has no option but to add his code to Miss Trulove's and the safe swings open. Don Estrada takes the bundles of cash, dropping them into a large bag that Al holds open. He then tosses a grenade into the safe and shuts the door. They stand and listen to the muffled boom. The safe and contents as dead as TheLynX now. Don explains,
"If this goes any further we will be back to close you all down. Hillbilly Motherfuckers!"

Subsequent examination of CCTV reveals no useful information as the Angels wear banadana's over their mouths and, basically, all look the same. Helena PD will not prove particularly interested.

****

Lucy had travelled up to Bozeman Montana with Little Joan. They stopped off at English Bob's and had time at the beach. In Bozeman, Howard had fixed her Telecaster. He had moaned,
"There are not geeetars young lady. These are slabs of wood and screws. You need a Gibson!"
"It's what you get used to Howard. You need guitars that tell you stories"
"Your Nick Lucas telling you stories still?"
"He sure is Howard!"
"How did you do this? Someone stepped on it?"
"That's right!"
Howard clicks his tongue and sighs,

"I told you young lady – kill 'em – any judge would let you off! Don't tell me it was another boyfriend?"
Lucy is quiet.

Back home, Little Joan continues her dancing, her singing, her fascination with water, she loves books and stories. She looks through a telescope at the ships crossing The Bay, the island where the "badees" are sent but her favourite views are the moon and stars. She wonders about all that. She is amazingly good at her sums. Like all children, everyone loves her. Aunty Ronee, Uncle Mike, Uncle TMan, Uncle Gnome, Uncle Tiny. Her favourite babysitter though is Uncle Don. Lucy Smith smiles to herself as she watches Little Joan turn to melodrama every time there is the sound of a motorbike stopping outside the house. She always dramatically puts a finger over her lips and opens her eyes wide in over-acted tension,
    "The sound of a Harley-Davidson can only mean one thing……..", she pauses and peers around corners with wide eyes, "………………it's Uncle Don!"
Lucy Smith smiles wryly as Little Joan ambushes Uncle Don with her water pistol. He theatrically staggers to his knees and she finishes him off with a headshot.

Lucy looks at the moon too. The witness to so many turning points in her life. She wonders if Boris's theories correlate the moon and Craniumonian "fate whirlpools"? She'll ask Bozzer next time she sees him. She sits and strums Nick Lucas one night, waiting for a ghost to deliver a song and, sure enough,

Your Ghost

https://badpeoplethemusical.bandcamp.com/track/your-ghost

Your ghost is cooking in the kitchen
Your ghost tells me when I got bad breath
Your ghost sets the night wind whistlin'
To warn me not to worry bout death

Your ghost is never suspicious
Your ghost always tells me death is not the end

Your ghost is never vicious
Your ghost don't like my new boyfriend

So I ain't scared of the Devil
And Jesus is not the answer
My hopes are never dis-shevelled
I don't even worry bout cancer

He's my life protector
I bless the day I met him
He's my biopic director
How could I ever neglect her?
How could I ever neglect her?

I'm a life defector
A death instructor
There ain't no woman luckier
I can't wait to see yer
I can't wait to see yer

So – death doesn't scare me
These memories were me
I can't die early

Your ghost tells me Saturn is the nicest planet
Your ghost never needs to telephone me
We have always been telepathic
So I can never be lonely

He's my life protector
I bless the day I met him
He's my biopic director
How could I ever neglect her?
How could I ever neglect her?

I'm a life defector
A death instructor
There ain't no woman luckier
I can't wait to see yer

I can't wait to see yer

So – death doesn't scare me
These memories were me
I can't die early

****

Felicia and Speedy are often seen at Dirtkickers gigs. Speedy
no longer with the SFPD. The eventual hearing about her
"assault" on Lathan concluded she was not suited to modern
day police teamwork. Her hearing was delayed and delayed
because no-one could find Lieutenant Lathan and, in any case,
Speedy was long gone by the time they reached their meaning-
less verdict. Felicia got her a start modelling and she has moved
to the dark side and even been known to drive around in the
Porsche, although most often on her faithful Kawi. Felicia
("Flea") and "Speeds" are inseperables. At least they are when
not working. Felicia has extricated from her penthouse flat in
the city and from the marriage to Rich Guy. The two women
live happily in the Sausalito residence. It's not that they don't
like men but just that they like each other better. Mike Remo is
one guy they both like a lot though. They like him to take them
to the all night muso café in Sausalito if The Dirtkickers play
any gigs close by. Mike struggles to keep a straight face when
they each cling to one of his arms when they walk in. You have
never heard a silence like it! Mike thinks they see him as the
Leonard Cohen of Skulk and who would argue under these
circumstances? What happens when they return to Flea and
Speed's residence, however, is outside the scope of this volume.
(You can however find a full and detailed account in "The
Sidewinder: Special Edition" available direct from Max Morpheus at $200).

****

**The remainder of that summer, Mike Remo, TheThunderman,
TheGnome, Lucy Smith, Ooljee, Ajei, The Fatback and THE
SIDEWINDER play gigs around SF**. They rundown song after
song after song. They build on the existing following for The

Dirtkickers and The Snakekings also become a sought after gig around The Bay Area. They even get attention from record companies and the media. Ooljee, Ajei, The Fatback and The Sidewinder smile on it all. Parasite media and parasite money means less than nothing to them. Mike and Ooljee form a bond, the majesty and scope of which is, again, outside the scope of this volume. They know the truth though, like a BorisTheCranium equation that will not be denied, and Ooljee and Ajei cannot remain in the Parasite City. Mike Remo is kind of opposite, he cannot live without the city and the city cannot live without him.

So, one sad day Ooljee and Ajei have to leave. They have regained the family land in Montana and it will be returned to The Reservation. Time brings them happiness. Perhaps as a result of Lucy Smith's original reckless act? Was that a rogue free-act? A random "quantum-event" born out of existentialism in a predominantly deterministic universe where every effect has a previous cause? You'd have to ask Boris The Cranium or Jean Paul Sartre, and smart money should be on the former even though his papers and theories still reside in the unread back archives of the scientific establishment. Well, anyway, all that aside, Mike Remo does visit Montana and Ooljee does visit SF. Ooljee seems to become younger and younger. Ajei is happy playing more SnakeRock with The Fatback and The Sidewinder. They build followings in Montana, in and around the Navajo Nation and sometimes even venture back to the City.

****

James Smith is more settled these days. Talk about the "Butterfly Effect"? Lucy Smith's Montana misdemeanour has created a disturbance that was somehow amplified out of all proportion. Like a 100 Watt Marshall stack – is that amount of amplification ever necessary? But then......was it Lucy's act that started it all? Surely it was Seth Snake's drunken breaking of her guitar that started this chain of fate events? Recklessly smashing a Gibson Nick Lucas guitar is surely deserving of capital punishment? The rest has been the result of that particular butterfly? James rests his case and wonders how the heavenly jurors are going to respond to his unquestionable logic? His theories are suddenly disturbed,

"Where does a man get a drink around here? You crazy limey bastard!"

James turns around to see Marv stood there smiling. James smiles back and stands to greet his friend; nervously wondering how he will react to the bad news about drinks!

****

And what of The Sidewinder and The Fatback? Well. No-one really knows. They return to The Nation. They appear. They disappear. Rogue agents of groovesnake rock. When they appear in San Francisco they gig with The Dirtkickers, but generally thay play on and around native American reservations. Ajei is the bass glue holding together their particular brand of hypnotic groove. Every note she issues has purpose and attitude, still. Catch one of their gigs if at all possible.

****

And what of Skulk Rock? Well, it continues to grow, nurtured by the guiding principles of Michael J Remo. Built on the groove foundation of The Thunderman and The Gnome embellished by the songs of Mike Remo and Lucy Smith and James Smith. You don't believe me? Ask Bob Dylan where he gets songs and he might tell you that a ghost will come to him and give him the song? Ask Boris The Cranium if there can be parallel universes?

There is a growing movement of "Skulkers" these days. Even other bands within the genre. They generally adopt the Skulk Rock salute and understand how to control their innate greed. These bands, and The Dirtkickers themselves, generally shun the increasingly desperate mainstream frantic to "sign them". Mike always politely tells them to "Fuck off! We do ok on our own! You gotta beware of greed Man!". One or two Skulk bands have even sacrificed themselves to the altar of money, record producers, executives and their "deals" and thus passed

from the realm of Skulk. They never last. They are bled dry and
shrivelled by the parasites.

True Skulkers know the truth.
Bad People will inherit this earth as the white parasites contin-
ue to eat themselves.
NO FUCKING BULLSHIT.

Let's Go

https://badpeoplethemusical.bandcamp.com/track/lets-go

So – let's go
Let's go and take a look
At the memories that we took
All along the merry way
And I know
There is no turning back
This is a one way track
And that that is that
Precious memories
You better try to keep
And try to share
Even if no-one cares
Snap shot history
Write a book for them to see
Cast it all into stone
So you can never be alone

This is a picture
A picture that we took
One day in a seaside city
Of American history
It was a different world
Going where the gravity hurled
The fate of our behaviour
Fruit of our endeavour
We watched as our silver fell
Into a a wishing well
A whole world to tell,

it's in a wagon train bound for hell
Cos wishes don't come true
Even if they are legally due
You got a contract to the good
Printed out and signed in blood

Just one time, In San Francisco
That time – where did it go?
Why did God have to make it so?
Susceptible to earthquakes you know
On Highway 101
You got to run and run and run and run
Like some kinda Kenyan
In perpetual motion
This world needs a U-turn
Let the parasites burn
Because they never learn
Too dumb to discern

So let's go
And do what we do best
Forget the rest
Cos they don't know
They don't know
What life is all about
They just shout
And cry in greed
All the stuff that they think they need
Just sell your car
And get a guitar
Get some drums
Get a bass
And chase and chase and chase
And let's go let's go
Let's go...

K O F R

Printed in Poland
by Amazon Fulfillment
Poland Sp. z o.o., Wrocław

57992002R00157